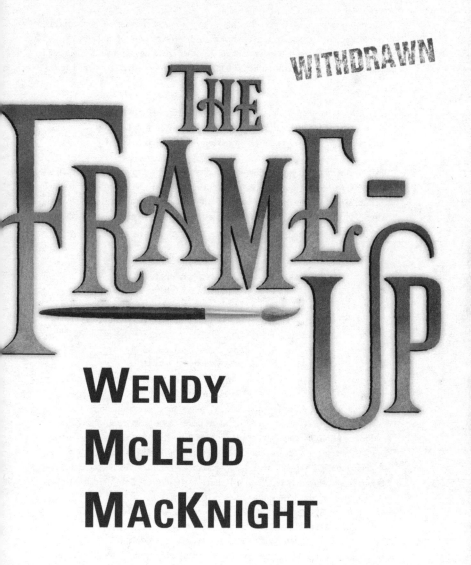

THE FRAME-UP

WENDY McLEOD MacKNIGHT

GREENWILLOW BOOKS
An Imprint of HarperCollinsPublishers

The Frame-Up
Text copyright © 2018 by Wendy McLeod MacKnight
Map illustration copyright © 2018 by Tu Anh Dinh
Pages 371–372 constitute an extension of the copyright page.

The text of this book is set in 12-point Joanna MT.
Book design by Paul Zakris

Library of Congress Cataloging-in-Publication Data

Names: MacKnight, Wendy McLeod, author.
Title: The frame-up / by Wendy McLeod MacKnight.
Description: First edition. | New York, NY : Greenwillow Books, an imprint of HarperCollins Publishers, [2018] |
Summary: "Twelve-year-old artist Sargent Singer must team up with some very unusual partners to thwart a theft of the masterpieces in the Beaverbrook Art Gallery"—Provided by publisher. Includes facts about Lord Beaverbrook, the gallery's founder.
Identifiers: LCCN 2018008792 | ISBN 9780062668301 (hardback)
Subjects: | CYAC: Art—Fiction. | Supernatural—Fiction. | Fathers and sons—Fiction. | Beaverbrook Art Gallery—Fiction. | Art galleries, Commercial—Fiction. | Art thefts—Fiction. | Mystery and detective stories. |
BISAC: JUVENILE FICTION / Art & Architecture. |
JUVENILE FICTION / Mysteries & Detective Stories. |
JUVENILE FICTION / Social Issues / Friendship.
Classification: LCC PZ7.1.M2587 Fr 2018 | DDC [Fic]—dc23 LC record available at
https://lccn.loc.gov/2018008792

18 19 20 21 22 PC/LSCH 10 9 8 7 6 5 4 3 2 1

First Edition

GREENWILLOW BOOKS

To Barry and Sydney and Forrest, with love
To my mother, forever behind the frame

A painting is never finished—it simply stops in interesting places.

—Paul Gauguin

CHAPTER ONE

Mona Dunn was late. She leaped from one painting to the next, her damp hair flying like streamers on a bicycle, her dress darkened here and there by still-soggy undergarments. She'd known there wasn't enough time, even without the calamity, which had involved a stranger farther down the beach, whose presence had trapped her in the water thanks to an ill-thought-out decision to jump in wearing only her undergarments. Her mistake cost her twenty minutes. She would be the last to arrive at Lord Beaverbrook's monthly meeting, just like last month and the month before. Lord Beaverbrook would not be pleased.

Breathless, she arrived at the meeting location: Salvador Dalí's *Santiago El Grande*, one of the largest and most dramatic paintings in the art gallery, with its massive horse and rider soaring toward the heavens. Located in the Orientation Gallery, near the entrance, it was a crowd-pleaser. Lord Beaverbrook was already speaking. After slipping through the picture frame into the meeting, Mona dipped behind Andre Reidmor, hoping his voluminous cloak would hide her.

"I should like to remind you of the many important events that will occur at the Beaverbrook Art Gallery this summer," Max Aitken—aka Lord Beaverbrook—read from his notes. Though his head was down, he added, "Good of you to join us, Mouse." Max's pet name for Mona was Mouse, because according to him she was everywhere and nowhere and never seemed to get caught.

Every head swiveled in her direction. Her friends, Madame Juliette and Edmund, flashed sympathetic smiles. Clement Cotterell stuck out his tongue. The horse and rider peered down and gave her hard stares. Mona curtsied, and then fixed her attention upon Max, pretending the attention did not bother her in the least. Papa called it her imperious look, and it often served her well.

"To continue," Max said, flicking a bit of dried paint off the lapel of his jacket, "the art restorer arrives today."

A murmur rolled across the crowd like a wave. Mona saw Juliette give Edmund a fearful look. No one liked being restored. It was a messy, tedious business, and it meant spending several days or weeks trapped in a work-room in the basement.

"Now, now," Max growled, waving the buzz away as if they were bees bothering him at the breakfast table. "You all knew this was coming. Everyone has to do their share if we are to remain a top-tier art gallery."

"But I was only just restored!" Lady Cotterell called out, swaying as if she might faint. Painted by a Dutch artist in the seventeenth century, she had a delicate temperament, thanks to being trapped in a painting for nearly four hundred years with crying baby Frances, three rambunctious children, and a husband who complained constantly about being stuck at the Beaverbrook Art Gallery in New Brunswick, Canada, when his dream was to live at the Louvre in Paris.

Lord Beaverbrook didn't glance up. "Madame, your painting was last restored in 1973."

"It was that long ago?" Lady Cotterell whispered to herself.

"As I said," Max continued, "I do not yet have the exact schedule, but here is the restoration list as I know it today: *The Cotterell Family, Madame Juliette dans le Jardin, Hotel*

Bedroom, Merrymaking, and Mona Dunn."

There was such an uproar after "Merrymaking" that Mona barely heard her name.

"Where will we spend the evenings while we're being restored?" a swarthy man Mona didn't recognize shouted. Despite having lived in the gallery for nearly sixty years, she still ran across residents who rarely left their paintings, especially a painting like Merrymaking, with its dozens of people both inside and outside the White Horse Inn.

Max shrugged, but as faces began to purple, he added, "Calm down. Sir Thomas Samwell has agreed to host folks over at Bacchanalian Piece while Merrymaking is restored. Satisfied?" He waited for the grumbling to trickle away. "Be prepared to go downstairs at a moment's notice. Keep your paintings organized. Now if you'll allow me to continue, I do have other news."

Someone started to speak, but was hushed. No one really wanted to cross the Boss, the residents' nickname for Max.

"The gallery will host a fundraising party on Friday night. Attendance is down this year, as are donations. As you well know, operating a world-class enterprise like this requires lots of money, and I expect you to look sharp during the party. No pained faces, please and thank you, regardless of the ridiculous things the guests say."

A few snickers volleyed their way around the meeting. Everyone had a handful of gallery patron horror stories.

Max acknowledged the laughter with a quick grin. "Also, the museum will host several weeklong summer camps, but with a twist: the final night of each week will include a sleepover—"

"What is this sleepover thing?" Andre Reidmor asked. His painting was almost six hundred years old, and he'd been on loan to another gallery when the last sleepover was held, in 1998.

"The children taking part in the art camps get to spend the night in the gallery at the end of the week," Mona whispered, even though, if truth be told, she was a little afraid of the stern-faced giant bear of a man who strode about in his fur-trimmed green velvet cape.

"Why would they do that?" he demanded. "It sounds bothersome, ya?"

Mona remembered the last sleepover fondly, an opinion not shared by Sir Charles, who railed against allowing "rambunctious ragamuffins" to spend the night.

Max's booming voice silenced all opposition. "Enough! Director Singer is of the opinion that such activities encourage family participation in art. Family participation means more income. Surely we can put aside our personal feelings for the good of the gallery?"

"He means the good of Lord Beaverbrook," someone muttered.

Mona twisted around. The speaker was British author W. Somerset Maugham, who was being held in the arms of a man Mona didn't recognize. Maugham winked at Mona, and she grinned in return. She liked Maugham. It was too bad he had the misfortune of being a sketch of a head. While Mona's painting only showed her from the waist up, her artist had thought of the whole of her, which meant when she left her portrait she was a complete person. Maugham's artist had focused solely on the head; Maugham could only leave his painting if someone remembered to go down to the workroom in the basement and get him. At least he could talk. No one liked the sketches of body-less hands; they tended to creep up at the most inopportune and frightening times.

Max pulled out his pocket watch. "It is almost six thirty a.m.," he said. "The security shift change will be occurring soon. I suggest we all return to our paintings. Have a good day." A few people near the front clapped, hoping Max would notice and think kindly of them in the future. Then, like theatergoers after a performance, everyone shuffled off toward the frame, where they lined up, chatting and laughing as they waited for a turn to step into the narrow passages behind the walls that magically led to the gallery's various rooms and their individual paintings.

Before Lord Beaverbrook himself could leave, a man emerged from the shadows behind him and whispered something in his ear. Mr. Dusk was Beaverbrook's right-hand man; he lived in *Hotel Bedroom*, located in the Hosmer Pillow Vaughan Gallery. His artist, Lucian Freud, was world-famous, and the painting had brought countless visitors to the gallery. But Freud had painted Dusk as a gray, shadowy figure, and because of that, most of the residents of the gallery gave him a wide berth. Max nodded as Dusk spoke and then held up a hand.

"Wait up!" he called. "Mr. Dusk here has reminded me I've forgotten something."

Those already out of the painting poked their heads back in, while everyone else turned their attention back to the Boss.

"The gallery director's son is arriving today," Max said, smiling.

"I didn't know he had a son," someone said. Mona nodded. She hadn't known either.

"He does indeed," Max said. "A twelve-year-old lad named Sargent. Apparently he's quite an artist. I assume he will participate in the art camps. Director Singer is very excited. And that is definitely that. Off you go!"

Mona was shoved along toward the frame and had nearly escaped when Max's booming voice caught up with her. "I would see you, Mona Dunn!"

Mona sighed. She'd been right; she wasn't getting off scot-free this time.

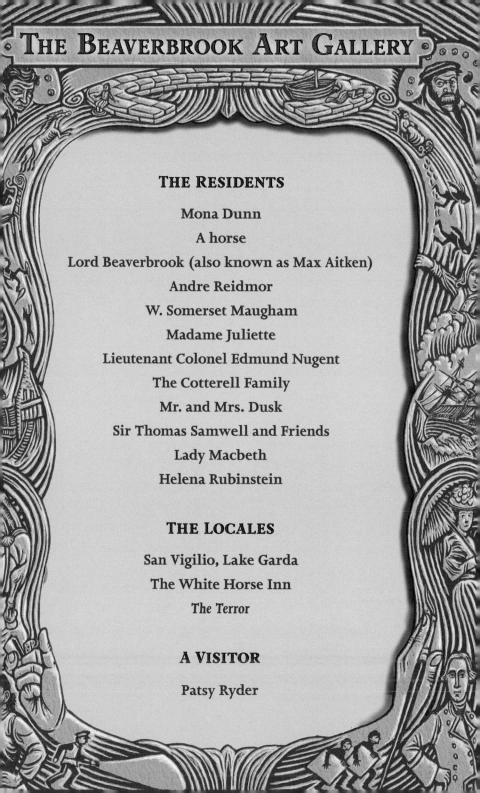

The Beaverbrook Art Gallery

The Residents

Mona Dunn

A horse

Lord Beaverbrook (also known as Max Aitken)

Andre Reidmor

W. Somerset Maugham

Madame Juliette

Lieutenant Colonel Edmund Nugent

The Cotterell Family

Mr. and Mrs. Dusk

Sir Thomas Samwell and Friends

Lady Macbeth

Helena Rubinstein

The Locales

San Vigilio, Lake Garda

The White Horse Inn

The Terror

A Visitor

Patsy Ryder

Mona Dunn, William Orpen, 1915. Oil on canvas.

Santiago El Grande, Salvador Dalí, 1957. Oil on canvas.

MAX AITKEN, LORD BEAVERBROOK

Portrait of Lord Beaverbrook,
Graham Sutherland, 1951.
Oil over conté on canvas.

Sketch of Lord Beaverbrook
Graham Sutherland, 1950.

ANDRE REIDMOR, GALLERY RESIDENT

Andre Reidmor, Bartholomäus Bruyn the Elder, 1540. Oil and tempera on panel.

W. SOMERSET MAUGHAM, AUTHOR AND MAX'S OLD FRIEND

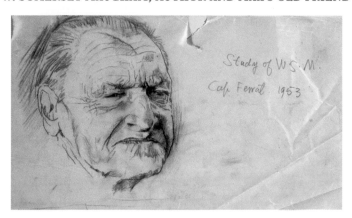

Somerset Maugham, St. Jean Cap Ferrat, 1953. Graham Sutherland, 1953.

Madame Juliette dans le jardin, Eugène Boudin, 1895. Oil on panel.

Lieutenant Colonel Edmund Nugent, Thomas Gainsborough, 1764. Oil on canvas.

The Cotterell Family. Left to right: Sir Charles, Lady Cotterell, Baby Frances, Lizzie, Clem, and Charles. Jan Mytens, 1658. Oil on canvas.

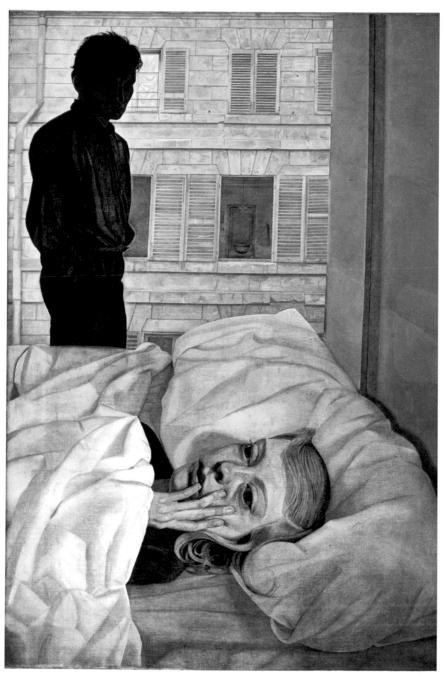

Hotel Bedroom, Lucian Freud, 1954. Oil on canvas.

Bacchanalian Piece: Sir Thomas Samwell and Friends.
Left to right: Sir Thomas Samwell, John Neal, Captain John Floyd
William Wilmer, William Piers, Caesar, and General Louis deJean.
Philippe Mercier, 1733. Oil on canvas.

LADY MACBETH, GALLERY RESIDENT

Lady Macbeth Sleep-Walking.
Eugène Delacroix.
1850. Oil on canvas.

HELENA RUBINSTEIN, GALLERY RESIDENT

Helena Rubenstein,
Graham Sutherland, 1957. Oil on canvas.

San Vigilio, Lake Garda, John Singer Sargent, 1913. Oil on canvas.

THE WHITE HORSE INN

Merrymaking, Cornelius Krieghoff, 1860. Oil on canvas.

THE TERROR

The Crew of the HMS Terror Saving the Boats and Provisions on the Night of 15th March (1837),
George Hyde Chambers, 1838. Oil on canvas.

Patsy Ryder, Jack Humphrey, date unknown. Oil on canvas.

CHAPTER TWO

Sargent Singer's stepfather, Bill, hummed as he eased the Mercedes into the drop-off zone for Terminal B at La Guardia Airport. It was six thirty in the morning on the last day of June, and Sargent was exhausted, not from getting up early, but because he hadn't slept at all.

"Are you sure this is the right terminal for Air Canada?" his mother asked, her knuckles white from clutching Sargent's ticket and boarding pass.

"Yes, Sarah," Bill said. He leaned forward to pop the trunk and then climbed out of the car.

Sargent was wriggling across the back seat to the door closest to the curb when his mother placed a hand on his arm. He froze, anticipating more motherly advice. In the past week, she'd subjected him to three serious sit-down discussions. Obviously that wasn't enough to convince her he'd be fine; she'd also tucked six pages filled with emergency phone numbers, email addresses, a detailed travel itinerary, a map of emergency exits on the airplane, and a summer reading list into the front pocket of his knapsack. She hadn't been this worried when he'd gone to Paris last summer to study at the Sorbonne.

But this trip was different. He was going to visit his father, and anything to do with Isaac Singer made his mother a wreck.

Sargent shook off her hand. "Mom, I gotta go."

He was free of her grip, but not from her intense blue eyes. "I know. Look . . . if it doesn't work out—"

"Mom, I'll be fine." Sure, he hadn't spent much time with his father over the years, but the guy ran an art gallery and Sargent was a painter. They'd have that in common, wouldn't they?

"I know, but if he starts acting strange . . ."

Sargent couldn't tell what part of the queasy feeling in his stomach was due to his mother's worries or his own. "Mom, stop. *He* asked *me* to spend the summer."

His mother sniffed. "Spending the summer is very different from spending a weekend."

Like he didn't already know that. No way were they rehashing his history with Isaac again. Not here, not now. He wouldn't have the guts to get on the plane. "Bill's waiting; I gotta go." He watched her turn, roll down her window, and hold up a finger to her husband.

"One minute, darling!"

Bill tapped his watch. "Let him go, Sarah. Security can take a while. We don't want him to miss his flight."

Afraid that missing his flight was exactly what his mother had in mind, Sargent scrambled out of the car and joined Bill, who drew him into a warm hug.

"Have a great summer, pal," Bill said, thumping Sargent on the back. "Don't worry about your mom. By the time we're back in the city, she'll have forgotten she even has a son."

Bill meant it as a joke, but it stung a little. Sargent was the child of his mother's first marriage and had been an only child for almost seven years before she'd remarried. Then his mom had two more kids—twins Ainsley and Ashley—and Sargent was forced to share her not only with Bill, but with a couple of Disney princesses come to life.

While Sargent was happy to hole up in his bedroom with his paints or a good book, the twins were like his mom and Bill—nonstop talkers who loved being the center of attention. It was like they were this perfect family of four, plus awkward him. Sargent was going to miss them all, but the thought of a little peace and quiet with no one bugging him to paint their nails or play Sleeping Beauty was appealing.

"I heard that!" His mother joined them on the sidewalk. Despite her obvious distress, she still looked impeccable, and Sargent was sure she'd reapplied her lipstick before getting out of the car. "Ignore Bill, Sargent, he's just being silly. Now listen, text me when you are past security, when you board, and when you land in Toronto and Fredericton. Okay?"

Sargent nodded, knowing there'd be texts waiting for him at every stop along the way. If he didn't respond, she might call out the FBI or something.

"Sarah, give him a hug. We can't stay in this spot much longer." Bill thumped Sargent on the back, then circled around and climbed behind the wheel.

"Maybe I should go in the terminal with you. . . ."

"Mom . . . come on. I don't need you to come in with me. The Air Canada lady is waiting for me at the desk. If you come in, it'll just drag things out. Please."

Eyes glistening, Sargent's mother held him in a vise-like grip that seemed improbable for someone so tiny. "Fine. I love you, sweetheart. Be good. I hope everything goes well with your father. Remember, I'm just a phone call away."

Sargent could feel a lump forming in his throat. While he wanted to spend the summer with his dad and get to know him better, part of him wanted to stay home, too. Home was familiar, safe. Afraid he might cry or, worse, chicken out of going, he nodded and fled through the revolving door and into the airport.

CHAPTER THREE

It wasn't easy being a kid at the Beaverbrook Art Gallery. Days stuck inside a painting, strangers gawking at you, living with the same people who told the same stories for years on end, making friends with visiting paintings only to have them leave. But the hardest part for Mona Dunn was that everyone expected her to act older than her thirteen years because she was a hundred-year-old painting. It wasn't fair.

Clement Cotterell intercepted Mona on her way to meet Max. "Come find me tonight. Unless you're grounded," he added saucily. "I want to share some sick beats I'm working on."

"Clem . . ."

"Don't Clem me—I gotta stay current! You might be content to live like you're still in 1915, but it's the twenty-first century, Mona. I see those fellows coming in with their music. I hear what they're playing. And I'm down with it."

Mona rolled her eyes. Clem's seventeenth-century look—puffy silk shirt, fawn-colored frock coat, short pants, hair that waved past his shoulders—bore no resemblance to his inner twenty-first-century hipster self. Over the past four hundred years, nine-year-old Clem had experienced every phase known to the history of childhood. It was hard to keep up.

Clem was Mona's partner in crime, but their age difference made him more a pesky younger brother than a true confidant. He poked her in the ribs and swaggered off toward the passage where his family stood waiting, his mother loudly fussing over the baby and the upcoming restoration project.

Madame Juliette and her fiancé, Lieutenant Colonel Edmund Nugent, were speaking with Max when Mona presented herself for her scolding.

"And you are certain this will not affect our matrimonial plans?" Edmund asked Max.

"I don't see why it should." Max turned to the shadowy

man lurking to his right. "Make a note, Dusk. Madame Juliette's work needs to be completed by July thirty-first, no exceptions."

Dusk scribbled a note in the small notebook he always carried.

Madame Juliette offered the two men a relieved smile. "Thank you. As you know, August fifth is our preferred date."

Mr. Dusk grinned, a flash of white teeth splitting the gray. "We'll do our best, Juliette."

Edmund glared. A product of the eighteenth century, Edmund disliked such familiarity. A proper gentleman did not use a lady's first name.

August fifth was an important date in the gallery calendar that summer. The entire building would be shut down for twenty-four hours while a new art installation was mounted on the roof. It was the ideal time for the wedding, which was to be held in *Santiago El Grande*, the very painting where they stood.

Mona looked from Madame Juliette to Edmund and sighed. It would be a grand wedding. Edmund, in his red military frock coat with the golden piping and brass buttons, was the epitome of dashing, thanks to his chivalrous eighteenth-century manners and his elegant oak walking stick. Madame Juliette was equally refined, an Impressionistic picture of flowery sweetness in her silk skirt the color of pale butter, her frilly white parasol held at a jaunty angle, the ever-present nosegay of red roses in one hand. Their wedding would be so romantic.

Best of all, Mona would be a part of it, standing up with Madame Juliette. It was the Beaverbrook Art Gallery's first wedding, and it was the talk of the paintings. The only disappointment for Mona was what she'd be wearing. William Orpen had painted her wearing her favorite dress at the time, a plain pleated affair the color of toffee with snowy buttons marching down the front. If only she'd chosen her white silk chiffon; *that* was a proper bridesmaid's dress. To be fair, at the time she'd had no idea she'd have another life behind the frame, one where she could wear only the clothes she'd been painted in.

Talk of the wedding had made her forget she'd been called to account with Lord Beaverbrook, but his throat clearing reminded them all.

"Perhaps we should stay," Madame Juliette whispered to Edmund. Mona gave them a grateful smile, but Max would have none of it.

"That will be all."

Mona watched her friends depart. "You needn't be so abrupt, sir," she said.

Max scoffed. "I thought I was downright agreeable, Mouse."

"Fifteen minutes, Lord Beaverbrook," Dusk said.

"Right, right. Go on, Dusk. Miss Dunn and I will be but a moment."

Dusk didn't move. He hated to miss the Boss dressing someone down.

"I believe I dismissed you," Max said, turning his wrath on Dusk instead. Mona smothered a smile as Dusk bowed and hurried away.

Max turned his attention to Mona. "How long have we known each other, Mouse?" he said, reaching into his pocket and extracting a fat cigar.

"My whole life," Mona said. This was true. Like Max, Mona's father, James Dunn, was a native son of New Brunswick. The two men had been close friends.

"I believe you were a young girl the first time I met you at your parents' estate," Max mused, taking a puff of the cigar.

"You weren't a lord then." She could recite Max's life's story by heart; he'd shared it with her dozens of times.

"You are correct. I did not become Lord Beaverbrook until 1917."

"I bet I tried to show you my ponies." The Dunn estate

was in the country, where Mona spent her days riding her beloved horses.

Max shook his head. "If you did, I don't recall. Enough reminiscing—you are taking advantage of me, miss."

"Me, take advantage of you? Impossible!" She grinned slyly.

"You know you are. We are family friends, Mouse. And with your father's portraits on loan for the summer, I consider myself your guardian. It doesn't do to have you traipsing in late as if you own the place—which, by the way, you do not. I'll not be played for a fool."

Mona hadn't considered how her tardiness might appear to others. "I'm sorry, Max. You know how I am. I take a walk and get caught up in my own fairy stories and then all of a sudden, I realize the time and run like the devil and still I'm late! I shall try harder, I promise."

"What's today's excuse?"

"I decided to take a quick swim on my way here. I was sure the painting was empty, but then suddenly someone was on the beach. I couldn't get out of the water because I was in my undergarments! By the time he left, my teeth were chattering and my toes were blue!"

As Mona wove her tale of woe, Max's face twitched and contorted. Finally his laugh escaped as a grand snort, and then Mona was laughing, too. It took several minutes for them to compose themselves, at which point Max stood up.

"You are a goose, there's no denying that. No more tardiness, Mouse, and no more adventures. I want this to be a quiet summer. The only excitement I want is for someone to hand Director Singer a fat check. Is that understood?"

"Understood," she said, executing a perfect curtsy.

Max pointed toward the frame and Mona scampered off, stopping to cross her eyes at the horse and rider before she left, who responded in kind. It was going to be a grand day, she just knew it. She'd survived Max, her dress was dry, and the summer sun streaming in the front door and the gift shop windows was making little diamonds of rainbow light on the polished maple floor.

As she stepped into her own portrait, she waved at Edmund. His portrait, and the painting of the Cotterells, was directly across from her own. He was already in place, leaning on his walking stick, and waved back, mouthing, "Everything okay?" He smiled when she nodded. She settled herself on her stool and waited for the first visitors to arrive.

CHAPTER FOUR

Three hours later, Sargent was in Toronto. He'd survived customs and the trek to the far reaches of the terminal to reach the gate for his Fredericton flight. Now he was slouched so far down in his seat that his long legs stuck three-quarters of the way across the aisle. He wasn't used to the five inches he'd grown since Christmas; he'd almost tripped three people already. His mother would be horrified that he wasn't sitting up, but he was too exhausted to care.

"Is the plane on time?"

The voice was booming and distinctive—as if someone had given a hippopotamus a British accent—and Sargent couldn't resist turning around to see who was speaking. He was mistaken about the hippopotamus part: the voice belonged to an elongated weasel, a man with bony arms and legs, a pointy chin, a forehead that never ended, and black beady eyes. His baggy T-shirt and trousers were covered with greasy stains and blotches of color. Sargent had a similar outfit in his suitcase. Whoever this guy was, he painted with oils and acrylics.

The blond woman behind the check-in desk didn't bother to look up. "We'll board soon."

"My boarding pass says we board at ten oh five," Weasel Man said. He glanced around the room in a bid to find other disgruntled passengers, and his eyes lit on Sargent, who looked away, afraid the guy might speak to him.

Weasel Man had the attention of the blond woman now. "I'm sorry, sir. We've had a delay, but the plane will still arrive on time. Take a seat. We'll board momentarily." She received an exasperated snort in response.

Sargent shook his head and hoped he wasn't seated anywhere near the guy on the plane.

Fifteen minutes later Sargent struggled down the narrow aisle in the cramped airplane, keeping his head low to avoid the open overhead bins. A glance to the right showed him he'd made it to row twelve. His seat was sixteen B and he counted ahead, groaning when he caught sight of a receding hairline.

"You can move to the empty seat across the aisle," Weasel Man said as Sargent stuffed his knapsack under the seat in front of him and began to buckle his seat belt.

"Pardon me?"

Weasel Man cocked his head in the direction of the empty seat across the aisle. "I said, why don't you go over there?"

Sargent gave him a blank stare. "I can do that?"

"Of course. I do it all the time. Then we'd both have more room."

Having been given a spot on a lifeboat leaving the *Titanic*, Sargent didn't have to be told twice. He unbuckled his seat belt, reached for his knapsack, and was just standing up when a man in a navy business suit dashed down the aisle toward them. Sargent knew where he was headed and he thumped back down, ignoring Weasel Man's curses. After stowing away his knapsack and rebuckling, he closed his eyes and waited for takeoff.

"People should be on time for their flights," Weasel Man said. "Are you from Fredericton?"

Sargent opened his eyes and shook his head. "New York City."

"Of course—you're wearing black. Everyone in New York City wears black."

Sargent glanced at his hoodie, jeans, and Vans: all black. Black was simple, and way cooler than the uniform he was forced to wear at private school.

"I'm from Shropshire, though you can hardly hear it in my accent. I live in Geneva now."

"Switzerland?"

The man nodded. "You must go. It's a wonderful city."

"Cool." Sargent leaned back as the airplane raced down the runway and thundered into the sky. Maybe Weasel Man would be quiet now that they were in the air.

No such luck. "Why is a lad from New York City going to Fredericton?"

"My dad lives there."

"Interesting. What does he do?"

"He's the director at the Beaverbrook Art Gallery." Normally the mention of an art gallery ended conversations. Then Sargent remembered the paint stains and held his breath.

Weasel Man flashed a genuine smile. "This is a coincidence. I'm going to Fredericton to work at the Beaverbrook Art Gallery this summer."

Of course he was. "Oh yeah?"

Weasel Man stuck out his hand. "Archibald Sneely." Sargent took the sweaty hand, and they exchanged a limp handshake.

"Sargent Singer."

"Your name is Sargent Singer?"

"Yup." Sargent waited for the other shoe to drop.

"Your parents named you Sargent Singer, after the artist John Singer Sargent?"

"Uh-huh." Adults, especially those in the art world, always made a big deal out of his name. It sucked. Luckily, kids his own age usually had no idea who John Singer Sargent was. He watched Sneely's face and waited for the novelty to pass. To change the subject, he decided to ask his own question. "So, what are you doing at the Beaverbrook?"

"I'm an art restorer. Your father has wanted me to come for a while, but I'm booked two or three years in advance. It's finally his turn. I'll be restoring five of the gallery's masterpieces."

"Cool."

"I'm like Dr. Frankenstein—I bring paintings back to life!" Sneely guffawed, slapping his bony knee.

Sargent swore he could hear spooky organ music in the background. "I paint. Last summer I studied at the Sorbonne in Paris."

"I am impressed, Mr. Singer. How old are you, anyway?"

"I'll be thirteen in November."

"If you were at the Sorbonne when you were eleven, you must be gifted. You should come observe me at work. Perhaps I can convince you to abandon painting for art restoration."

Sargent nodded and closed his eyes, lulled by the plane's white noise. Soon enough he woke with a start to the shudder of the airplane's wheels hitting the tarmac. Sneely was peering out the window at a buff-colored brick building.

The pilot's voice crackled over the intercom. "Welcome to Fredericton!"

There was no going back now. As the other passengers gathered up their things, chatting amiably to one another, Sargent began to chew at a ragged cuticle. Isaac would be waiting for him right inside those doors. He hadn't seen Isaac—except on FaceTime—in six months. Had he made a mistake coming here?

CHAPTER FIVE

When Isaac had first moved to Fredericton, Sargent had to look it up on Google Earth, because who'd ever heard of New Brunswick, Canada? Except for the one time he'd been forced to accompany Isaac to Albuquerque to see his dying grandmother, their visits had always occurred in New York City. Isaac would fly in for a day or two of uncomfortable bonding, then leave. So it had surprised Sargent when, during Isaac's Christmas visit, he'd insisted that Sargent's summer belonged to him.

"He's twelve years old, Sarah!" Sargent had overheard Isaac tell his mother as they stood in the exquisitely decorated foyer waiting for Sargent, who was going with

Isaac to a hockey game. "I've paid my dues. Sargent's growing up. He needs his father. And I've proven myself to you, haven't I? Enough is enough. I'll take you to court if I have to."

Sargent, hidden in the shadows of the living room, held his breath. This was just like the other awful conversation he'd overheard when he was eight years old. What kind of dues had Isaac paid? He waited for his mother to argue. When she did not, when she called for him instead, he shuffled forward. Only seven feet of expensive Oriental carpeting divided his parents, but it might have been an ocean with Sargent in the middle as an uncharted island.

"You can have him for the summer," she'd whispered. Then she had fled, leaving Sargent to follow a jubilant Isaac out the door.

Now here he was, wondering how he'd survive eight weeks in the middle of nowhere with a man he barely knew.

"Is your father picking you up?" Sneely asked, bringing Sargent back to the present.

"I guess so."

"Perfect, he can bring me into town, too. Save the gallery the price of a taxicab."

Great. More time with Sneely. Following the crowd

into the terminal, Sargent caught sight of Isaac and hesitated, all prickles and gawkiness in the midst of happy reunions. Isaac pulled him into a tight hug that lasted too long. When Sargent was finally able to escape, he realized he was looking straight into his father's eyes.

"You grew!" Isaac said, delighted.

Self-conscious, Sargent blushed, as if growing was a skill he'd mastered since he'd last seen Isaac. He'd forgotten all about Sneely until a phlegmy throat cleared itself nearby.

"Isaac Singer?" Sneely said, shoving his hand between father and son.

"Yes . . ."

"Archibald Sneely." Isaac looked confused, but then the name registered, and he took Sneely's hand.

"Of course, of course . . . that's right. I knew you were arriving today!"

"Not only have I arrived, I was fortunate enough to sit with your fine lad, who, I might add, was so considerate as to offer your assistance in getting me to my hotel." Before Isaac could respond, Sneely added, "My suitcase is the vintage Louis Vuitton. I must excuse myself and visit the loo. I'll meet you gentlemen out front." And then he was gone, leaving Isaac and Sargent staring at each other beside the baggage carousel.

"Odd duck," Isaac said. "Although the last one was from Romania and he was odd, too. Do you know what a Louis Vuitton suitcase looks like?"

Despite Sneely's insistence that Sargent sit up front with Isaac, this proved impossible, thanks to Sneely's storklike limbs, which could not be folded into the coupe's back seat.

"The curse of the tall," Sneely said as he took a seat next to Isaac and pulled out his phone. "I shall make it up to you, young Sargent—I promise."

Isaac had chosen a route that skirted the St. John River, a wide azure ribbon flanked on either side by a sea of trees: furry spruce, prickly pine, maples painted in every hue on the color wheel between green and maroon. Here and there a lone elm reached upward, its soaring branches reminding Sargent of the arched columns in the cathedrals he'd visited in France. While Central Park had lots of trees, it seemed to Sargent that New Brunswick was nothing but trees. He imagined mixing dozens of shades of green to do the scene justice.

"Gorgeous, huh?" his father asked over his shoulder. "They call Fredericton the City of Stately Elms. There are tens of thousands of trees all over the city. Did you have a good flight?"

"I had to get up at five o'clock." Sargent cursed how petty he sounded.

"Who drove you—Mom or Bill?"

"Both. Bill's mother is visiting so she stayed with the girls."

"That must have been an interesting drive." When Sargent didn't respond, there was an awkward pause. "Grade six went okay?"

"Seventh grade."

"Right, right. Wow, seventh grade already. Time flies. Your sisters are well?"

"Yes." Because Sargent and Isaac rarely saw each other, their conversations always followed the same pattern: school, Ainsley and Ashley, art.

"Are you still working with your art teacher, Mr. Leon?"

"Mr. Leonard. Twice a week."

"That's fantastic."

An uncomfortable silence settled between them now that Isaac had exhausted his topics. Sargent wished Sneely would stop texting and start talking again. He was odd, but lively.

"We're close to the gallery now," Isaac finally said. "This is Waterloo Row. I don't live far from here, only a couple of blocks from the gallery in an apartment in an old house. This street is considered the most desirable real estate in the city, thanks to the river and the Green, which stretches for miles."

His comment caused Sneely to look up. To their left, stately houses lined several blocks, but it was the view to the right that explained why people wanted to live here. A grassy swath ran parallel with the river, its trees thinned to expose sparkling water and to make room for a pedestrian walkway. Everywhere he looked, Sargent saw people running, strolling, and biking.

"Very pretty," Sneely said.

The car dipped below an underpass, and when it emerged Isaac pointed to the right. "There it is—the Beaverbrook Art Gallery!" He pulled into a metered parking spot in front of the building so his passengers could take a good look. Sargent rolled down his window and stuck his head out.

The Beaverbrook wasn't huge—at least not compared to the major galleries in New York City and Paris—but there was something about how the architect had situated it high on an embankment beside the river, forcing visitors to look up as they approached, that was impressive. The building itself looked like a series of connected boxes built of sandy bricks interrupted here and there by tall banks of windows. Two sets of wide concrete steps led to a recessed entryway, over which BEAVERBROOK ART GALLERY 1958 was spelled out in steel.

Isaac pointed to a building to the left. "There's your hotel, Mr. Sneely." He hopped out and went around to the trunk to get the art restorer's luggage. Sneely climbed out and grabbed his suitcase.

"I'll have my secretary—her name is Martine— schedule us a meeting for later this afternoon," Isaac said. "Unless you'd prefer we wait until first thing tomorrow morning so you can rest?"

Sneely looked appalled. "I don't do mornings. If you don't mind, I'd like to go in now and take a look around."

"Right now?" asked Isaac. "I'd sort of planned a lunch for Sargent. Why don't you check in at the hotel and I'll meet you back here in an hour?"

Seeing the scowl on Sneely's face, Sargent climbed out of the car. "It's okay. I'd like to take a quick look myself. We can eat lunch afterward." He hoped Isaac couldn't hear his gurgling stomach.

Isaac gave him a grateful nod and dug around in his pocket for some change to put in the parking meter. Then Isaac and Sargent followed Sneely, who was dragging his suitcase up the front steps. It was time to see the gallery. Sargent hoped it wasn't too lame. Fredericton was small, after all; he shouldn't expect anything remarkable.

CHAPTER SIX

Mona liked where she lived in the Beaverbrook. She hung in the Harriet Irving Gallery, the room to the right of the gallery's entrance. Thanks to her location, she always knew when tour groups arrived, could overhear staff conversations (and juicy gossip), and was often the first painting visitors saw. The only downside was that the constant traffic allowed little opportunity to relax her shoulders or take a few good blinks. Still, she was grateful for her prime spot when she heard Director Singer introduce his son and the art restorer to his assistant curator, Janice Hayes. Finally, something exciting was happening! Janice was prone to nervous laughter, and judging from the giggles that floated like soap bubbles into Mona's gallery, meeting Sargent and Sneely was almost more than she could bear.

"The gallery has two levels." Director Singer was saying. "We're on the main level, which has six galleries: the Canadian Gallery to our left, the Orientation Gallery and the McCain Gallery straight ahead, and to our right, the Harriet Irving Gallery, the Sir Max Aitken Gallery, the Vaulted Gallery, and the Hosmer Pillow Vaughan Gallery. I always start with the Harriet Irving Gallery," he said, stepping into Mona's gallery.

Mona had expected Director Singer's son to be younger, so she was startled by the lanky boy who trailed his father around the corner. He looked like Director Singer, though his dark eyes, too-long hair that needed taming, and black clothing struck Mona as mysterious.

As he often did, Director Singer pointed to her portrait first. "Mona Dunn, my golden girl. You know her father was originally from New Brunswick?"

Sneely shook his head while Sargent stepped forward and read the small sign attached to the wall next to her portrait. "William Orpen. British, 1878–1931. *Mona Dunn*, 1915. Oil on canvas." He stepped back. "She's so lifelike."

"Ah, the Orpen." Sneely turned to Sargent. "One of the paintings I'm restoring."

Mona was used to being defined by the artist who'd painted her. William Orpen was renowned for his portraits of the rich and famous, and she'd spent several hilarious days with him during her sitting back in 1915. None of that showed in the painting, however; Orpen had insisted she look enigmatic, like the other Mona—Mona Lisa.

"Someday you'll be just as famous," he'd told her and her parents when he'd unveiled the final portrait. That day had yet to arrive.

"You said her dad was born in New Brunswick?" Sargent asked, eyes still fixed on Mona. His gaze was so intense, it was hard for Mona to keep her composure. Most people looked at her with glassy-eyed stares before moving on to the next painting. Who was this strange boy?

Isaac nodded. "Sir James Dunn was born three hours north of here, in Bathurst. He was a wealthy industrialist and a friend of Beaverbrook's."

Sneely looked around. "Ah yes, Sir James Dunn. I understand the gallery has several portraits of him: two by Walter Sickert, two by Salvador Dalí—impressive."

Isaac smiled. "It is impressive, isn't it? We're very proud of them. Unfortunately, those paintings aren't here this summer. They, and the Dalí portrait of Dunn's wife, are on loan."

Sneely tsked, then slunk closer to Mona, his pointy chin almost touching the canvas. "Dunn chose excellent artists. Orpen was at the top of his game when he painted this girl."

Isaac beamed at Mona. "Mona Dunn was the apple of her father's eye. She was thirteen years old when this portrait was painted. I've heard she owned thirty-five horses."

"Whoa, she must have been rich," Sargent said. "I like how Orpen painted her."

"I do, too," Isaac said. "He surrounded Mona with darkness so we'd be drawn to her."

"What happened to the real Mona?" Sargent asked.

A cloud passed over Isaac's face. "She grew up and married, had a child, was considered the most beautiful girl in England in her day. But then she died tragically at age twenty-six."

Sargent sucked in his breath. "How'd she die?"

"From peritonitis, which is an inflammation of the abdomen caused by bacteria. It was common in those days and led to organ failure."

Sargent winced, which pleased Mona. She was always thrilled to hear the story of the original Mona, even the part about her death. It was romantic and tragic, but best of all, theoretical, since Mona in the gallery was forever thirteen years old. Mona in the painting would live on indefinitely, if cared for properly.

Sneely stepped back. "She needs a good cleaning— see those minor abrasions here and there? If you like her now, Sargent, just wait till I'm done. She'll go from good to excellent."

Mona bristled at the man's arrogance. She wasn't looking forward to being restored, even if it would be nice to be upgraded from good to excellent in the quarterly condition reports Director Singer had to prepare for every painting as part of his chief curator duties.

Barney Templeton, the museum's janitor, slipped into the gallery. Mona liked Barney—he was shy and pleasant. He'd almost made it across the room when Isaac spotted him.

"Barney, come meet my son and the art restorer who'll be working here this summer." The janitor put down his bucket and, wiping his hands across the front of his coveralls as he came, hurried over.

"Hullo," he said, extending a hand to Sargent and Sneely in turn.

"Mr. Sneely is one of the finest restorers in the world," Isaac said. Sneely and Barney bobbed their heads at each other.

Barney smiled at Sargent. "We've heard all about you.

I hope you enjoy Fredericton."

Sneely headed toward Edmund's portrait with greedy eyes. "I'd prefer to explore the gallery alone," he called over his shoulder. "I want to feel entranced when I examine the artwork, not distracted."

It was all Mona could do not to wrinkle her nose at the man's rudeness. She could tell from the way Sargent's eyes bugged out that he shared her opinion.

"Um, certainly," said Isaac. "We'll catch up later." Sneely did not respond.

Mona watched Director Singer and his son leave, biting back a sigh. Sargent Singer seemed interesting, and was obviously named after John Singer Sargent, the painter of her favorite piece in the gallery, *San Vigilio, Lake Garda*. She hoped he'd come back soon.

The midafternoon tour was the most trying at the gallery. By three o'clock tempers flared, especially within families, worn out after long car rides or visits to shopping malls and water parks. Children, forced to experience culture by well-meaning parents, were shuffled from room to room, the refrain "Don't touch!" ringing in their heads. The guides, or docents as they were more properly called, tried to remain chipper, but at three o'clock, it was difficult.

Sargent, who had returned to the gallery after lunch, decided to take the tour while he waited for his father's meeting with Sneely to end. Though Sargent was actually interested in the tour, by the very first painting, *Santiago El Grande*, he was already regretting his decision.

"That guy on the horse is naked, Buzz," a young boy who Sargent guessed to be about seven years old, squealed to his older brother.

"Look Bernard — his feet are dirty. I bet they stink!" offered Buzz, reaching to put a sticky hand on the canvas.

"Don't touch the paintings, boys." Amy the docent sounded on the verge of tears.

"Listen to the lady, boys," barked their father, a balding man of indeterminate age, whose wrinkles were a stark contrast to his Taylor Swift T-shirt. "Behave, or no movie!"

Bernard ignored the hollow threat. "The other guy flying there, the guy with all the gold stuff around him, he looks like he's wearing a diaper!"

"I bet he's got the squirts," was Buzz's delightful addition to Bernard's thoughtful analysis.

"It's not a diaper," muttered Sargent as Amy launched into the historical and religious significance of the painting. He knew Amy was wasting her time. It was easy to imagine a later scene where the boys were sprawled out on the hotel bed playing video games, complaining about how dull the gallery was except for that painting of "the dude in the diaper."

Amy shepherded the group around the corner and into the Harriet Irving Gallery. Sargent smiled when he saw Mona again. He took a seat on a nearby bench to study her.

"How much longer is this stupid tour?" Buzz was clearly on his last legs, and they were only at the second painting.

"Um, about thirty minutes more," said Amy.

The brothers marched over to Sargent and plopped down beside him.

"Who are you?" Bernard demanded as Amy happily began to walk the father around the room without the boys in tow.

"Sargent." He continued to stare at Mona, hoping they'd realize he had no interest in talking to them.

"Sergeant, like in the army? I have a whole box full of soldiers at home."

"Yeah, we shoot and kill everything!" Buzz added, pulling out an imaginary rifle, aiming it at the paintings, and picking them off one by one.

"It's spelled S-A-R-G-E-N-T, not S-E-R-G-E-A-N-T."

"That's stupid," Bernard said, wiping his nose on his T-shirt. "Couldn't your ma spell?"

Sargent swallowed the urge to shove Bernard off the bench. "Of course she could spell."

"I wish I was named Sergeant," Bernard said. "When I grow up I'm going to be in the army and kill people."

"Great."

Bernard beamed, having completely missed the sarcasm in Sargent's voice.

"I'm going to be a truck driver," said Buzz. "Next vacation Dad's taking us to the monster truck races, which'll be way better than this stupid place."

"He's right," Bernard said. "This place sucks."

Buzz pointed at Mona. "It does suck. Look—even that stupid girl in the picture there thinks it sucks. Hey, lady!" he yelled at Amy, who winced. "You should let this girl out. She hates it here! Can we go now, Dad?"

Fortunately, the father nodded. "Thank you, miss. I think we'll cut this short. There's a hot tub at the hotel that's calling my name."

"You're welcome," Amy said, trying not to appear too thrilled. "I'll just walk them out and be right back," she said to Sargent. "Okay?"

"See ya!" Buzz hollered. He stuck his tongue out at Mona and chased Bernard out of the room, hollering that he would too climb the leopard statue outside, even if it was against the rules.

Sargent watched them go with relief, happy to continue the tour with Amy alone. Out of the corner of his left eye he sensed something moving. He turned in time to catch Mona Dunn sticking out her tongue at the receding backs of Bernard and Buzz and gasped, as did she. A blink of the eye later, she'd returned to her normal pose. Shaking, Sargent stood up and approached the portrait. Everything looked normal. Thinking this was some kind of practical joke, he peeked around the side of the frame, looking for a hidden camera. There was none.

Whistling, he sauntered out of the room, then ducked back in quickly to try to catch Mona moving again. She did not. He positioned himself in front of her and made a series of funny faces to see if he could get a reaction. No reaction. Finally he gave up and stared at her in wonder. Had he imagined it? And if he hadn't, what did that mean? Was Mona Dunn alive?

CHAPTER SEVEN

It was nine o'clock that same night. Frank Stewart, the gallery's rotund security guard, was settled in front of his bank of security cameras, listening to a baseball game on the radio. Every hour on the hour, Frank walked the gallery, and in between, he watched the cameras for signs of intruders. What he didn't watch were the paintings. After twenty years on the job, they were old hat to him, although their staring eyes still creeped him out.

Truth was, Frank never glanced at the paintings as he made his rounds, and the residents knew it. Still, they were careful not to move when he walked past, and since the cameras didn't record sound, the residents were able to speak freely so long as Frank was in his office. No, Frank was only interested in intruders, and so he did not notice that the entire Cotterell family, along with Edmund and Juliette, were bunched around Mona in her portrait.

"Whatever will you do, Mona?" Lady Cotterell asked in despair, moving baby Frances from one hip to the other. "You have been found out!"

Mona drooped. She'd come close to being caught several times over the years—hadn't they all? It wasn't uncommon for the paintings to show their boredom or frustration when the visitors' backs were turned. It was dangerous, but the thrill made the dreaded three o'clock tour bearable. But this was the first time someone had seen her move. It was disastrous.

"I bet the director's son thinks he imagined you sticking out your tongue," Clem said, trying to be helpful.

His mother shook her head. "Did you not see how he peered at her afterward, all the faces he made, the way he tried to look behind her painting? Clearly he suspects something."

Madame Juliette placed her arm around Mona's sagging shoulders. "I heard him tell Janice he was exhausted. After a good night's sleep, he will blame what he saw on being tired."

Edmund nodded. "That's it exactly!"

"Maybe he'll think the gallery's haunted," Lizzie Cotterell offered.

"Or that he's gone crazy," young Charles Cotterell added.

"Thank you for trying to cheer me up," Mona said. "But I have placed us in grave peril."

"Indeed, you have not!" Edmund protested. "The situation is unfortunate, but hardly catastrophic. He is young; if he shares what he has seen, his father will think he is telling tales."

"Maybe he'll be too scared to stay in Fredericton," said Clem. He pushed through the group and stood at the edge of the frame, absentmindedly running his fingers along its elaborate gilt. "Hey, I'm going for a walk. I'm sick of being cooped up."

"Whose painting will you visit, Clement?" his mother demanded.

"I thought I'd go see Madame Rubinstein," he said. Madame Rubinstein was Helena Rubinstein, a Polish émigré famous for creating a cosmetics empire. She loved children, and the tables in her portrait were always covered with the most delectable sweets.

"You won't tell her about what happened, will you?" Mona said.

"Course not—I'm no snitch. Why don't you come with me, stop moping?"

"Maybe," said Mona. Really though, all she wanted was to be alone.

"Take your brother and sisters, Clement," his mother said. "I simply must have a respite." She looked over at Sir Charles, who was staring into space, wholeheartedly disinterested in Mona's woes and only present because of his wife's nagging. "Sir Charles, shall we take a turn?"

He nodded, clearly desperate to escape the cramped portrait. With cries of "Good luck!" and "Don't worry!," the Cotterell family departed.

"Do buck up," Edmund said, patting Mona on the head. "He struck me as an affable chap. Even if he does suspect you are alive, I'm sure he will not break your confidence. That would be most ungentlemanly!" Nothing outraged Edmund more than a loose tongue.

"But I broke the most important rule. . . ."

"Accidentally," said Juliette in her most soothing voice.

"It doesn't matter." Mona's voice was barely above a whisper. "Don't you see? Max has kept us safe all these years, thanks to his rules. And I broke the most important one. 'Under no circumstances are residents to interact with humans or move about when there are humans in the building.' I was cross at those boys for mocking me. I let my vanity get in the way of our safety. Really, I must go and confess to Max immediately."

"You shall do no such thing!" Edmund thundered. "The Cotterells will not break your confidence, nor shall we. This will blow over with no one the wiser. Now," he commanded, pulling Mona to her feet. "You must engage in vigorous exercise to take your mind off today's misfortune. Juliette and I were planning on taking a walk. Will you not join us?"

Mona managed a half-hearted smile. "You are kind! But I thought I'd go sit on the pier—"

"At *San Vigilio, Lake Garda*," Juliette finished for her. "That is a fine idea, chérie. There is nothing so comforting as being outside when one is feeling out of sorts."

Mona followed her friends out of the frame. They took a left, while she veered right, hurrying in the direction of the one place in the gallery that always cheered her up.

For as long as she could remember, the pier in John Singer Sargent's *San Vigilio, Lake Garda* had been Mona's special place. Her father had taken Mona and her brother, Philip, to Lake Garda for a fishing trip in 1911, and it had been one of the happiest weeks of her life. Stepping into the painting, she paused, as she always did, to drink in the shimmery blues, greens, and golds of the water. She waved at the two Italian women in the distance, who spent their days swapping stories and recipes.

Signoras Rossi and Bianchi had lived away from Italy for more than a hundred years, and yet they still had learned only a handful of English, the most widely spoken language of the Beaverbrook Art Gallery, despite Max's request that all residents learn enough English to communicate with one another. Mona thought there was something rather sweet about their dedication to the old ways. In the decades since she'd arrived at the gallery, Mona had taken it upon herself to learn their language, along with French, Spanish, and a little Portuguese. Signoras Rossi and Bianchi appreciated her efforts and always rewarded her with biscotti and other delicious treats.

Mona sat on the stony pier and dangled her feet in the lake, trying to decide if she should grab a fishing pole. As she stared at the lapping waves, a ridiculous thought presented itself to her: did Sargent Singer like to fish? Horrified, she shut her eyes, but there was no escaping the memory of him staring with such intensity at her portrait, making those funny faces, looking at her as if she was alive. That was the worst, him looking at her as if she were a real person. A human being had not looked at her like that in more than a hundred years, and for some inexplicable reason, that caused a sharp pain in her chest. Sighing, she stretched out on her back and watched the clouds float by. In the distance, gulls called. Waves slapped against the stones with a slosh. It was peaceful and it was lonely. She closed her eyes and slept.

It was dusk when Sargent and Isaac emerged from the restaurant where they'd gone for supper. The meal had been good, but Sargent was drained by Isaac's attempts at conversation. He'd lost count of the awkward silences and the number of times Isaac had asked if he liked his chicken. Plus, the Mona Dunn incident was freaking him out.

"I suppose you're wondering what you're going to do all day while I'm at work, huh?" Isaac said. They'd crossed Queen Street and were making their way down to the Green for an after-dinner stroll along the river. "I'm afraid I don't have any vacation until August."

Sargent hadn't wondered, so he said nothing. He'd expected to spend his days sleeping in, surfing the net, and watching TV, reading the odd book and doing some drawing for good measure.

When Sargent didn't respond, Isaac kept going. "The Beaverbrook offers four weeklong summer sessions every July."

Sargent slowed to a stop and looked warily at his father. No way could he do this.

Isaac sensed his reluctance. "Look, I know you've

been studying for years and you have tons of talent, but it would give you something to do—"

"With kids who aren't interested in art?"

Isaac took a breath, his voice strained when he responded. "In fact, a lot of the kids are talented. And we have excellent instructors here in Fredericton. Including me."

Sargent flinched. He could tell he'd offended Isaac. But he couldn't share the real reason he didn't want to participate: summer camp was the worst. It always seemed like everybody but him already had friends and someone to sit with at lunch. But as awful as eating by himself was, the instructors fussing over him was way worse. "Let's see how Sargent tackled this exercise!" rewarded him with nothing but exasperation from the other kids. Except for Paris last summer, Sargent had refused to attend summer camp for years. But telling Isaac the truth wasn't an option. He'd have to suck it up, even if it meant July would be the worst month ever.

"Sorry. You're right," he whispered.

The heaviness between them lifted. Isaac beamed. "I promise you'll have a blast."

Sargent pictured endless lonely and boring days and managed a nod.

"And hey—you know what else?"

"What?" Please don't let it be worse than summer camp, he thought.

"At the end of every week, the campers have a sleepover in the gallery. We'll watch movies and play games. How cool is that—nighttime at the museum!"

Even though the idea of hanging out all night with kids who didn't like him was a nightmare, the idea of spending the night in an art gallery was intriguing. "Cool," he said, trying to sound enthusiastic.

They began to walk again, but this time the silence was comfortable. Soon they arrived at the Beaverbrook. "You know, I really love working here," said Isaac. "A gallery this size has endless possibilities, and the paintings are world-class."

"Yeah, I can't believe they have a John Singer Sargent and that amazing Dalí."

"Impressive, huh? Do you mind if we pop in for a second? I need to get a document."

Sargent followed his father to the back door and watched him swipe his security pass over a metallic box. There was an electronic beep, and they stepped inside. As Isaac veered right toward his office, Sargent pointed to the stairs.

"Can I wander around?"

Isaac looked uncomfortable.

He thinks I'm some little kid, Sargent thought. "I promise I won't touch anything. Mom lets me explore the Met by myself."

Isaac winced at the mention of Sarah. "Fine. I won't be long anyway. Just make some noise so the ghosts know you're coming."

Sargent's mind flashed to Mona sticking out her tongue. "Is the Beaverbrook haunted?"

The expression on Isaac's face was unreadable. "My office was actually Lord Beaverbrook's bedroom when the museum first opened. Some people say he still walks the galleries now and then, keeping an eye on things. You never know. . . ."

It was a code red. The word spread from painting to painting like a wildfire: everyone back to their paintings—NOW. Luckily, Sargent had plugged in his music. Had he not, he would have heard the residents' scurrying and rustling as he climbed the stairs to the main level. He knew that museums turned off the lights after hours in order to protect the artwork, but it was still creepy to walk through the galleries with only the dim after-hours light fixtures in the hallway to guide him. At one point, he was sure he sensed something moving, but when he turned to look, the man in the painting—ANDRE REIDMOR, the sign on the wall beside him read—was perfectly still.

Edmund had seen Juliette home, despite her protestations that such chivalrous behavior was unnecessary given the circumstances, but cursed his own gentlemanly ways when he caught sight of Sargent walking along the hallway toward him. Wearing a bright red uniform and living in an immense frame was proving to be most inconvenient; his absence would be noted right away. He was furious that Max had not warned them that Director Singer and his son might return that evening.

He hurled himself into his painting just as Sargent entered the gallery and managed to get himself sorted out before Sargent looked up. Of course—the boy was back to see Mona. He glanced across the room toward her portrait and almost cried out. Mona was missing!

CHAPTER EIGHT

Sargent couldn't breathe. How could the portrait of Mona Dunn be empty? He circled the gallery, checking to see if anyone else was missing. Something seemed off about the Cotterell family painting. Had Lady Cotterell always held a rose? Was the baby supposed to face left or right? Mostly he tried to come up with a reasonable explanation for Mona's absence. Maybe Sneely had taken the painting to be restored and the gallery had hung another canvas with a similar background in its place. He laughed out loud, relieved. *You're just tired and feeling weird about coming to Fredericton. It was time to look at something else.*

San Vigilio, Lake Garda hung at the very end of the Vaulted Gallery, and Sargent approached it slowly, thrilled to finally see it in person. From a few feet away, a funny shape on the pier in the painting caught his eye. He stepped closer and leaned in to see what it was, then jumped back. Mona Dunn was curled up on the pier, fast asleep. Which was impossible. He squeezed his eyes shut and reopened them. She was still there.

He watched, spellbound, as her small chest rose and fell, accompanied by faint snores that reminded him of the sound made by baby birds. In books, people pinched themselves to make sure they weren't dreaming, so he gave it a try. Nothing changed, which led him to one fantastical conclusion: Mona Dunn was alive and able to leave her painting. How this could be, he had no idea. He needed to find Isaac. Someone else needed to know about this.

Just then, Mona opened her eyes, saw Sargent's enormous (to her) black ones staring at her, and cried out. Shocked, Sargent yelped and jumped back. Mona scrambled backward on the pier, coming dangerously close to the edge on the other side.

"Watch out! You're going to fall in!" cried Sargent.

Mona caught herself in time, never taking her eyes off Sargent.

Heart thumping, Sargent held up his hand. "I'm sorry I scared you."

Mona scooted forward and began to pull on her stockings and shoes. "You startled me," she corrected. She stopped tying a shoe to look up at Sargent. "Please . . . promise me you won't tell a soul you saw me here. I will be in such trouble!"

Could he keep this secret from his dad?

Mona could tell he was hesitating. She stood up and tried again. "No one knows about us."

"Us" implied that more paintings than Mona Dunn's were alive. "No one knows" meant that Sargent had just uncovered one of the world's greatest secrets. What would everyone think if they found out that paintings were alive? How excited would his dad be? But the desperation in Mona's eyes and voice couldn't be ignored.

"I won't tell."

Mona's shoulders relaxed, and the smile she gave him was genuine.

"Thank you. I must go now."

"Wait—will I see you again?"

"I don't know!" she called over her shoulder as she ran to the frame and disappeared.

Stunned, Sargent stared at *San Vigilio, Lake Garda*. One

minute she'd been there, the next she was gone. How would she get back to her painting? In the distance, he heard Isaac call his name and jumped. As he ran toward the stairwell, he veered left and peeked into Mona's gallery. She was back in her portrait, seemingly lifeless. He ran for the stairs, not noticing the shadowy figure watching him from the painting in the Orientation Gallery.

"There you are," Isaac said when Sargent rejoined him at the bottom of the stairs. His satchel was stuffed with papers. He caught Sargent staring at them and groaned. "I have to finish my speech for a fund-raiser the gallery's hosting this weekend. I need to add some statistics, help people understand how important the gallery is, how helpful their donations will be."

Sargent raised a skeptical eyebrow. "You think statistics will get people excited?"

Isaac laughed. "Don't look at me like that! I just need to figure out a way to increase the gallery's revenues, that's all. Costs are going up, and we need more money for programming and exhibits. Actually, the gallery is having serious financial issues, and I'm under a lot of pressure from the board to turn that around. I hope the fund-raiser will help."

Sargent pictured Mona Dunn sleeping on the pier. If people knew that the paintings at the Beaverbrook Art Gallery were alive, you'd have to beat them away with a stick. The gallery would never have to worry about money again.

CHAPTER NINE

The code red was over, but everyone stayed in their paintings. Mona wasn't surprised. By now, everyone in the gallery must know she'd been caught out of her frame. They were probably holding their collective breath, waiting to see what Max would do. There would be consequences. She wasn't surprised when Dusk arrived.

"The Boss wants you." Dusk flashed a simpering smile, enjoying the role of messenger.

Mona eyed him with distaste. She'd spent the last sixty years giving Dusk a wide berth. Dusk was akin to a fine gray mist, apt to show up at any time and spoil a lovely day. He blended in with the rabbits' warren of passageways and portals that crisscrossed the space behind the frames. It was impossible to count the number of times he'd simply materialized out of nowhere. She wasn't about to go anywhere with him, especially tonight.

"Tell him I'll be along soon," she said, trying to ignore his intense stare.

He bowed deeply. "I wouldn't keep him waiting. He's in a mood."

Mona's father had taught her early about the importance of hiding one's emotions. "You mustn't show weakness," he'd told her one soggy afternoon in 1912, when she'd been tossed from a feisty mare. "If the horse senses your fear, she'll know she's in charge. Only one of you can be in control, Mona, and it must be you." When she'd protested, argued the horse was too large, he'd held up a hand. "Size means nothing. One stout heart can slay a hundred dragons." Later, after a successful ride, his only praise was, "One dragon down." She'd never forgotten the lesson.

"Max is just another dragon," she told herself now. She stood up, smoothed her dress, and gave a thumbs-up to Edmund and the Cotterells, who watched her with anxious expressions.

Appropriately, Max's portrait hung in the Sir Max Aitken Gallery, which opened off the Vaulted Gallery. When

Mona arrived, she heard him deep in conversation with Dusk and stepped back. No way was she talking to Max if Dusk was there. No, she'd wait in the painting next door, a good-sized canvas titled *Bacchanalian Piece: Sir Thomas Samwell and Friends*, until Dusk left. A masterpiece of the early eighteenth century, it was the gallery's equivalent of a party boat, and the raucous belly laughs emanating from the painting told her the party was in full swing. Thanks to the keen ears of Sir Thomas's faithful servant, Caesar, the rowdy partygoers had never been caught, and Mona often wondered how they kept their composure when Frank was on the move.

"Hey-ho, it's Miss Mona," Sir Thomas called as she stepped into the picture. "What brings you to my home on this fine evening, m'dear? John, have someone fetch a chair!"

John was Captain John Floyd, once an officer in the First Dragoon Guards, who obligingly hollered, "Chair!" Mona knew no chair would be forthcoming; none ever was, because the men could never remember to get one. The rest of the people at the table—Caesar; Parliamentarian John Neal; the two Williams, William Wilmer and William Piers; and General Louis deJean (affectionately called the Guitar General, as his guitar never strayed from his side)—were in no shape to find their own chairs, let alone one for Mona.

Mona curtsied. "Thank you, Sir Thomas, but it is unnecessary. I am waiting on Lord Beaverbrook, who is engaged at present. I thought it more pleasant to wait here with you."

Sir Thomas stood up, smoothed his silvery velvet britches and navy frock coat, and raised his glass. "Gentlemen, let us bestow our warmest welcome. To Miss Dunn!"

Glasses were raised like torches in the tranquil evening light. The group drank to Mona's health a dozen times. Hosting duties fulfilled, Sir Thomas hiccupped and sank into his chair.

"*Pourquoi est-ce que vous attendez Monsieur Aitken?*" General deJean inquired.

"I am waiting on Max because I am in a spot of trouble," Mona replied. Had the news not reached them?

Captain John eyed the ruby liquid in his glass with a crooked smile. "Come for your sentence, have you?"

"Pray tell us what you did, and we shall pass our own, friendlier, judgments," one of the Williams said. Mona was embarrassed to admit that after fifty years, she was still unsure if this was William Wilmer or William Piers. Really, it was poor manners on her part not to remember.

"Oh, do!" begged the other William. "We shall be infinitely fair!"

"I think I shall leave the task to Lord Beaverbrook," she said. "But I do have a question for you." Leaning forward and using her most conspiratorial whisper, she asked, "In the last three hundred years, have you ever heard tell of anyone who lived behind the frame being able to leave? You know, join the ones who do not live in paintings."

Captain deJean's eyes were sympathetic. "C'est un rêve, ma chérie. A dream." He set his guitar aside and took Mona's hand.

"Some wish to interact with those outside the frame," Caesar said, taking a melancholic sip of wine. "We come into our paintings with our original souls and memories, but sometimes it does not seem enough. I miss the real world at times. Alas, it is impossible to return."

"Do you not think Max is able to do it?" Mona asked. She'd often wondered how he knew everything that was going on at the Beaverbrook.

Caesar shook his head. "Max is larger than life, but he is not larger than his painting. No one can leave his painting."

They were interrupted by the arrival of Agnes, Madame Rubinstein's maid, who carried an invitation for the group to join her mistress for some good cheer.

"Hear, hear!" roared the table. The partygoers stood up, toasted Mona's excellent health, begged her to treat their table as if it were her own, and staggered away.

Mona had no intention of eavesdropping, but the sudden quiet, coupled with the raised voices next door, made it unavoidable.

"She must be sent away," Dusk was saying. "For her protection and our own!"

Max's growl reminded Mona of a pug she'd had as a girl. "I don't share your opinion."

"Pah! Your perspective is colored by affection. We have too much at stake. You will regret it if you ignore my advice."

"I often regret listening to your advice," Max countered.

Mona leaned closer. Were they talking about her?

"Bury your head in the sand if you like, Lord Beaverbrook, but mark my words: something very bad is afoot now that the boy knows Mona is alive. Now I'll leave, for you are irritated."

Mona shrank back into the shadows, lest Dusk choose to stop in at Sir Thomas's on his way by. He did not. Counting to fifty, she steadied her knocking knees and stepped into Max's painting.

CHAPTER TEN

Prior to meeting Mona, the only magic Sargent had believed in was his ability to draw and paint things that looked like exact copies of whatever his subject matter was. But now everything was different, including him. Suddenly, he'd become the keeper of the world's biggest secret. Unless there were other magical secrets. Who knew? Maybe Santa Claus and the Easter Bunny were real, too. He was never going to be able to look at the world in the same way.

His mind a tornado of questions and theories, he replayed his encounter with Mona over and over until he'd picked apart every moment. Around three o'clock in the morning, he gave up trying to sleep and turned on the light. He desperately wanted to wake Isaac, tell him what had happened; Mona's secret was so huge it was making him shaky. But he'd made a promise. He reached for his phone. There was a text from his mother reminding him to call her. He typed "OK" and hit send. Then he searched "haunted paintings." Maybe someone else had seen one, too.

There were lots of entries, but most were written by crackpots. The rest were movie plots or fan fiction. Paintings coming to life and tormenting people was a popular theme. Mona Dunn didn't strike him as the tormenting type. He scrolled on until another link caught his eye. It was a website that celebrated the uncanny. He wasn't sure what uncanny meant, so he looked it up. The definition gave him goose bumps, for it described uncanny as something mysterious, eerie, or supernatural in nature. Mona Dunn was uncanny, very uncanny.

He returned to the website and found an image of a magazine article from the 1950s. It was supposedly written by an anonymous art gallery director who refused to share his or her name or where they worked for fear they'd lose their job. Sargent read the article twice, his heart pounding. Whoever the author was, he'd experienced exactly what Sargent had experienced. The last part of the article sealed the deal.

At first it was mere whispers. I'd hear noises coming from the paintings and blame it on the air-conditioning, or my overtaxed imagination. Then late one night I returned unexpectedly to the gallery. I heard noises and went to investigate. I crept down the hallway and peeked around the corner. Half of the occupants of the paintings in my entire gallery were standing in one of the largest paintings, chatting and eating cake. It appeared to be someone's birthday. There was a rousing chorus of "For He's a Jolly Good Fellow," and several people, including one of Picasso's jesters, made a speech. It was as if I had happened upon a fairy circle, and it was all I could do to contain my impulse to step forward, announce my arrival, and join in the festivities. Instead, I backed away and left, shaken.

That night I went home and paced for hours. I am not a superstitious individual, nor am I prone to flights of fancy. In fact, I am a man of science, despite my love of all things creative. Surely there was a logical explanation for what I had seen, apart from the obvious—that I was losing my mental capacities. Then it hit me: I remembered my high-school physics and the first law of thermodynamics: energy cannot be created or destroyed; it can only be changed from one form to another.

I have come to believe that some of the artist's energy or the energy of the person or scene being painted is transformed into the painting at the time of its creation and lives on. There is no other explanation, save the hand of God, but as I have said, I am a man of science. Whether all original pieces of artwork are suffused with this energy, I do not know. Nor will I subject my own paintings to experimentation so I might prove *my theory. They deserve to live their lives, as I deserve to live mine. I am merely grateful that I was granted a glimpse into their world.*

Sargent read the article twice before turning off his phone. He knew, absolutely, that the author was correct. Hadn't he sometimes had a strange euphoric sensation when he was painting, especially when the work was going well? All that energy, all that concentration—it had to go somewhere, right?

Mona Dunn had said she would be in trouble if people found out about the paintings being alive. In trouble from whom—human beings or the other paintings? Then there was Isaac's comment about ghosts in the gallery. Maybe those ghost stories began when someone accidentally heard a painting speak or saw something unexpected in a painting, just like he had. Maybe all ghost stories were related to paintings being alive. The thought boggled his mind.

What would happen if people found out about the world that existed behind the frames? Would they be scared? Excited? People didn't always do the right thing. Sometimes people destroyed what they feared. He had to keep Mona's secret, do whatever he had to in order to keep her and the other paintings safe. And maybe, if was lucky, he might get to know her better.

CHAPTER ELEVEN

Max was occupied with paperwork when Mona entered his portrait. One of the true mysteries of the Beaverbrook Art Gallery was how the all-knowing Max conducted his business. After several long seconds, he removed his reading glasses and placed them and the papers on a nearby marble-topped table. His expression was serious, the usual Cheshire Cat grin absent.

"Kept me waiting, eh? Why'd you stop next door?"

Mona shrugged and flashed a sly smile. "Trying to avoid you for as long as possible, I suppose."

Max arched a bushy eyebrow.

She decided it was best to plunge in. "Look, Max. I am

dreadfully sorry about falling asleep and getting caught by Sargent Singer. I . . ."

Her voice trailed off when she saw the fury building on Max's face. She'd been in trouble before but had never felt afraid.

"Mona Dunn, this is a dangerous game you are playing." Max's eyes were cold, unyielding.

Mona blanched. "I don't know what you mean."

"I think you do."

"It was an accident!"

"Was it? You are a wild girl, and your father and I have allowed you freedoms that most girls your age would never have."

"What freedoms? I'm trapped in this art gallery and can't leave!" Even as Mona spoke, bitterness swelled up inside her, the bile of thousands of repetitive days.

Max studied his rough hands. When he looked up, his face had softened. "I'm sure it is difficult to be eternally thirteen, to live forever among the same people. It makes sense that you would long for other company and other experiences from time to time."

Mona said nothing.

"This gallery was my dream, Mona." He stared beyond her to the paintings that surrounded his own. "I wanted to give something back to New Brunswick, something special and important that would outlive me. I spent years choosing paintings, strong-arming friends for donations of cash and artwork. You know the original Max kept a bedroom here?"

Mona wondered where the story was going.

Max closed his eyes. "At first I was afraid to tell the original Max I was alive, but then I realized he would be pleased."

Mona's eyes narrowed, and she watched him as a mouse watches a cat. "Pleased?"

"Pleased that he—I—would live on long after his human body was spent, pleased that he would not be forgotten. And I was right. He was happy. But we both realized that the paintings must have rules to live by if they were to be safe, so we drafted them together on the very night I revealed myself to him. Until today, they have never been broken."

Despite the urge to hang her head in shame, Mona forced herself to keep eye contact with Max. "I told you, it was an accident," she said.

"In my experience, youthful exuberance does not always end well for the youth."

"Are you threatening me?"

"Consider it a warning. If you and the boy do not behave, I will have you sent you away."

Mona knew he could achieve this, though she had no idea how. White-hot tears pooled in her eyes, and she blinked them back. "You wouldn't dare! Papa would be furious!"

"Wouldn't I? It would be easy to send you to your father and stepmother for the summer."

"But I'm to be restored! I'm to stand up with Juliette at her wedding, I—"

"You are here at my pleasure, Mona Dunn. Never forget that."

Mona had seen evidence of Max's cruelty before but had never experienced it firsthand. There was poor W. Somerset Maugham, banished ten years ago to the basement workroom for some mysterious affront against Max. And hadn't her father shared stories of how Max's business successes often came at the expense of others?

Stunned, she stumbled toward the exit. She paused at the frame and looked back, desperate to show him she would not be broken. "I shall never forgive you, Lord Beaverbrook, not as long as I live. We are no longer friends."

Without reacting, Max picked up his papers and began to read again. A furious Mona departed, vowing to ignore Lord Beaverbrook, regardless of the cost.

Rules for the Residents of the Beaverbrook Art Gallery

As written by Max Aitken, Lord Beaverbrook, and the Portrait of Lord Beaverbrook, *night of August 12, 1959*

1. Under no circumstances are residents to interact with humans or move about when there are humans in the building.

2. Do not get caught outside your painting.

3. Do not go into someone else's painting without his or her permission.

4. Issues requiring attention are to be directed to the Portrait of Lord Beaverbrook.

5. Paintings wishing to travel between the main floor and the basement must pass through Santiago El Grande.

6. Failure to abide by these rules will result in punishment and possible banishment.

7. Rules subject to change without notice, as per the will of Lord Beaverbrook.

CHAPTER TWELVE

Sargent slept late. It was nearly noon when he opened his eyes, and it took him several seconds to register where he was. Right . . . Isaac's spare room. He dressed quickly, wandered out to the kitchen, and stopped. The apartment's walls were covered in artworks. Were they alive, too? Quaking, he gathered up the nerve to speak.

He began with a sketch of an old man sitting in a rocking chair. "Hello! Nice day, huh?"

No response.

"Um, hi, my name's Sargent. I'm staying here for a few weeks," he said to a painting of a woman arranging flowers.

Still nothing.

"Woof!" he barked at a Labrador retriever.

Were they afraid of him? He was about to try a young child sitting under a tree when he noticed a note on the kitchen table: *At work. Walk down for lunch.* He didn't have to be asked twice. He'd try again with the apartment paintings later.

It was nice that Isaac's apartment was only two blocks from the Beaverbrook. Five minutes later, he was standing at the front desk, chatting with Janice.

"Your dad says you've signed up for our summer sessions," Janice said, sounding kind of squeaky.

Thinking about camp started the butterflies again. "Yeah, I guess."

Janice studied his face for a moment before responding. "We're going to have a lot of fun. I promise. I mean, it's not Paris, but I guarantee you'll learn something."

Sargent's face burned. Why had Isaac told Janice that he'd gone to Paris last summer? Mortified, he looked around, his eyes resting on a Salvador Dalí mug on a shelf in the gift shop.

"I'm happy to have the chance to get to know you, Sargent. Your dad is so proud of you."

When he turned back to Janice, he noticed her neck was all pink and blotchy. "He's talked to you about me?"

"All the time. Anyway, I'm just glad you're here." Janice took a deep breath. "Your dad's out at a meeting but should be back any second. You can wait in his office." She pointed to the stairwell directly in front of her desk and handed him a security pass. "The basement level of the gallery is mostly staff space. There are two galleries to the right: the Oppenheimer Gallery, which kind of wraps itself around the education room where we'll have our sessions, and the Contemporary Gallery, where we'll have our sleepovers. To get to the staff area or the back door, you need to swipe through the security doors. There's a set to the left at the bottom of the stairs and another set off the Oppenheimer Gallery. If you use the closest doors, keep going straight down the hallway, past the kitchen and some workrooms, then turn right. You'll see your dad's secretary, Martine, at the end of the hall. If she's not there, go in. You can return the pass later."

Sargent was desperate to see Mona, but the rowdy laughter of a tour group stopped him from taking a detour. Downstairs, he spotted Barney sitting in the staff kitchen, nursing a mug of coffee.

He stuck his head in the door. "Hi, Barney!"

"Hiya, Sarge. Listen, if you ever want the real tour of the gallery, let me know."

Intrigued, Sargent stepped into the kitchen. "What do you mean, the real tour?"

"I mean the tour where I tell you all the deep dark secrets of the Beaverbrook Art Gallery. I've worked here for a quarter of a century. I know all about its gory past."

"Gory past" implied murders, mayhem, and other exciting possibilities. Maybe Barney knew the paintings were alive. "Cool. I'll try to find you later."

As Sargent stepped back into the hallway, Barney called after him. "Take a look in the workroom on your way by. Sneely's in there, and he's putting on quite a show."

It was easy to find the workroom. Sargent simply followed the bellowing.

"Don't they know that's not the brand I like?" Sneely was shouting. "And this—this is outrageous! This is art restoration, not car mechanics!"

Sargent knocked, was directed to enter, and found himself in a spacious workroom. The walls were lined with paint-splattered shelves stocked with rows of varnishes, paints, blank canvases of various sizes, and dozens of new and used brushes. A piece of art was tacked up in one corner. Straining, he saw it was a sketch of a man's head, the words *Study of WSM, Cap Ferrat (1953)* penciled beside the face.

"W. Somerset Maugham," Sneely said, an impressive

trick given he was rummaging in a packing crate. "Famous British novelist. I don't suppose you've read *The Razor's Edge?*"

"Nope."

Sneely stood up. "They always forget something, you know." His right arm swept the air. "I send a detailed list and they always forget something."

"What did they forget?"

Instead of responding, Sneely began to lay his restoration tools on the table with the precision of a surgeon in an operating room. These included Q-tips, brushes of every shape and length, skinny metal tools that looked like scalpels or what dental hygienists used to scrape your teeth. A strange-looking contraption that appeared to be half microscope, half ophthalmologist's machine was attached to the edge of the table. Sargent guessed its long arm must be able to pivot to wherever Sneely needed it to in order to better see the painting he was working on. A nearby easel held the *Merrymaking* painting.

"Does this need a lot of work?" Sargent asked, studying the diminutive figures in front of the inn. He especially liked the two men driving a sleigh; the horses were painted perfectly.

"No, which is why I'm starting with it first. I like to

begin with the easy ones, get a rhythm going. It needs cleaning, and I'll strengthen the canvas where it threatens to tear from age. I don't expect to have it here for more than three days, unless I get an unexpected surprise."

"What do you mean?"

"In my experience, the paintings themselves show me what needs to be done," Sneely said, adjusting the arm of his microscopelike machine. "A good art restorer listens to his paintings."

Was Sneely being serious? Now that Sargent knew Mona was alive, he couldn't help but wonder if anyone else at the gallery knew as well. "They talk to you?" he said, trying to sound casual.

Sneely scooped up some brushes and guffawed. "That's a good one."

Trying to hide his embarrassment, Sargent leaned over the table. A canvas with the unmistakable perspective lines of *Merrymaking* sat in the center.

"What's that?"

"I always sketch a rough copy of the painting I'm working on. Sometimes I even paint the copy if the work is complicated. *Merrymaking* is straightforward, so it won't be necessary."

"That's a lot of extra work."

"Work is my middle name. Off you go. I've given you

your first lesson; now I must listen to Merrymaking."

Sargent could hear Sneely's obnoxious snicker all the way down the hall.

No one was around, so Sargent went straight into Isaac's office. The long couch under the window was inviting, but he took a seat in the impressive leather chair behind the desk. Books lined the walls in uneven, colorful pillars, interrupted now and then by stacks of paintings three or four deep. More paintings hung on the wall. Two pictures hung at eye level to the left of Isaac's computer: a photograph of three-year-old Sargent and a sketch of Lord Beaverbrook's head. Sargent shivered. Beaverbrook looked like he was staring at him.

He turned his attention to the desk. It was littered with paper: reports, newspaper clippings, letters, and all kinds of evidence of Isaac's disorganization. Every birthday card from Isaac came weeks after the fact, and he was always late when they FaceTimed. On the other hand, his mom's desk was spotless. No wonder they'd divorced.

The letterhead on a piece of paper on top of the mess caught his eye: the Albuquerque Museum, a place he'd gone to when he and Isaac had visited Grandma Singer. When he read the subject line, "Request to display your work," he couldn't resist reading the letter.

Dear Mr. Singer, the letter began. Sargent noticed that Mr. Singer was crossed out and someone had written *Ike* in blue ink. Hardly anybody called his father Ike. Whoever was writing this letter must know him well.

It is with great pleasure that I invite you to submit two pieces of your work for inclusion in our upcoming New Mexico Artists exhibit scheduled for next spring. As a native of our fine state and a talented artist, and now an art gallery director and curator, you are exactly the type of artist we wish to present to our patrons and visitors.

Though I understand you have not exhibited lately, the quality of your work merits your inclusion. I am especially hopeful you can show my personal favorites: Sarah in the Morning *and* The One Who Makes My Heart Sing. *It would be a joy to share them with our patrons. I look forward to hearing from you at your convenience.*

Sincerely,

Art Tomlinson, Gallery Director

Sargent read the letter twice. Isaac was an artist? Why hadn't Isaac told him he painted? How come he didn't know these paintings existed? He pulled out his phone, feeling weird when he typed "Isaac Singer, artist" into Google search. The first hits were about Isaac's job as director and the Beaverbrook Art Gallery. But the eleventh was promising: Isaac Singer Art Show, Soho Gallery. Soho was a neighborhood in New York City. His click opened a newspaper article.

Isaac Singer's new show, A Changed Man, opened last evening at Gallery Dumont. It has been three years since Singer's last show; he explained that the delay was due to his becoming a husband and father. Perhaps he should have become a family man sooner, for it is clear he is now an artist fully in control of his vision. The paintings present scenes of domestic life: his wife, Sarah; his new baby, Sargent; their cat, Chou; and their small apartment in the Village.

But there is something dark about this domesticity. Shadows fall in alarming ways, colors bleed into shades of gray and umber, and a contented smile seems angry when viewed from another angle. The Isaac Singer view of domesticity leaves the viewer conflicted, but his work makes us hope it's not another three years until his next exhibit. Daily at the Gallery Dumont until November 30.

Sargent returned to the search page and clicked on images. The screen filled with thumbnails of at least two dozen paintings, most scenes of his parents' old apartment, a place he had no memory of but recognized from his baby pictures. The picture of his mother was most surprising; her long braids and lazy smile were not the mother he knew now. He kept clicking until he found The One Who Makes My Heart Sing. It was him as a newborn baby, crying, surrounded by darkness.

Sargent shut off his phone. He'd lost his appetite. Why was his dad keeping these paintings a secret from him?

CHAPTER THIRTEEN

When Mona was a young girl, her parents had returned home after a long trip with a trunk full of souvenirs and treasures from the South Pacific. Mona's favorite had been a pinky-silver conch shell, roughly the size of her head, a shimmery iridescent pearl coating on the inside. Papa said if you put your ear against the shell, you could hear the ocean. Mona would sit for hours, listening to the gentle *whoosh*, imagining sandy beaches and warm breezes. Sometimes, sitting in her painting, watching the real world unfold outside the frame, she had the unsettling sensation that she was back in her bedroom, listening to an imaginary ocean.

But parties were different. Even her falling-out with Max couldn't dampen her enthusiasm for the fund-raiser. She adored it when the gallery hosted events. Unlike normal visiting hours, when most patrons hushed themselves as if they were in a funeral parlor, parties were bubbly, exuberant affairs. By the time the staff was finished, every room had a table topped with flowers, flyers about upcoming exhibits, and information packets explaining how to become a gallery member—and potential donor.

Mona's favorite part was the guests. The women were peacocks in their cocktail attire—long gowns, sequin skirts, little black dresses—and the sounds of their high heels clicking as they walked was mysterious and grown-up. Over the years, she'd thrilled at the changing styles; the long sheaths and teased hair of the 1960s had given way to slinky gowns and flipped hair in the 1970s, and then to shoulder pads and fat curls in the 1980s. Since then, styles had gotten simpler, but Mona missed the drama. The men's tuxedos had changed as well, but the men never did: they were forever adjusting their collars as if their bow ties were nooses.

Every party had at least one or two attendees who considered themselves art experts. Gallery residents called them the know-it-alls. It was humorous to watch them barge their way into conversations, eager to share their knowledge. Early in the evening, Mona was the focus of two glamorous couples, only to be rudely interrupted by a Mr. Harmsworth, who elbowed his way through the group until it appeared as if the others were admiring him, not Mona. He looked like a bulldog, thanks to his thinning hair, massive jowls that flung about as he spoke, and the buttons straining to contain his barrel chest and protruding belly.

"You do know who this is?" tonight's know-it-all sputtered.

"Mona Dunn," one of the men said, pointing to the sign on the wall.

"No, no, I mean: do you know who she is?" Harmsworth paused dramatically, and the couples glanced at one another in confusion. Mona had seen this before. Soon they'd be plotting their escape.

Isaac and Janice strode into the gallery, with a bashful-looking Sargent, yanking at the bow tie around his neck, in their wake. Their arrival was a gift to the two couples, who scurried away.

"There you are, Harmsworth!" Isaac stepped forward, arm outstretched. "I've been looking all over for you." He tilted his head toward Sargent. "This is my son, Sargent, who's visiting me for the summer. This is the assistant curator, Janice Hayes."

Harmsworth bowed deeply and kissed the back of Janice's hand with his horribly moist lips. "Enchanted, my dear."

"Oh my," Janice said, peering down at her hand. Mona wanted to gag.

Harmsworth gave Sargent a disinterested nod. Sargent responded with a half-hearted one, then bugged out his eyes at Mona.

Isaac flashed Sargent a "what the heck?" look and turned to Harmsworth. "How about we go see the Dalí now?"

"Ah, the Dalí, I know quite a bit about Salvador Dalí. He—" Harmsworth's voice was swallowed up by the buzz of the crowd as the group headed toward the Orientation Gallery.

The idea of Harmsworth holding court in front of *Santiago El Grande* almost made Mona giggle. One of the gallery's legends was that Dalí's soaring horse had once asked an obnoxious visitor to leave. Maybe tonight it would happen again.

It was nearly midnight. Most of the partygoers and staff had gone, but Mona could hear Sargent and his father chatting with Mr. Harmsworth and Janice. Then their voices became distant and she heard the sound of footsteps on the stairs. She settled back into her painting, only to be surprised two minutes later when Sargent wandered into the gallery. Mona watched him stop in front of Edmund's portrait. Despite Max's warning, she wished he'd visit her, too.

Frank stuck his head into the gallery. "Where's your dad, Sargent?"

"He and Janice took Mr. Harmsworth down to Dad's office."

"Thanks, I just need to ask him about something before he leaves."

Sargent circled the room twice. When he arrived at Mona's portrait, he pulled out his phone and began to type, not looking up.

"I don't want to get you in trouble," he whispered between clenched teeth. "I just want to talk. There's a blank canvas in the cloakroom in the basement. My dad's going to be at least twenty minutes because Harmsworth's such a windbag. If you're able to get into the canvas, meet me." Without glancing up, he left. Mona counted to a hundred, then slipped out of her painting.

One of the greatest challenges for the gallery's residents was that, when going from the main level to the basement, they were required to stop at Max's gatekeeper,

Santiago El Grande, whose horse and rider required the solving of a riddle as a sort of toll. Mona's riddle-solving abilities were excellent, but the excitement of meeting Sargent made her thinking dull.

"Would you please repeat the riddle again?" she asked, tapping her right foot against the edge of the frame. If she didn't hurry, Sargent might have to leave before she got there.

The horse peered down at her. "Very well," it said. "As I was going to St. Ives, I met a man with seven wives. The seven wives had seven sacks. The seven sacks had seven cats. The seven cats had seven kits. Kits, cats, sacks and wives— How many were going to St. Ives?"

There was obviously a kink in her brain—she could not solve it. The horse was clearly delighting in her exasperation, if his toothy grin was any indication. So far as Mona knew, he was the only talking animal in the gallery, though there were rumors that a herd of cows sang opera once a month in another painting. She began to pace. There was no making a run for it; that was a sure way to get caught by Max. And there was no bargaining with the horse, for he allowed no exceptions. A person could not go downstairs unless they solved the riddle, something Mona seemed incapable of doing.

"Think, Mona, think!" she muttered. "Seven wives,

seven sacks, seven cats, seven kits . . . oh, and there was a man, too, wasn't there?"

"Give up?"

Mona scowled and was about to comment about how ironic it was for a horse to be so catty, when a familiar blond head poked into the painting.

"Come find me if you want to go for a swim later," Clem said, adding, "And the answer is one person. See ya!"

Of course! The person met them on the road, which means they were heading *away* from St. Ives! "One person was going to St. Ives!" she cried, triumphant.

"No fair. She had help," the unhappy horse told his rider.

Mona held up her hand. "I've answered your riddle. The rule says we must solve riddles to pass through your painting. It doesn't say we can't have help."

The horse and rider exchanged looks, but allowed her to pass. As she left, Mona could hear them discussing how to eliminate this loophole, but she could have cared less. She was going to see Sargent!

CHAPTER FOURTEEN

Sargent was sitting in the corner of the cloakroom when, with a gentle *whoosh*, Mona popped into the canvas propped against the wall next to him.

"Whoa—how'd you do that?"

Mona shrugged. She didn't know how, but she liked how impressed he was by the feat. "Hello."

"I didn't think you'd come." Sargent smiled.

Mona arranged herself cross-legged on the sea of white canvas, tugging at the hem of her dress so it covered her knees. "Me either. I am in so much trouble for being caught out of my painting. Lord Beaverbrook is furious; he's threatened to send me away if it happens again."

"Lord Beaverbrook? But he's dead!"

Mona raised an eyebrow.

"Oh, right. He's a painting, too," said Sargent, cheeks flaming. "Why'd you come, then?"

"Because I haven't talked to someone outside of a frame for a hundred years."

"Wow," was all Sargent could muster.

Something washed over Mona, something she couldn't describe, but which reminded her of the anticipation of Father Christmas's arrival when she was very young. For the first time in decades, she had no idea what was about to happen, and she savored the feeling.

Sargent's curiosity had plagued him since he had met Mona five days before. "So, are all paintings alive?" Sargent asked.

"All the paintings at the Beaverbrook are alive, and the paintings that come here for special exhibits are alive, so I guess the answer is yes."

"Like, how do you even exist? Are you magic?"

"I don't know. Maybe. A lot of the paintings here believe it's the magic of creation. You know—when artists work, they try to capture the soul of the person or thing they're painting. But they also put some of themselves into the painting, too. I guess all that energy brings us to life."

Sargent responded with a vigorous nod. "I get it. Sometimes when I'm painting, it's like I can feel this jolt of electricity, especially when things are going well." He paused. "Whoa—that means the stuff I paint is alive, too. That's so creepy. It's like what the guy on the internet said."

"What guy on the internet?"

Sargent's mouth fell open. "You know about the internet?"

Mona smirked. "Everyone knows about the internet, Sargent. I see it on people's smartphones every day. Plus, I met a fellow from a visiting painting at one of Max's meetings a couple of years ago, and he told me all about it. It sounds amazing."

"I guess you can't be alive for a hundred years and not know a bunch of stuff," Sargent mused. "I found an article written by a guy who discovered the paintings in his museum were alive. His theory is pretty much the same as what you just said. You said there are meetings?"

Mona rolled her eyes. "Max—Lord Beaverbrook—holds resident meetings every month. It's his way of keeping us in line. They're so boring."

"I think it's cool. What I don't get is how this is still a secret. I mean, more people than me must know paintings are alive. And how come my own paintings aren't alive?"

Mona shuddered. "I hope no one else knows. Max expends considerable effort to protect us, which is why he's so cross. It puts us at risk when someone from outside the frame learns about us. Maybe your paintings haven't woken up yet. Sometimes it takes a while for a painting to come to life. Or maybe they don't want you to know they're alive. Maybe they're afraid."

"But I'd never put you or any other painting at risk!"

Mona reached out as if she was placing her hand on a pane of glass. "I know."

Visibly relieved, Sargent continued. "Will you get older?"

"I'll always be thirteen, always wear this dress, always be behind the frame." Her voice caught a little.

"Do you sleep? Eat?"

"Sometimes. We don't need to, but it's nice to close your eyes and dream a little. Lots of the paintings have food in them, so the residents still eat, but mostly because it makes them feel more alive." Mona bit her lip.

Sargent thought of the artwork in the gallery. "It must be so cool, getting to go into all those paintings. I'd love it."

A ripple of sadness crossed Mona's face. "Most of the time it is, but sometimes it feels like we do the same thing over and over. We visit one another at night, talk about our day—"

"Your day?"

"You know, what visitor said what silly or rude thing or belched or scratched inappropriately. My friend Clem keeps track of what people say. He's so funny, I wish you could meet him. . . ." Her voice trailed off. It was sad that Sargent would never get to meet Clem.

"How do you get around?"

"There are passageways between our paintings, and sometimes we can jump from painting to painting, unless we're completely wrapped up. It's mysterious even to us."

"But you can't step out of the frame?"

Mona's jaw clenched. "No." It was time for her to change the subject. "It's my turn to ask questions. Are you enjoying your visit? I was so surprised when I heard you were coming. I didn't know Director Singer had a son."

Sargent winced. "I'm not surprised." He fixed his eyes on a poster tacked to the wall. It was stupid, this tightness in his chest, all because Mona didn't know Isaac had a son.

Mona could tell she'd hit a sore spot. "Your parents are divorced?"

"Yup. Yours?"

Mona shook her head. "They didn't divorce until after I was painted."

"That must have been nice, living with both of your parents." Sargent thought of the happy look on his mom's face in Isaac's painting. He'd never seen her look at Isaac with anything other than distrust and barely contained anger.

"I suppose so, but my parents left me with a governess for weeks at a time," said Mona. "It was dreadfully lonely, even with my brother and sister for company. And we never ate dinner with them; we were brought in to say good night, or sometimes we had tea with them."

"I don't remember ever living with Isaac. He didn't visit me at all until I was six or seven. When I was younger, I used to tell people that he was dead. Stupid, huh? But it was easier than answering their questions." He forced himself to look at Mona, relieved when he saw her sympathetic nod.

"Papa was rarely home, but he did take a keen interest in my riding. The strange thing is, I've become much closer to my father since we came to the Beaverbrook, probably because there are four portraits of him here, and one is always stopping by to visit or tell me what to do."

Sargent's eyes widened. "Seriously? There are four

versions of your father here? That would drive me around the bend! This summer is the first time I've stayed with my father for more than a weekend. I was kind of nervous about coming, but I want to get to know him. I'm glad there's only one of him, though."

Mona giggled. "I'm so used to having four fathers here that I forget how odd it is! Do you have any brothers or sisters?"

"Two five-year-old half-sisters who try to make me play dolls and have tea parties."

"There are some little girls in other paintings that I take care of sometimes. They keep me on my toes. You sound like a good brother."

Most of the time Sargent thought he was a lousy brother, but he didn't want to say that to Mona. "I guess. It's hard, because they have such a great dad. Sometimes I feel jealous."

He waited for Mona's reaction, and was reassured when she offered him a crooked smile. Leaning forward, she whispered conspiratorially, "My father's third wife, Lady Dunn, has a portrait here in the gallery. I don't like her at all. You're fortunate that she's away for the summer so you don't have to look at her snooty face." She looked so guilty Sargent laughed.

"She's not nice to you?"

Mona shrugged. "As nice as she is to anyone. You want to hear something funny?"

"What?"

"After my father died, Lady Dunn married Max. In real life. Can you believe it? Now they all live at the gallery. It is quite scandalous! They don't talk about it, but everyone else does."

Sargent snorted. "That makes my family seem almost normal. What do you do for fun?"

Mona's lashes dropped down to her cheeks. "Not much. Most of the children here are from old paintings and aren't any fun."

"What about before, when you were alive?"

"I didn't have a lot of friends then, either," Mona said, her voice suddenly wistful. "I was tutored at home with my brother and sister."

"I guess we have something in common, then, because I only have one good friend, Cory. He lives in my apartment building. We hang out and watch movies or play video games. I know lots of kids, but I have a hard time talking to people. I can never think of what to say."

"You're talking to me," Mona reminded him, her crooked smile back.

Sargent returned the smile. "I guess I am, aren't I? Maybe we could be friends." He stopped, amazed and embarrassed that he'd dared to say out loud what he'd wanted to say since they'd first met.

Mona was so taken aback she could hardly speak. "That would be wonderful!"

Isaac's voice reverberated down the hallway. "Sargent!"

"I've got to go," Sargent whispered, untangling his legs and standing up. "See you later."

Watching him leave, Mona's heart leaped and sank in equal measure.

She had always thought of her life as having two parts: the part before she was painted, and the part after. Now there was a third: the part where she had a friend named Sargent Singer.

CHAPTER FIFTEEN

It was well after midnight, but Sargent was so full of energy after talking with Mona that it was all he could do not to swing from tree branches or holler at the stars as he walked home with Isaac. The world was full of magic! He and Mona Dunn were friends!

Isaac was too busy analyzing the fund-raiser to notice. "I still can't believe Harmsworth came to the party," he repeated for the fifteenth time. "I never thought he'd show."

Sargent couldn't imagine anyone being excited about Harmsworth. "Who is he, anyway?"

"John Jacob Harmsworth. He's from Montreal. His

father was originally from New Brunswick, and the family keeps a summer place about an hour from here, in St. Andrews. Over the years they've made healthy donations to the gallery, but not lately."

"What does he do?"

"Rumor has it he manages the family holdings. His father was a tire magnate—made millions selling tires and then sold his company to a huge American conglomerate and made even more money. Harmsworth is said to have one of Canada's finest art collections."

Sargent had no idea what a conglomerate was and didn't really care. "Why'd you take him downstairs after the party?"

"I was telling him how my office was originally Lord Beaverbrook's bedroom, and he was desperate to see it. Then he wanted a backstage tour. Said he's always dreamed of building a Harmsworth Gallery, but that it's too complicated. I suggested he consider building a Harmsworth Wing at the Beaverbrook. We're going to talk more next week."

"I liked your speech." Ignoring the statistics, Isaac had given a heartfelt speech about the important role art played in society and how the Beaverbrook made New Brunswick a world-class place because it was filled with world-class art that inspired and delighted residents and visitors alike. The partygoers had cheered, and then reached for the donor envelopes.

"I was so nervous. The party was a big deal. I need to turn things around if I want to keep my job. Those donations and Harmsworth could fix everything. What do you think of Janice?"

"She seems nice."

Isaac stopped walking. He turned to Sargent and began to speak very fast. "I need to tell you something. Janice is my girlfriend. We've been dating for six months. It's strange dating someone I work with, but I really like her. I might even get up the nerve to ask her to marry me."

Isaac's face was all shadows in the dark night, but Sargent knew he expected a response.

"Um, that's great," he said.

But it wasn't great. Something hard knotted itself in Sargent's stomach. Isaac had been dating someone for six months, was even considering proposing to her, and he hadn't bothered to tell Sargent until now? Before his mother had married Bill, she'd spent months making sure Sargent and Bill liked each other. Isaac was telling him this momentous news like it was no big deal. First Isaac's secret life as a painter, now this. Why didn't Isaac want to tell him things?

"Thanks, Sarge. I don't know about you, but I'm exhausted. Let's get home."

Suddenly drained, Sargent trailed Isaac back to the apartment.

Mona agreed to go for a walk with Edmund and Juliette after the party, mostly because she needed to know if her cloakroom rendezvous with Sargent had gone undetected. It appeared it had, for only Edmund mentioned Sargent's name.

"Did that boy attempt to speak with you earlier this evening?" he asked as they walked the pier at *San Vigilio, Lake Garda*.

Mona was no liar, but she was creative. "He was typing on his phone."

"Odd," Edmund mused with a sideways glance at Juliette.

"Not at all, he—" Mona began, then stopped. "That's strange."

"What is strange, chérie?" Juliette asked.

"There, behind that cypress tree. It's Dusk."

Juliette and Edmund followed Mona's pointing finger to a spot halfway up the terraced hillside, where the skinny trunk of a lone cypress tree was doing a poor job of hiding Dusk.

"What the devil is he doing up there?" Edmund raised a hand. "Halloo, Dusk!"

Dusk started, then turned and began to climb the hill. At the summit, he glanced back. The sun was behind him, and he cast a long shadow. He crested the hill and was gone.

"How curious," Juliette said. "I believe he was watching us."

"I'm certain he was," said Edmund. "Should I go after him?"

Mona stared at the now-deserted hilltop. "It would be a waste of time, Edmund; he's long gone. I suppose Max has him spying on me, making sure I don't step out of line again."

"Max is only trying to protect you," Juliette said. When she saw the face Mona pulled, she laughed. "Come, let us forget Monsieur Dusk. Perhaps a gelato would take your mind off Max."

"There's the spirit," Edmund said. "I would favor a gelato myself."

One of the stucco villas lining the shore housed a café renowned for its wonderful Italian desserts. Rossi's was a favorite of the residents, not only for its food but for its ambience, nestled as it was between the hills and the lake. A weathered wooden sign in the window said

TODAY'S SPECIAL: CHOCOLATE GELATO, but in fact the proprietor, Signor Rossi, had run out of chocolate gelato the very afternoon John Singer Sargent had completed the painting and had been unable to restock it since. The food and wine that existed at the time of its painting was forever magically replenished, but what did not exist could not be had, which was why Clem begged Max regularly to find a way to get a painting with a pizzeria.

Only one of the eight tables was occupied when they walked in. Signor Rossi stood behind the countertop, drying a glass. His tanned face, scored with the lines of numerous sunny days, broke into a grin when he caught sight of Mona, his favorite customer. He tossed the striped cloth on the counter and hurried to greet them.

"Ciao!"

"Ciao, Signor Rossi," Mona said, her grin matching his.

He turned to Juliette. *"Bellissima!"* He kissed her on both cheeks, then did the same to Mona, adding a pat on her head like an exclamation mark. Edmund stiffened—he loathed being kissed—and tried a preemptive bow, hoping to discourage Rossi. It didn't work. Signor Rossi waited until Edmund was upright, grabbed his face with both hands, and gave each cheek an enthusiastic smack. He ushered them to a table overlooking the lake. "What can I get you?"

"Lemonade would be lovely," Juliette said.

"I think I would enjoy a lemon gelato," Edmund said. "Mona?"

Rossi sighed. "Mona wants chocolate. She always wants what she cannot have."

Mona sighed dramatically in return. "I suppose I could live with lemon."

Signor Rossi kissed her on the forehead and rushed off, humming.

A middle-aged couple, wearing simple clothing from what Mona guessed to be the nineteenth century, sat at a nearby table. The man wore woolen breeches, a striped shirt, leather suspenders, and a pair of worn leather boots. He looked familiar. The woman, who was what Edmund politely called sturdy, wore a long gray skirt made of rough wool and a white cotton blouse buttoned up to her chin. Her friendly smile revealed a mouthful of rotting teeth.

"Evenin'," the lady said. Her voice reminded Mona of thick honey.

Edmund stood up and bowed deeply. "Lieutenant Colonel Edmund Nugent, at your service. My companions are my fiancée, Madame Juliette, and Miss Mona Dunn, heiress. Which painting do you call home?"

The man stood up and bowed awkwardly. "Argyle

Smith, cap'n. Me wife's name's Bertha. We live in Merrymaking."

"Ah. Then you find yourself at sixes and sevens, what with the restoration."

"It's a welcome change, if you ask me," Bertha said. She took a last spoonful from her dish, slurped loudly, then stuck her spoon into her husband's half-full one. "I keep the rooms up at the White Horse Inn, and Argyle's a trapper. What with the restoration work, everyone inside the inn who ain't seen by the public got to leave. The rest of the poor buggers are stuck in that stuffy workroom whenever the art restorer's about. Really, the restoration is a lark for Argyle and me. We left the night after the restorer began and been touring about ever since, visiting other paintings, meeting new people, like regular tourists."

"How marvelous for you," Juliette said.

Before Bertha could respond, Rossi was back with their order. He waited for Mona to eat her first spoonful so he could receive his usual reward of a sticky lemon kiss. The conversation ceased as Mona and Edmund dug in, but it was impossible not to overhear the Smiths.

"It was odd, that's all I'm sayin', Bertha."

"Explain it to me again so's I can understand. You say the art restorer was talking to a painting?"

Mona put down her spoon, ignoring Juliette's warning look. Edmund stopped eating, too.

"He kept saying, 'Stop whispering!' in a shrill voice. One of me mates what stands outside the inn said he kept tugging at his hair. Makes my blood run cold to think of it."

"He's an odd bird. Could he be talking to Mr. Somerset Maugham?"

"If he was, I never heard Mr. Maugham speak in return."

"How could you, your ears so full of wax and superstition."

Argyle ignored the dig. "He's made a copy of us, you know. It's not a good one, but it does look like the inn. Did you not notice it when we left? I think he's making a copy to sell."

"Are you accusing him of being a forger? Those be strong words, Argyle."

"I'm not accusing him of anything. But I do wonder about him, that's all, and I'll be glad when *Merrymaking* is back in its rightful place upstairs. C'mon—off we go."

Bertha and Argyle stood up, chairs squeaking as they scraped across the wooden floor. After a nod to Signor Rossi, they headed for the door, bobbing their heads at Mona's table.

"Sacré bleu!" Juliette said. "I do not want to be restored now! We must speak with Max!"

Edmund held up his spoon. "Steady. We cannot allow the fear-mongering of ill-educated individuals to form our opinions. However, to ease your mind, I shall inquire around, determine if there is any veracity to the story we have overheard. Remember, they live at the White Horse Inn. For all we know, Argyle was under the influence."

Juliette nodded but set her glass of lemonade aside. "I should like to go home now."

Waving good-bye to Signor Rossi, Mona followed her friends out the door. As they hurried toward the frame, she replayed Argyle and Bertha's conversation in her head. Like Juliette, she'd do anything not to be restored. Except talk to Max. She would never talk to Max.

CHAPTER SIXTEEN

Sargent and Isaac were not the first to arrive at the gallery on Monday morning. Raised voices were coming from the main level. They rushed upstairs to investigate, surprised when they found John Harmsworth and Barney Templeton standing quietly in front of *Santiago El Grande*.

"This is a surprise," Isaac said. "I wasn't expecting you until later today, John."

"My bad," Harmsworth said, giving Isaac a vigorous handshake. "When I woke up this morning, the sun was shining and I was desperate to see your paintings again. I was waiting on the front steps when I saw Barney walk by, and I begged him to let me in."

Barney shuffled from side to side. "I'm sorry, Mr. Singer. I'm not supposed to do that."

"No harm done, eh, Isaac?" Harmsworth patted his ample belly. Sargent noticed Harmsworth's shirt cuffs were frayed and his shoes scuffed and worn. For a rich guy, he sure didn't dress like it.

"I'm off to breakfast, Singer. Care to join me?" asked Harmsworth.

"I wish I could," Isaac said. "But our summer camp starts today, and I said I'd help set up."

"Yeah, you did," said Sargent. No way could he go to the education room by himself.

"Sargent can help me," Barney offered.

Isaac handed Sargent his briefcase. "Do you mind?"

Sargent minded a lot, but what could he say? Annoyed to find himself abandoned, he watched Isaac follow Harmsworth out the main entrance, then trailed Barney down the stairs.

At the bottom, Barney pointed left. "The chairs are in the room beside the kitchen. Do you have a security pass?"

Sargent flashed the pass he'd yet to turn in.

"Great," said Barney. "We need nine chairs. Bring them to the education room."

The hallway was murky thanks to the early hour. Sargent was surprised to see light seeping out from underneath the door to Sneely's workroom. Without thinking, he knocked.

"Is that you again, Barney?" Sneely called. He sounded like he had a cold.

"It's Sargent, Mr. Sneely."

There was a pause. "Go away. I'm busy."

Before Sargent could respond, he heard Barney call his name, and he hurried to grab the chairs.

Barney and Sargent plopped down into adjoining chairs when they finished setting up the room.

"Thanks for your help," Barney said. "Bet you're looking forward to today."

"I guess." Sargent tried to sound enthusiastic. "What's up with that guy Sneely?"

Barney shook his head. "I'd steer clear of him if I were you. I know I do."

Sargent was confused. "But—"

Barney's cell phone rang, and he stepped out into the hallway. He looked troubled when he returned. "I'm off. Tell Janice to call me if she needs anything. Have fun!"

Sargent settled into his chair to wait. Today would be anything but fun.

At ten o'clock, Janice ushered in the seven other campers. Sargent was jittery, a feeling that intensified when he realized that the seven newcomers were, in fact, old-timers, having taken numerous courses together over the past few years. They giggled and whispered as they took their seats, at which point they all turned and stared at him. Great.

Janice surveyed the room, a loopy grin plastered on her face. Dressed in a painter's smock and jeans, and almost levitating with excitement, she kept smiling at Sargent. He leaned back and let his hair flop over his eyes, wishing he was anywhere else.

"Hi, guys! Before we get started, let's do some introductions. I know most of you know one another, but maybe you could say your name, your age, and why you're enrolled in this summer camp, as opposed to the awesome bowling camp you might have gone to." That got lots of chuckles. "I'll go first. Janice Hayes, Assistant Curator. I have a master's in museum studies from George Washington University, and I've worked at the Beaverbrook for three years." She pointed to a boy wearing expensive basketball sneakers. "You first."

The guy looked at the others with a lazy grin. He struck Sargent as someone who felt comfortable anywhere. "Marcus Carty. I'm twelve years old, and I'm taking this course because my mom's making me."

"That is so not true, Marcus!" Janice scolded. "You have a lot of talent."

"Me next," said the pretty girl with dozens of twisty coils cascading down her back. "Alice Johnson. I'll be twelve in October and I love to draw." She nodded to the girl sitting next to her.

Besides Marcus and Alice there was Abby Gilman, ten years old with a mouth full of metal; Troy McGinnis, eleven years old with green hair sticking up everywhere and a burning desire to write and illustrate comic books; Adam Polchies, who was eleven and planned to be a movie or theater set designer when he grew up; Emma Brooks, twelve years old with a notebook filled with sketches of clothing designs; and nine-year-old Alex Doucet, who giggled when she told them she wanted to be a children's book illustrator. Finally it was Sargent's turn.

Brushing the hair out of his eyes, he muttered, "Sargent Singer. Twelve years old. I paint."

"Sargent Singer? As in John Singer Sargent, the artist?" Alice asked.

Sargent's cheeks flamed. He nodded, waiting for the smart remarks. Instead, he was surprised when Troy said, "Cool, man," and everyone turned back to Janice. He took a deep breath to slow his racing heart. He'd survived introductions, now he just had to survive lunch.

Janice clapped her hands. "Great! Okay . . . details. We'll eat lunch together out on the Green so long as it's not raining. There's a fridge in the corner where you can store your food."

Sargent pictured all that green grass, impossible to hide in.

"If you need to go to the washroom, it's straight down the hall and to your left past the stairs. We finish every day at four o'clock, except Friday. Remember, Friday's the sleepover: We'll have pizza in here, then we're taking over the Contemporary Gallery next door for our movie and sleepover. I might even have a surprise or two up my sleeve!"

Alex raised her hand. "What movie are we watching?"

"Harry Potter, the first one. You know, because the paintings are alive!" A ripple of excitement rounded the room. You could never see Harry Potter too much. Sargent had forgotten about the paintings being alive at Hogwarts. Wait till he told Mona. Too bad she couldn't watch it too.

"This week's session is all about what types of mediums we choose to use when we create art," continued Janice. "Typical mediums include paint in all its forms; charcoal or graphite; crayon; chalk; sand; markers; and pastels. Those are only examples, not an exhaustive list—always use your imagination! The mediums we choose usually dictate the techniques we use."

"Do you mean like how it was hard for me to do a detailed portrait of Alice last summer using watercolor?" Emma said.

"Exactly! Here's your morning assignment: I want you to take your notebooks and go around the gallery. Look at the paintings, see what mediums the artists used. Take your time, and be prepared to tell me what the piece of art might have looked like if the artist had used a completely different medium. Spread out! I'll be wandering around, keeping an eye on you. If you need to talk, whisper. Now—follow me!"

For the next hour and a half, the campers wandered from room to room in groups of two or three. Sargent had ended up with Troy and Adam, who, when they discovered he still had a security pass, insisted he sneak them into the staff area so they could ride the freight elevator up to the main level.

"This is the coolest thing ever," Troy said as they pulled down the metal grate that was the elevator door.

"I haven't been on this yet," Sargent said, bouncing up and down on his heels, worried they'd be in trouble if they were caught. He was relieved when it clanked to a stop. No one was around when they stepped out into the large storage area that was behind the Canadian Gallery. They slipped through the hidden door unnoticed and continued on their way.

"It's like we're sneaking up on everybody," Adam added. "You could really scare the crap out of somebody if they didn't notice that door."

Troy and Adam were like a comedy team. By the time they reached Mona's gallery, Sargent was sure his stomach would explode from laughing so hard. Still, when he saw Mona's portrait, he was speechless. It was even more spectacular now that he'd actually talked to her.

"This is my guy," said Troy, plopping down on the floor in front of Edmund. "He reminds me of a superhero, with that red suit of his."

"Or Santa Claus, 'cause of the white hair," said Adam. "I like what Gainsborough painted around him, although the sky is that weird green the sky turns right before a tornado hits."

"Yeah, he should be like 'Oh, no—me and my perfect hair are going to blow away!'" Troy trilled in a falsetto voice.

Sargent grinned up at Edmund. What was he thinking? "The sign says this is oil on canvas. What would it be like if he was just drawn with charcoal or pencil or something?"

"You wouldn't know how sick that suit is, for starters," said Troy, "so I think you might not think the guy was all that impressive."

"Yeah, and if he'd used watercolors or acrylics, he wouldn't look so lifelike," Adam said. He nibbled at the eraser on the end of his pencil as he continued to watch Edmund. "Hey, you know what?"

Sargent looked up at Edmund's face. "What?"

"This talk about superheroes makes me think we should watch *Superman* as one of our next movies."

"I've never seen a Superman movie," Sargent confessed.

"Man, you have some catching up to do! Maybe Janice can get it for next week."

"You guys will be back next week?"

Adam laughed. "We're the Beaverbrook Rats; we take everything the gallery offers. We're all here for the next four weeks. We were the only kids last summer. You'll get used to us."

"But the question is . . . will we get used to you?" Troy said, scooting his butt across the floor so he was now in front of Mona. "Hello, Mona. It's me, your lover boy."

"You're lucky she can't climb out of that painting and smack you," Sargent said, joining Troy on the floor at Mona's feet.

"I wish she would. I'd give her a big smooch."

Sargent snorted. "Seriously?"

"You don't know Troy," Adam called over his shoulder. "He's girl crazy. He's in love with Mona, one of the Cotterell girls, Taylor Swift, and basically any cute girl with a pulse."

"That's a lot of love," Sargent said.

"I'm a lot of man," Troy said. "Hey, you know what? I think Mona would make a good character in a comic. Maybe I'll do one of her and buddy over there," he said, pointing back at Edmund. "They'll be superhero crime fighters by night, portraits by day."

At lunchtime, Sargent watched everyone rush off without him. He was shuffling toward the door when Troy poked his head back in. "Yo, Sarge—sit with us. I got a lot of questions!"

Alice's face appeared. "He means he's got lame jokes to share with you," she said tartly.

"She's not wrong," Troy conceded.

Relieved, Sargent ran to catch up. Adam had saved the three of them a spot on one of the blankets Janice had provided. They spent the lunch hour laughing at Troy's stories and running commentary about everything, and making Sargent tell them all about New York City. Alice shared the plot of the novel she was reading, horrified when Sargent said he'd read Tolkien but none of the Narnia books.

"I'm bringing you *The Lion, The Witch and the Wardrobe*," she said, and Sargent knew there'd be a quiz about it in the future.

"You're a Beaverbrook Rat now, Sarge," Troy said as they headed back after lunch.

Sargent couldn't believe being called a rat could make a person so happy.

After a debriefing with Janice about the morning's activity, they got their week's assignment: do a copy of their favorite painting using a different medium than the one the painting was done in. Troy immediately picked Edmund, but Sargent was torn. If he chose Mona, he'd get to spend time with her, but that might make the other paintings suspicious and get her in trouble. In the end, he chose to do *The Cotterell Family* so at least he could be in the same room as Mona. When Janice dismissed them at four o'clock, Sargent was sorry; he didn't want the day to end.

A few minutes later, Sargent stood in the hallway outside Isaac's office. Martine was so deep in conversation with Janice and Amy that none of them noticed him standing there.

"Is Isaac going to show his paintings in Albuquerque?" Amy asked.

Sargent, who'd been staring at his phone, suddenly began to pay attention.

"No. He says he doesn't own the paintings," Janice said.

Martine nodded. "I have to call the museum tomorrow and decline."

"It's too bad. He's—" Janice caught sight of Sargent and flushed. "Anyway, I should go. Night everyone!" She grabbed her purse and hurried past Sargent.

Sargent watched her receding back. He'd forgotten about the letter from the Albuquerque Museum. But if Isaac didn't own the paintings, who did? There was one person who might know, but he probably shouldn't ask her: his mother.

CHAPTER SEVENTEEN

The first day of camp had been a success, but even after living with him for a week, Sargent still struggled to think of things to talk to Isaac about. Every night they sat side by side on the couch, eating takeout and watching television, having awkward conversations about the gallery or something in the news. Tonight's dinner was Thai food, served with a side of Harmsworth.

"I had a great meeting with Harmsworth today," Isaac said.

"Yeah? Is he going to donate money?" Sargent glanced across the room at Isaac's desk, which was buried in financial statements from the gallery. Most nights, Isaac spent hours poring over them. Math wasn't Sargent's favorite subject, but even he knew that all those negative balances weren't a good thing.

Isaac crossed his fingers. "It's looking good. He's so interested in the gallery that I can't help but think he's planning a sizable donation." He stopped talking and stared blankly at the television for several seconds. "I don't know what I'll do if he walks away. . . ."

"Why would he walk away?"

The question seemed to catch Isaac off guard. "What? Forget I even said that. I'm just borrowing trouble. Hey, how was camp today?"

"I really liked it."

Isaac beamed. "I knew you would! Were the other kids impressed by your talent?"

This was Sargent's least favorite question ever. His parents might be polar opposites, but they sure thought alike, at least in terms of Sargent and painting. He took a long drink of water before responding. "We haven't done much work yet. You said the others kids are good, too."

"They are. But you have exceptional talent, Sargent."

"I guess. . . . What about you? Do you ever paint?"

Isaac seemed surprised at the question. "Um, no. I haven't painted for years."

"How come?"

"I don't know. I guess I got busy."

Sargent watched Isaac's face, looking for a clue. "Did you used to paint a lot?"

Isaac pretended to be interested in a commercial about a truck. As the seconds ticked by, Sargent wondered if he should repeat the question. Then suddenly Isaac said, "What's up with all the questions about me and painting?"

Sargent tried to sound nonchalant. "Just wondering where I got my talent from."

Isaac's shoulders relaxed, and he leaned back against a throw pillow. "Your mother would probably say it was from her. She studied art history at Harvard, but she could have been a professional illustrator if she'd wanted."

Sargent nodded, thinking of the homemade birthday cards his mother gave to each member of their family every year. Last year, she'd drawn Sargent in front of the Eiffel Tower to commemorate his trip to Paris. Her drawings *were* good.

There was another pause. Sargent tried to think of how else to ask Isaac about the paintings.

Finally Isaac clicked off the television and turned so he was facing Sargent. "I need to talk to you about something."

Sargent sat up straight and waited.

"I've been thinking about our conversation on Saturday night. I shouldn't have sprung that stuff about Janice on you. It was thoughtless. I guess I've gotten so used to being alone that I forget I have someone to share my news with."

Sargent stared up at the painting of the old man on the rocking chair and wondered if the old man was listening to their conversation. "No big deal."

"Thank you for saying that, but it's kind of a big deal, at least for me. I owe you an apology. I invited you here for the summer so we could get to know each other. It's hard for us to do that if we aren't completely open, you know, sharing our news and all. I'll try to be better about that."

Some of the pressure on Sargent's chest eased. "Janice is a lot of fun."

He could hear the gratitude in Isaac's voice when he responded. "You are going to love her! And she's so talented. If it's okay, I could invite her to have dinner with us tomorrow night? Honestly, I am a lousy cook. Janice has been feeding me for months."

Sargent pictured the garbage can filled with empty pizza boxes and takeout cartons. A home-cooked meal would be good. Every time his mom had asked what he'd been eating since he'd arrived, he'd had to change the subject.

Isaac jumped to his feet and reached out a hand to Sargent. "How about we go for a walk before I have to face those wretched financial statements again?"

Sargent allowed himself to be pulled to his feet. "Sure." It still bothered him that Isaac hadn't told him about his paintings, but he guessed they had to start somewhere.

CHAPTER EIGHTEEN

By eleven o'clock on Monday night, Mona was fuming. Two things were making her cross: Troy making cow eyes at her all day long and the news that all residents were to remain in their paintings until at least midnight because Sneely had decided to work late.

In fact, Sneely's unpredictable working hours were getting on everyone's nerves. He'd completed his work on Merrymaking and returned the painting to its rightful spot earlier that day, but no one was able to attend the grand reopening of the White Horse Inn because Sneely was still in the building. By the time he finally left, the exodus from the paintings was of biblical proportions.

"Want to go for a swim?" Clem called out to Mona, who was on her way to Helena Rubinstein's portrait. She waited for him to catch up, noticing he'd rolled up his sleeves in an attempt to make them less floppy, more like how Adam and Troy wore their shirts.

"I'm sorry, Clem—I'm in a beastly mood. I thought I'd go see if Madame Rubinstein had any biscuits and a friendly ear."

"Mind if I tag along?"

"Not at all. What did you think of the campers?"

"I'm glad Adam and Troy came back this summer; they're players." Clem was famous for adopting the latest lingo used by visitors.

"Players?"

"Cool dudes. It was all I could do not to crack up when they were talking. I heard what Troy said to you." He poked her in the ribs and cackled.

Mona stiffened. "It was tolerable when he was eight, but now that he's eleven, it's unseemly." She stopped and drew Clem into a tiny alcove. "Never mind the campers, I have an interesting story to tell you. Guess who I saw in *San Vigilio, Lake Garda* last night?"

"Who?"

"Dusk!"

"Creepy Dusk? What was he doing there?"

"I think he was spying on me. When Edmund hailed him, he ran away."

"Did Edmund chase him?"

"He wanted to, but we reckoned Dusk would be long gone. Later, when we visited Rossi's café, we overheard an intriguing conversation between a couple that lives in Merrymaking."

"What was so intriguing about it?"

"They hold the suspicion that Mr. Sneely might be an art forger." She said the sentence slowly to make it more dramatic, which she knew Clem would appreciate.

"Whoa! What makes them think that?"

Before she could respond, they heard someone coming toward them. Mona recognized Dusk's voice immediately, and she and Clem shared a wide-eyed glance. Hearts hammering, they retreated farther into the shadows just before Dusk and Argyle Smith passed by. It was clear from Dusk's chalky-gray face and Argyle's glare that there had been some kind of quarrel. Mona and Clem waited for the men's footsteps to die away before hurrying away in the opposite direction.

"They looked real mad," said Clem.

"The other man is Argyle Smith. He's the husband of the couple I just told you about."

"The couple who thought the art restorer might be an art forger?"

Mona gave an emphatic nod.

"Papa told me the art restorer's working on Dusk's painting now," Clem said. "Maybe Dusk's scared."

"Or maybe Dusk's part of a scheme and is worried Argyle Smith is on to it. Max is concerned about the gallery's finances. Maybe he's having forgeries made to sell."

Clem looked unconvinced. "Max would never do that."

It did seem too much, even for Max and Dusk. "Probably not, but I think we ought to slip down to the workroom and take a quick look around."

Thankfully, the riddle at *Santiago El Grande* was simple. "What loses its head in the morning and gets it back at night?" the horse asked when they arrived.

"A pillow," Mona and Clem said together.

The horse eyed them suspiciously. "Did someone tell you the answer?"

"You asked me the same riddle last week," Mona snapped. "Get some new ones!"

"Rude!" the rider called down.

Clem jumped in. "Mona doesn't mean to be rude. She's just cross because the art restorer stayed so late."

The horse and rider exchanged significant looks. "He's not to be trusted," the horse said. "And that's all we'll say."

Intrigued, Mona looked up. "Has Mr. Dusk gone back downstairs yet?"

The horse whinnied and shook its head. "No. He was agitated when he came through earlier. It took him ten minutes to solve a simple riddle."

Mona tugged at Clem's arm. "We must hurry if we wish to be gone before he returns!" She gave the horse and rider a perfect curtsy. "My most sincere apologies, kind sirs."

Only a night-light was on when the two friends popped into a blank canvas propped against the wall. Mona noticed another canvas lying on the table, and even in the dim light, she could see it contained the distinct outline of Hotel Bedroom, including the shadowy shape where Dusk stood in the painting's background. The original was propped up on an easel nearby. Dusk's wife was in her usual spot, lying in bed and staring at nothing with her vacant eyes. Dusk was gone.

"Strange, isn't it?"

Startled, Mona and Clem looked around, assuming Dusk had returned.

"Up here."

It was Somerset Maugham, high up in the corner of

the room. "I wondered how long it would be until someone else arrived. This room has been a veritable beehive of activity tonight."

Mona smiled up at the sketch. "Oh, Mr. Maugham, you gave us a start! What do you mean, this room has been a veritable beehive of activity? It seems so quiet."

"Things aren't always what they seem. People—from both inside and outside the frame—have been coming and going all day."

"Who?" Clem and Mona asked together.

Maugham's black eyes glittered as he spoke. "Strange, I've been stuck in this lonely workroom for years, and now suddenly people can't get enough of me. If you must know, Mr. Sneely and Mr. Singer were here, as was a strange portly man. Oh, and Barney Templeton. Of course, Mr. Dusk and his wife are here—though heaven knows where Dusk is now—and even Max popped in. It's been a thrilling day."

"Why were they here?" Clem said. "The Dusks and Sneely make sense, but the rest?"

Maugham's eyes widened. "I'm not sure it's safe to say."

"You can trust us to keep a secret, Mr. Maugham. It's only us, and her," Mona said, motioning toward Mrs. Dusk.

Maugham's eyes narrowed. "It's never just us and her," he whispered. "We live in a world where someone is always watching. The paintings in this gallery have lived here for decades. They get bored, you know, they cause mischief. . . ."

"Are you bored?" Clem asked, eyeing Maugham with suspicion.

Maugham snickered. "Me? Never! But then I have a tremendous imagination. I'm writing a new book, you know, a book about what happens in an art gallery when everyone goes home and someone makes copies of priceless paintings."

Mona's eyes widened. "Is that what's happening?"

"What do you think?"

Mona thought of Argyle Smith's comments to his wife. "I think Mr. Sneely is up to no good."

Maugham closed his eyes. "He's not the only one."

"Who else—"

"Hush! I hear Dusk coming! You mustn't let him catch you in here!"

Clem looked at Mona, eyes wild. "We can't leave; we'll pass him for sure!"

"There's another empty canvas behind the door," Maugham said. "Hop into that. I'll try to distract him so you can make your escape. I wouldn't want him to find you with me. Who knows what he might do to you?"

"He's right," Mona said, grabbing Clem by the hand and jumping to the other canvas. "Dusk told Max he wants me sent away. He must know I'm on to something!"

They made it into the canvas with no time to spare. Dusk was back, and Max with him.

CHAPTER NINETEEN

From their vantage point behind the door, Mona and Clem could only see Maugham. But they heard the *whoosh* of someone arriving, and then Max spoke.

"I suppose you know why I've come again." His voice was brittle.

Maugham responded with his prettiest smile. "You missed me."

"I did not. But there are rumors aplenty here, and I suspect you are a veritable Rumpelstiltskin, spinning lies and watching as they wreak havoc."

Clem tugged at Mona's sleeve, anxious to leave. She waved him off.

"Moi? You do me a great disservice. I am but a lonely old bachelor, trapped here thanks to your spitefulness. If others are fearful, the only person you should blame is yourself, or your shady sidekick. I don't blame people for being afraid. I am fearful, too."

Max laughed. "You've never been scared a day in your life, but you should be."

Maugham regarded Mona and Clem. Mona clutched Clem's arm, worried Maugham was about to give them away. Instead he smiled and looked back at Max and Dusk. "Why, I've even heard you've threatened to send paintings away that dare question your authority. What am I or other paintings to think when we are not allowed to question you, Max? Will you send us all away? How far are you willing to go to make people do as you say?"

There was a low growl, followed by Dusk's voice. "He's baiting you, Boss. Let it go. He's not going to tell us anything."

"I'll make him tell me," was Max's furious response.

"Temper . . . ," Maugham warned.

Mona had seen enough. Max and Dusk were out of control. She and Clem needed to get away before they were caught. Grabbing Clem's hand, she made for the passageway.

"That was scary," Clem whispered when they stopped

in a small landscape to catch their breath. "I thought Lord Beaverbrook was going to attack him! What do you think he would have done if he'd caught us in there?"

Mona shook her head, too upset to speak. The Max she had thought she knew was gone, replaced by this bully. She wiped a tear from her cheek and pulled Clem along.

"Where are we going?" he asked when they'd made it past *Santiago El Grande* and he'd solved another easy riddle—What comes down but never goes up? Rain.

"We need to go someplace where Max won't harass us. Let's go see Madame Rubinstein. It's a good thing we went down to the workroom, for now we know something terrible is going on, but oh, Clem, part of me wishes we never had!"

Luckily, Madame Rubinstein was home alone when they arrived. If she noticed Mona's red eyes, she kept her thoughts to herself. Instead, she opened her arms wide.

"There are my two chums," she cooed, hugging them each in turn. "What are you up to so late at night, my little *mysz?*" Mona loved it when Helena called her "mouse" in Polish, the language of Madame Rubinstein's youth.

"We're hoping for some treats and to ask if you've heard the gossip about the art restorer making forgeries,"

Mona said, having decided that being direct was the best course of action.

Madame Rubinstein chuckled and placed a heavily ringed hand on Mona's shoulder. "The paintings here are superstitious, that is all. They do not like his methods. But if Director Singer does not mind, why should I?"

"Do you think we can trust Sneely?" Clem asked.

"Is anyone trustworthy, Clement Cotterell? We are all human and therefore frail. Some of the residents are afraid because they love it so much here. Many of them did not have such pleasant lives as we did before we were painted. Some of them lived hardscrabble lives of woe, but then Max brought them here and now they are comfortable, safe, and happy. Do not forget: we are the immortals now. Our original selves have died. We are the ones who live on. There is much at stake. Perhaps they worry they will be stolen away and taken someplace that is not so lovely as the Beaverbrook Art Gallery."

"Has a painting ever been stolen from the Beaverbrook?" Mona asked. She hated to ask the question. It made her uneasy, as if she was putting a jinx on their happiness.

"I do not think so. But it is always a fear. You know the story of how Mona Lisa was stolen, yes?" She placed a china plate stacked with treats on the table. Mona grabbed one.

"I don't," Clem said, his mouth full.

"It was August 21, 1911. You had not been painted yet, Mona, but the other Mona, *Mona Lisa*, was already the most famous painting in the world. Despite the top-notch Louvre security, it appeared someone simply walked off with her."

"Someone just walked off with her?" Mona's chest tightened.

"Yes. Interestingly, Pablo Picasso was one of the first to be questioned by the police, although he was quickly ruled out as a suspect and released. As is often the case, the theft was an inside job. A museum employee, Vincenzo Peruggia, took her one night. It is rumored he worked with a con man, Eduardo de Valfierno, to get the painting to art forger Yves Chaudron. The plan was for Chaudron to make copies and sell them as if they were the original. Whether that is true or not, who knows? The art world has always been a source of gossip and speculation."

"Imagine someone having the audacity to do such a thing!" Mona exclaimed.

Madame Rubinstein tugged on one of the long ropes of pearls that encircled her neck. "Yes, with the original hidden away in Peruggia's apartment, it would have been easy enough to convince the greedy art collectors with their deep pockets that the *Mona Lisa* they were being offered—and that they could only hang in some private room in their house—was THE Mona Lisa. What is it about human nature that makes us want to own coveted things, regardless of the cost?"

When neither Clem nor Mona responded, she continued with her story. "As in most things, there was a slip-up. It made Peruggia nervous to have the painting in his apartment for so long and he decided to try to sell the painting to an art dealer from Florence, Italy, who tipped off the police. After two years of being stuck in a closet, Mona Lisa returned to the Louvre amid immense fanfare in 1913. The theft made her the most famous painting in the world."

She finished her story and patted their heads. "Now off with you. I am tired and it is nearly dawn. I think I shall have a little rest."

As she stepped back into her own familiar painting, Mona couldn't help thinking about the other Mona, stuck in a closet for two years. It must have been terribly lonely and frightening. What would she do if that happened to her? At least Mona Lisa knew people would be searching for her; she was the world's most famous painting, after all. Would anyone look so hard for Mona Dunn?

CHAPTER TWENTY

Janice was exactly what Sargent and Isaac's relationship needed. Besides her culinary skills, she was a wicked opponent at Scrabble (Sargent had never met anybody who had memorized every word that started with an X before) and adored watching sci-fi movies with him. Best of all, she kept the conversation moving.

The deathly silences were replaced by lively debate and long conversations about art, movies, and favorite books. So it seemed natural to Sargent to bring up Isaac's paintings one evening when he and Janice went for a walk while Isaac stayed home to get ready for a meeting he had with Harmsworth the next day. More and more,

Harmsworth was looking like the Beaverbrook's savior, and even though Sargent still thought the guy was a windbag, if he helped Isaac, that would be a good thing.

Janice had stopped in the center of the pedestrian bridge that crossed the St. John River—an old converted train bridge—and looked upriver. "Don't you wish you had your paints here so you capture this view?" she asked.

Sargent stared at the sky, marveling at how the splashes of color behind the setting sun were the same shade as the watermelon they'd had for dessert. "Do you paint a lot?"

Janice shook her head. "I dabble, but it's more frustrating than fun because I can't convert what I see in my head onto the canvas." She turned and smiled at him. "But you don't have that problem, do you?"

Usually Sargent would have mumbled something that downplayed his talent, but for some reason, he trusted Janice not to make a big deal about it. "No," he conceded. She nodded, and they turned back to watch the sun slip below the horizon.

"My dad can paint, too," Sargent said.

"He's very talented," Janice agreed.

"I heard you mention the Albuquerque Museum the other day."

Janice flushed. "I'm so embarrassed; I shouldn't have

been talking about that. That's your dad's business, not mine."

"But you think he should let them exhibit his paintings," Sargent said.

"I think your dad is amazing. I wish people could see his work and give him the recognition he deserves. Most people don't even know he's an artist. But he doesn't have the paintings, and for whatever reason he doesn't want to try to get them, so that's that."

Sargent didn't respond. He was too busy thinking about how thrilled Isaac would be, if he, Sargent, managed to get the paintings and have them sent to Albuquerque.

For the first time in his life, Sargent didn't just enjoy learning new skills, he enjoyed hanging out with other kids, too. It actually seemed to make his art better.

"You're really good, man," Troy said, glancing over Sargent's shoulder at the rough sketch he was making of *The Cotterell Family.* "You should be teaching this class."

Sargent looked aghast. "No way! I have a ton to learn. And everyone here is talented."

"Yeah, we are, but not like you are. You're like some kind of progeny."

"Prodigy!" Alice called out from the other end of the room. "Progeny means he's someone's offspring. Which is technically true of Sargent, but also of the rest of us, too."

"That girl is too smart for me," muttered Troy under his breath.

Sargent was making a copy of The Cotterell Family using crayon and pastels. He'd never done anything so adventurous before, but Janice's enthusiasm, and his fellow campers' lack of competitiveness, made him feel brave. Janice had laughed when he'd told her his plan.

"Terrific! We'll have to hold it up afterward so the Cotterells can see themselves in crayon." She leaned toward the painting. "You won't like that, will you, Lady Cotterell?"

Sargent sucked in his breath, waiting to see if there would be a response, but of course there was none. Sargent tagged along when Janice went to check on Adam, curious to see how his friend's work was coming. Adam was copying Sutherland's portrait of Lord Beaverbrook using a collage technique: part fabric, part torn paper, part painted pieces of paper glued on a board.

"In set design, you have to be able to make things look rich on a shoestring budget," Adam told Janice. It sounded cool. Sargent had always focused on painting. Maybe he'd try collage for another project.

He was the last one to leave the Harriet Irving Gallery

at the end of the afternoon. He'd avoided making eye contact with Mona all day, although he couldn't help but grin every time Troy said, "Mona, baby, I'm gonna make you a star!" He was stretching his arms above his head when a tour group trouped in, planting themselves in front of Edmund and the Cotterells. It was the perfect opportunity to say good night to Mona.

"We could meet Friday when I stay overnight," he whispered, keeping his eyes on his phone while he spoke.

"I'll try," Mona whispered, barely moving her lips. "Something strange is going on here, Sargent. Some of the paintings think Mr. Sneely is making copies of them to sell! I'm trying to get to the bottom of it."

Sargent glanced up, just as Janice poked her head in the door. "C'mon, Sargent, we're waiting on you."

Troubled, he nodded to Mona and ran to catch up with the others.

When Sargent arrived at Isaac's office a few minutes later after saying good-bye to the other campers, he discovered Isaac wasn't alone. A tiny woman, who looked like she might have been present on the first day the earth was created, sat opposite Isaac at the round table, both of them staring at a small painting on an easel.

Isaac looked up. "Your timing is perfect, Sargent. I'm

just about to do an appraisal for Mrs. Zelda Murray. We want to see if this painting is the real deal or a fake. Come have a seat."

Mona's comment fresh in his mind, Sargent plopped down in the empty seat on the other side of the table. Maybe he could learn something useful.

Zelda Murray held out a bony hand for him to shake. Sargent tried not to look at the protruding veins that seemed ready to pop through her translucent skin. He'd never met anyone so old. Her hair wasn't snow white; it was so white, it threatened to disintegrate. Their handshake was limp; Sargent was worried he might break her.

But Zelda Murray's smile was youthful. "Your father has been telling me what a talented artist you are, Sargent. And to answer your unasked question, I just celebrated my one hundred and second birthday in April."

Sargent's eyes widened. Flustered, he turned to the painting. "Is that a—"

"A Gauguin? I hope so," Zelda said. "My husband and I were avid art collectors, traveling the world to add to our collection. We were so enthralled with art we used to participate in the Pageant of the Masters in Laguna Beach, California."

"Pageant of the Masters?"

"The Pageant of the Masters is when people come and pose as *tableaux vivants*, or living paintings. One year we did *Hotel Bedroom*. It was quite something. Imagine the fun, pretending to be a painting come to life, standing inside a massive picture frame."

Sargent nodded. He could imagine that.

"Apart from the Beaverbrook, Zelda has the most notable collection in the city," Isaac added.

Zelda lifted her chin. "It will be the Beaverbrook's when I die. If I die," she added mischievously. She pointed a gnarled finger at the painting. "As I said to you on the telephone, Isaac, this painting is the only one yet to be appraised. We were given it in the early 1950s by my uncle Edgar and were never sure of its authenticity. Not that it mattered; we would have kept it anyway, because we were very fond of Edgar. Now, as I prepare to pass my darlings on to you, I feel this little mystery needs to be sorted out."

Sargent had seen Gauguin paintings at the Metropolitan Museum of Art. But those paintings were bigger, from Paul Gauguin's time in Tahiti, and full of riotous colors and primitive figures. This painting was tiny, a black-and-white print of leaves and shadows. Gaugin had created it by making a woodcut, which meant he'd carved the image into a piece of wood, rolled ink over it, and then pressed the inky wood onto the paper. Sargent looked at his father, questioning.

"Gauguin certainly used woodcuts to make his prints, so that's the first bit of good news," Isaac said. "But then," he added, "I am sure you and your husband knew that, Zelda."

Zelda smiled. "We knew a little about art."

"A little . . . ," Isaac murmured, lifting the print off the easel. He pulled a handheld loupe, a tool that looked like a miniature telescope, from his pocket and began to study the painting.

"How can you tell if a painting is real?" Sargent said.

"It's not so difficult if you know what you're looking for. For example, if the piece was never trying to pass itself off as a real thing, there is often a C in a circle down in the corner."

"A C?"

"It's a copyright symbol that tells us the painting is a copy. This painting doesn't have that."

"And . . ."

"Another way is to hold it up to the light." Isaac lifted the painting up so the late-afternoon light shone through it. "In a fake, you're often able to see the entire image on the reverse, because they copy the original, stroke for stroke. Most artists don't work like that; they make mistakes or change their mind along the way, so the back looks quite blobby, like this one.

"Then I ask myself: did Gauguin do this type of work? The answer is yes. Then I check to see if I can see little dots in the picture, which would indicate the painting was printed." He leaned in so close to the surface of the painting with his loupe that Sargent worried he'd touch the paper.

Sargent held his breath. "Any dots?"

"Nope. Now if this was an oil painting and it was fake, you might see evidence of mechanical brushstrokes. Some art forgers have quite sophisticated methods nowadays."

Zelda was as riveted as Sargent. "Do any of them ever try to paint a forgery from scratch?"

"Oh, sure," Isaac said, turning the picture over again. "And some of them are very good. In fact, some are so good it's impossible to tell the difference. Mechanical brushstrokes are easier to spot, because you'll see a brushstroke going in a direction that's inconsistent with what's being painted. Or the brushstrokes look too similar; an artist can't be that perfect. Where the best forgers are beaten is usually in technique and color. It's nearly impossible to replicate an old color, and of course we have photographs of the original to compare it with."

Sargent hadn't seen Sneely's copy of Merrymaking, so he

had no idea how it had been done. He needed to go see Sneely, find an excuse to look at what he'd been working on, and check it out with his newfound knowledge.

Isaac took a deep breath. "Zelda, I couldn't find an official record or reference to your picture, but that's not unheard of. Artists often do small studies that they sell or give away to friends. In my opinion, this is indeed a Gauguin and should be insured for at least five hundred thousand dollars."

Zelda clapped her hands in delight. "I knew Uncle Edgar wasn't the type to buy a copy! Thank you, Isaac, you've made my day."

She turned to Sargent and took his hand. "A pleasure meeting you, Sargent." This time, Sargent wasn't afraid of breaking Zelda. He was pretty sure she was unbreakable.

CHAPTER TWENTY-ONE

Mona had thought she would love seeing Sargent every day. Instead it was torture. Since the day he'd spent sketching the Cotterells, their interaction had been nonexistent. It was already Thursday, and he hadn't stopped by once since Tuesday. Now and then she'd catch glimpses of him racing around the gallery with his new friends or leaving with Isaac at the end of the day. She wasn't envious that he was having a good time—of course he should have fun—but Sargent's fun only reinforced how dull her own life was.

Meanwhile, Troy had become her constant companion, chatting away about nothing and pressing on her last nerve like a buzzing housefly she couldn't swat. Just as bad was Mr. Harmsworth, who'd spent the week peacocking around as if he owned the place. His visits to stare at her were unsettling. The only break in the monotony was that Max had called a meeting.

This time, Mona planned to be late. She wanted to inspect *Merrymaking* when its residents couldn't see her nosing around. She knew it wasn't a forgery—if it had been, the residents would have been unable to return to it—but she wanted a good look at it before she looked at Sneely's copy in the workroom. The only problem was that she couldn't actually visit *Merrymaking*, for Papa and Max had expressly forbidden her to visit any painting containing a common public house.

Instead, she slipped into the painting on the opposite wall, Delacroix's *Lady Macbeth Sleep-Walking*. Though wandering into paintings of landscapes and crowded scenes was common, going into another resident's portrait without their permission was against the rules. It was like visiting a friend's bedroom when they weren't home. Though Mona knew she would be furious to find an unwanted guest in her own portrait, she justified the transgression by telling herself that she would only be a moment.

Sneely's work had made *Merrymaking* more vibrant, alive, as if the residents were newly painted. Mona couldn't imagine a copy could ever be so detailed. But if Sneely wasn't a forger, what was going on? And why were so many people suddenly visiting the workroom?

"Out, damned spot!"

It was Lady Macbeth! And while Lady Macbeth might not be awake, the servant and the doctor who dutifully followed her on her nightly sleepwalk were decidedly so. Mona dashed out of the frame and ran toward *Santiago El Grande*, praying she hadn't been spotted.

If she expected that Max would be gone by the time she passed his painting, she was wrong. His low growl echoed in the passageway behind his portrait. Why wasn't he at the meeting yet? Who was he speaking to? Mona strained to hear, but the voice was indistinguishable. Creeping forward, she pressed her ear up against Max's frame to listen.

"It's going all right?" Max said.

The person who responded was not in Max's painting, nor on the far side of the frame. Whoever was speaking was outside of the frame, standing in the gallery. Which meant Max was talking to someone from the world outside the frame! Mona's initial shock was quickly replaced by righteous indignation—how dare he chastise her for being caught by Sargent when he was engaged in similar behavior? It was infuriating!

Despite a burning desire to run into his painting and confront him for his hypocrisy, she held back. Max always said knowledge was power, best revealed at the right moment. She'd make him eat those words.

"Has he provided you with a dollar figure yet?" Max asked.

There was a garbled response, and then Max said, "You are doing an excellent job. I'll keep my people on the straight and narrow until you complete the deal. Everyone will be shocked."

Mona strained to hear the next comment, but the only words she could understand were "soon" and "sleepover."

Max chuckled. "Everything will work out. It always does. People won't like it if they have to move, but it doesn't hurt to be shaken up now and then, does it?"

Then . . . footsteps. The person was leaving. Mona dashed back along the passage, popping in and out of paintings, trying to catch a glimpse of whoever it was. Finally she saw dark pant legs heading down the back stairs. The only distinguishing feature was a pair of black sneakers, which was vexing; half the staff wore black sneakers. Frustrated, but knowing she had stumbled upon valuable information—if she could only make sense of it—she made her way to *Santiago El Grande*.

CHAPTER TWENTY-TWO

Mona spotted Clem at the far side of *Santiago El Grande*. She had to wriggle through the crowd to reach him, going past Sir Thomas Samwell and Andre Reidmor, who was holding Somerset Maugham's head in his arms. Reidmor gave her his best bearlike stare, all dark and dangerous, as she squeezed past, but Maugham winked and whispered, "Well done! Max never suspected you were there." Mona grinned. She was almost to Clem when someone tugged at her arm. Turning, she looked up to see Argyle and Bertha Smith.

"Hullo," Argyle said, bobbing his head. Bertha curtsied.

Mona was pleased to see them. "Hello! Are you happy to be back in Merrymaking?"

Bertha leaned in close, smelling of cabbage and corned beef. "It don't feel like home."

"Whyever not?"

"Too clean," Argyle supplied. "The first time a feller spilled his beer, you coulda heard a pin drop. They was afraid to mess things up. Never thought I'd see the day that would happen!"

"Surely it's not clean inside the White Horse Inn? How could Mr. Sneely manage that?"

Argyle shrugged. "Who knows? But the sheets was clean and the floors polished so's you could eat off them. I can't figger out how he done it. You can even see out the windows."

"There, there, ducky," Bertha said, rubbing Argyle's stooped shoulders. "It'll be a right royal mess soon enough. We can manage until then."

They were interrupted by intense clapping. Dusk was attempting to call the meeting to order. Mona whispered her good-byes and went to stand beside Clem, who nudged her and pointed to a spot in the painting behind Dusk. One of the body-less hands was creeping, crablike, along the side of the frame. Clearly, Dusk hadn't seen it, or he would have shooed it away. Mona listened to Dusk but never took her eyes off the hand.

"Good evening," Dusk said. "I'm pleased to see such a good turnout on such short notice. Lord Beaverbrook is here to discuss the rules for tomorrow evening's sleepover, and I suggest you pay particular attention. Failure to follow the rules could result in sanctions."

"What sort of sanctions?" someone called. Meanwhile, the hand cupped, as if it were listening with an imaginary ear for Dusk's response.

Dusk turned an odd pinky-gray color. "I'm not at liberty to discuss punishments."

Max stepped forward and nudged Dusk to the side. Mona wondered if Dusk knew that Max had spoken with someone outside of his frame.

"Good evening. I'm sorry to call another meeting so soon, but I thought it prudent given tomorrow evening's activities. But before I address that, I want to ask if the residents of Merrymaking are pleased with their restoration?"

There was lukewarm clapping. A man dressed in furs with a dreadful scar zigzagging across his cheek shouted, "It's too bloody clean, Beaverbrook!"

Mona had never seen Max look so irate. He leaned forward. "You there—Mr. Ryan, is it? Did you ever read my book about my early life?"

Mr. Ryan shook his head. "Can't read." He scratched at the stubble on his chin and grinned at his neighbors as if he'd said something clever.

Beaverbrook's smile was menacing. "Of course you can't read," he continued. "Not to mention you were long dead before I put pen to paper. If you had read *My Early Life*, you would have come across a passage. And if you had read that passage, you would know that one shows gratitude when someone like me does something generous for someone like you. One does not complain."

"What passage?" Mr. Ryan looked less emboldened now. He glanced at Argyle Smith.

Mona knew the passage. She could quote it from memory, and she recited it soundlessly now with Max. "On the rock-bound coast of New Brunswick the waves break incessantly. Every now and then comes a particularly dangerous wave that breaks viciously into the rock. It is called 'The Rage.' That's me." Max paused. "If you don't want the rage, I would advise you to be thankful for what you have received and keep your mouth shut."

The room was silent. Even baby Frances knew better than to cry. Max continued to stare at Mr. Ryan. "Do you understand what I'm telling you, sir?" Mr. Ryan nodded. Satisfied, Max turned his attention back to the task at hand. Behind him, the hand made the okay sign.

"Now. Tomorrow evening. The campers will remain in the education room in the basement until after they eat their pizza, which will be delivered at seven o'clock sharp. They will remain there until eight thirty, eating and playing games. Then they will move next door to the Contemporary Gallery to watch a movie and go to sleep. Therefore, all visiting and movement is limited to the period between seven and eight thirty. I apologize for the inconvenience."

"What if the art restorer stays late again?" Sir Charles Cotterell called.

"I understand he has an engagement. This is a difficulty, but we must be discreet. While every effort will be made to contain the campers within the Contemporary Gallery, they may need to use the facilities and, children being children, may engage in some shenanigans. Any other questions?"

"There are rumors about the art restorer," Mona said. "Are you confident he is simply doing his job and not engaging in any nefarious activities?"

Max squinted in her direction. "If all the residents of Merrymaking have to complain about is a spotless painting, then yes, I am confident in his abilities, Miss Dunn."

Mona would not be so easily put off. "But it is said he is making copies of the paintings."

"He makes rough copies to assist him with his work. Dusk's painting is down in the workroom now. Do you have any issue with the process, Dusk?"

"None," Dusk said, though his word was at odds with his tone of voice, which quavered. In the background, the hand wagged its index finger, as if it didn't believe Dusk, which caused a few chuckles.

If Max heard the laughter, he didn't acknowledge it. "If there is nothing more, I have other matters to attend to. Good night."

Max hurried off, something he'd never done before. Normally, he lingered, chatted with people, addressed private issues brought to his attention. The others were equally surprised, and shuffled off toward the sides of the frame. Mona noticed that Mr. Ryan was scowling. Max had made an enemy, not that he would care. Even Dusk seemed bewildered by Max's speedy departure. He spotted Mona and beckoned her over. Rolling her eyes, she did.

"Mr. Dusk?"

"I understand you were in the workroom the other night," he said.

Mona stiffened. "I stopped by to say hello to Mr. Maugham."

"Is that so? I understand you and Clement were asking a lot of questions."

"I understand the workroom is popular these days."
She could give as good as she got.

"The workroom is always busy. You wouldn't know
that because until recently, you've never concerned yourself with it. Regardless, I'd prefer you give it a wide berth,
at least until the restoration work on my painting is complete. My wife was upset by the noise."

Mona pictured Mrs. Dusk's vacant eyes. "I'm sorry. I
didn't realize she understood what was going on . . . ,"
she said, faltering. Mona had her faults, but cruelty was
not one of them. If she'd distressed Mrs. Dusk, she was
truly sorry.

"What my wife does or does not understand is none
of your business, Miss Dunn. Please, just do as I say. I'd
appreciate if you'd stay out of the basement completely
until Mr. Sneely finishes his work. I wouldn't want you
to be in the way."

Mona stepped back. "Is this Max's request?"

Something flickered across Dusk's face, but it passed
so quickly Mona couldn't grasp its meaning. "I am Max's
right-hand man."

Mona glanced upward to try to keep her temper in
check. The horse and rider were eavesdropping and
appeared as interested in the conversation's outcome as
she was. "I can go where I like."

"Yes, but will you be able to solve the riddles to get there? They can be difficult."

Mona stole another glance at the horse and rider. They stared back at her, inscrutable. Something was definitely going on. Max and Dusk wanted to block her from going into the basement. What were they up to? More and more, the gallery seemed like a prison, not a home.

Then something caught her eye on the ground behind Dusk. It was the hand, inching forward. Normally Mona would tell another resident if one of the hands was too close for comfort, but she was so vexed at Dusk she kept silent. Seconds later, the hand pounced, hopping up and tapping Dusk on the shoulder as if it wanted to ask him a question. Startled, Dusk cried out, trying to brush it off his shoulder.

Mona gave Dusk a grim nod. "They've not stopped me yet." She wheeled around and ran to the closest portal, ignoring Clem's calls, anxious to get away. She desperately wanted to run to San Vigilio, Lake Garda, but what if Dusk followed her there? Instead, she hurried back to her painting and lay on the floor to avoid being seen by prying eyes. Never had she felt so alone.

CHAPTER TWENTY-THREE

By late Friday morning, every camper's version of the painting they'd chosen to copy was finished. Janice had them haul eight easels out to the Contemporary Gallery, which they arranged around the room like a proper art exhibit. Sargent loved seeing everything displayed; it was like they were real artists. Isaac had come down to review their work and planned to take Sargent out for lunch at his favorite Greek restaurant, Dimitris.

"I love your copy of The Cotterell Family, Sargent," Alice said. It was good. Sir Charles and Lady Cotterell were rendered in neon shades, Clem and the other kids were gradations of purples and pinks, the trees and sky were colored in shades of orange and red. "It's kind of Andy Warholish."

This was high praise, and Sargent lapped it up. "I like yours, too. It's cool how you made *Santiago El Grande* a charcoal sketch," he said, tilting his head in the direction of Alice's work.

"It's okay, I guess. It's sort of predictable. You know, picking the most famous painting in the gallery to copy and all."

Adam joined them. "Technically, they're all pretty famous," he said. "Is it wrong to have a favorite? Because I love Troy's comic."

All week, the other campers had watched Troy write and ink his comic. Edmund's red military garb became a red skintight spandex suit, with a golden E monogrammed on the center of his chest in the style of an illuminated letter from a medieval book. Mona was his black-mask-wearing sidekick, complete with caramel-colored bodysuit, white cape, and tall black boots. Everyone agreed she looked kick-ass.

The plot was simple: Edmund and Mona were trying to stop a nefarious art thief named Salvador Dolly from stealing the crown jewel of the gallery, an imaginary painting from Troy's twisted mind called *St. John River Zombie Rumble*, which portrayed zombies attacking the Fredericton Garrison in 1750. His painting was a bloodbath, full of maimed soldiers morphing into zombies, and it took up two full pages in the comic.

"I love the last line," Sargent said, glancing across the room to where Troy was explaining his comic to Isaac. "'The paintings at the Beaverbrook Art Gallery will always be safe so long as I, Mona Dunn, have even one breath in my body,'" he added, adopting a falsetto voice.

Adam snorted. "Or when Mona karate-chops Salvador Dolly. I was like, yeah!"

Alice giggled. "The best part was when Edmund rode through the gallery on the back of the horse from *Santiago El Grande*."

Isaac was looking at Adam's Lord Beaverbrook collage. Touching Beaverbrook's forehead, he marveled at how Adam had managed to make wrinkles out of pink calico fabric. Sargent seriously doubted that Beaverbrook would enjoy having pink-flowered fabric for his face; from what Mona had said, he sounded like a bully. Which reminded him—he needed to see Mona; he had a cool idea. He glanced over at Isaac, who had yet to talk to Alice and Abby. He should have more than enough time to run upstairs before lunch.

The Harriet Irving Gallery was filled with older women wearing purple dresses and red hats. They gathered around the docent, Amy, who was telling them all about Edmund and the Cotterells' paintings, and their boisterous laughter was so infectious it made Sargent laugh, too. Every eye was on them, which made it the perfect time to talk to Mona.

Sargent stood in front of her portrait. "We're watching a movie in the Contemporary Gallery tonight," he said between clenched teeth. "It's really good—*Harry Potter.* You should come."

Mona had never seen a moving picture before. Now and then one of the art installations included a short film, but she'd never seen a Hollywood film, though she was aware of them.

"I wish I could, but I can't," she whispered. "Max has banned me from going downstairs. Plus we're only allowed to leave our frames between seven and eight thirty."

"That's not fair," Sargent hissed.

Mona said nothing, but her lower lip quivered.

Sargent thought quickly. "Listen, I'll stick a blank canvas under the front desk. Make sure you're in it by eight thirty. I'll bring you down right before the movie starts, then return you before the movie ends. No one will know. You'll love the movie. It's so good—Daniel Radcliffe and Alan Rickman are in it." Mona nodded, though she had no idea who he was talking about.

Amy stuck her head in the doorway. "Hey, Sargent, have you seen your dad?"

"He's downstairs. I'm on my way back down. Want me to go get him?"

"Mr. Harmsworth is here and wants to see him. Can you take him downstairs with you?"

"Sure." Sargent glanced at Mona. She hadn't said she'd come. He hoped she would.

Harmsworth was pacing in the front lobby. "Ah, Sal," he said, thumping Sargent on the back. "Good to see you again!"

"Sargent."

"Of course. I hear you'll be my beacon, leading me to your father. Lead on, Macduff."

Sargent didn't know who Macduff was, but he led Harmsworth to his father, who was studying Abby Gilbert's watercolor interpretation of Merrymaking. The watery hues gave it a different feel, making it look like a fairy-tale cottage instead of a common alehouse.

"John!" Isaac called when he spotted Harmsworth. "This is a surprise!"

"A welcome one, I hope," Harmsworth said, looking

around the room with a bemused expression. "I see your summer campers have vivid imaginations."

"They do indeed," Isaac said. "They're very talented. It's quite inspiring. Would you like me to show you their work and introduce you?"

"No time for that," Harmsworth said, turning back toward the door. "I thought we'd have lunch, chat about the inner workings of the gallery. You know, opening and closing hours, staffing levels, that sort of thing. I never make an investment unless I fully understand the business I'm investing in."

Sargent waited for Isaac to tell Harmsworth he already had lunch plans with his son, but instead Isaac replied, "I'd love to buy you lunch." Clearly he'd forgotten all about their plans. Sargent stepped aside, stung, as Isaac and Harmsworth headed for the exit.

Sneely appeared in the doorway, blocking the two men. His eyes narrowed when he saw Harmsworth. "May I speak with you, Mr. Singer?"

"I'm off to lunch, Archibald. Can it wait?"

The art restorer shook his head. "It's about the supplies I requested."

Isaac and Harmsworth were already squeezing past. "Talk to Janice, she'll fix you up."

Sneely grunted, then stalked away.

"I thought you were going to lunch with your dad," Alice said to Sargent.

"Me too." It was hard not to sound bitter.

"My mom made some amazing ratatouille last night. Want to share?"

Sargent gave her a grateful nod. "Thanks, I—"

Alice smiled. "No biggie. My dad forgot to pick me up once from the movies. I get it."

Sargent knew it shouldn't be a big deal, so why did he feel like Isaac was abandoning him for Harmsworth? Suddenly he missed his mom. But calling her in the middle of the day required an excuse . . . which was when he remembered Isaac's paintings.

"Ten minutes until lunch, guys!" Janice hollered.

"I'll be right back," Sargent mumbled. He stepped into the cloakroom for some privacy and dialed his mother, hoping he wasn't pulling her out of some important meeting. He was relieved by her cheerful hello.

"Hello, sweetheart! I was just thinking about you, wondering how you are. We haven't talked for two days and I've been worried. Is everything okay?"

Sargent grinned. His mother asked him that question every time they spoke.

"Everything's fine. Can I ask you something?"

"Of course. What's up?"

"Isaac got an invitation to show two of his paintings at the Albuquerque Museum. *Sarah in the Morning* and *The One Who Makes My Heart Sing*. But he's turning down the invite because he doesn't own the paintings. I wondered if you know where they are?"

He heard the sharp intake of breath. When she finally spoke, she sounded tense. "I know exactly where they are. They're in storage. They belong to you."

"Oh." Sargent wondered when she'd planned to share this information with him. It was strange to think of the paintings wrapped up and waiting in some storage locker. Then it hit him: those paintings could be alive, too.

"I'm surprised he didn't ask you for them," his mother said, echoing the question he was already asking himself. Why hadn't Isaac asked him if he could borrow them? Did he think Sargent wouldn't agree? A ripple of uncertainty snaked through his body.

"Why didn't you tell me about them before? I might have hung them in my bedroom."

His mother's voice turned icy. "They are beautiful paintings, but they are very painful to me, Sargent. When your father and I divorced, I felt it was important that the paintings of you and me stay with you, and your father reluctantly agreed. I did not think it was my place to tell you about them. They're your father's paintings, not mine."

"Yeah, but you have them," he pointed out.

"I don't have them. The storage company has them."

"Mom, come on. Why didn't you tell me about them?"

"To be honest, I'd forgotten about them. But they belong to you; if you want them shipped to Albuquerque, let them know. Just not to our apartment." She added, "I think it would be poor taste to hang a portrait of me painted by my ex-husband in the home I share with Bill."

Sargent thought about his conversation with Janice. He wished people could see Isaac's work again, too. Maybe it would inspire Isaac to pick up a paintbrush again. He pictured the two of them side by side, painting, and smiled.

"Can you ship them out to Albuquerque?"

His mother made a sound that he took to be a yes. Deciding it would be nice to talk about something else before they hung up, he changed the subject. "Does the Met have any paintings by William Orpen?" He heard his mother's long nails clicking on her keyboard.

"Two, a self-portrait and a graphite sketch of a woman dressing. You can see them on the website. Why are you interested in Orpen?"

"The gallery has a portrait of his, Mona Dunn."

The keyboard clicked again. "Oh, it's gorgeous. What

a lovely girl. What do you think of *Santiago El Grande*? I've always wanted to see it."

"It's good, I guess, but strange."

"That was Dalí. Darling, I have to go. Do you need anything else?"

"Nope. Thanks, Mom." Sargent hung up and smiled.

CHAPTER TWENTY-FOUR

Mona was fretting. Not because it would be difficult to slip into the canvas Sargent was leaving for her—that would be easy. The problem was her friends. Would they tell Max when she didn't return at eight thirty? However, if she could convince Edmund that she'd be back in her painting before the end of the movie, maybe he could convince the others to keep quiet.

Sargent's invitation was the most thrilling thing that had happened to her since she'd woken up in her portrait, alive. All the residents were desperate to see a moving picture. Wasn't that worth breaking the rules for? Lost in her thoughts, she was surprised when Director Singer and Janice entered the gallery, then realized they'd come to await the pizza delivery.

"Sargent really likes you, Janice. His visit is going better than I thought it would, and most of that's thanks to you."

Janice smiled. "I'm glad, he's a great kid. Have you had the talk with him yet?"

"I can't figure out how to do it." Mona thought Director Singer sounded nervous.

"It won't get any easier. And it will make things better, I promise. . . ."

Director Singer nodded. "You're right. I love you, Janice." Mona almost gasped when he pulled Janice in close and kissed her. Mona had never seen anyone kiss like that before. Edmund was much too proper to embrace Madame Juliette in front of others.

When they stepped back, Janice's eyes were shining. "I love you, too, Isaac."

"This is not where I was planning to do this, but . . ."

He was on his knees. Mona glanced across at Edmund and the Cotterells, all of whom were trying to look without being seen looking. Director Singer was about to propose!

Director Singer placed the ring on Janice's finger. She said yes, and then they laughed and hugged until the night bell rang. The pizza had arrived. As soon as they left, Mona wiped her eyes and waved at her friends. Lady Cotterell dabbed her eyes with a lacy handkerchief. Clem pretended to throw up.

At seven, the galleries upstairs came alive as residents hurried to get their business done within the allotted time frame. Mona waved Edmund over.

"I only have a moment," he said. "I'm off to see Juliette."

"I need you to do me a tremendous favor."

Edmund's face grew wary. "I cannot say yes until I know what it is."

"If I am not back by eight thirty, will you keep my absence a secret and ensure the Cotterells do as well?"

"Wherever will you be?"

"I have been invited to watch my first moving picture."

"Are you mad, Mona? Absolutely not! I forbid it! You shall get caught!"

"I shan't get caught. Oh, Edmund, you know how I want to see a moving picture. . . ."

He blanched at her imploring look. "Who crafted this plan, that boy?"

Mona bristled. "He's not 'that boy.' He is my friend. He has arranged this as a special treat for me. The movie is about Harry Potter. Even you have heard of Harry Potter,

Edmund. Can you not see clear to allow me one night of fun in my life?"

"This is madness, Mona." Edmund tapped his walking stick against the frame. "I would like nothing better than for you to see one of these moving pictures. But if you get caught . . ."

She put a hand on his arm. "I shan't get caught, Edmund. Please."

"I know I cannot stop you, but I beg you not to go."

"You will speak with the Cotterells, smooth the waters?"

He studied her face. "I will do my best, for it is clear you will not be dissuaded. But Mona, you must find peace with your life here. Sargent will leave at the end of the summer. He will grow old. You will not. The path you travel guarantees nothing but heartache."

Mona's eyes filled with tears. "Edmund, I know you are right, but still . . ."

"Then good luck, little one. I will do my utmost to help you. Be safe."

"I've got to wrap you up," Sargent whispered as he leaned under the front desk where Mona was waiting in the canvas. "Otherwise it's too risky."

Mona nodded. "The safest way for you to get me

down downstairs unseen is to go through the Canadian Gallery. There's a hidden door there that leads to the freight elevator."

"Okay! Remember: we leave when Harry heads for the train at the end." Sargent draped a drop cloth loosely over the canvas and lifted it gingerly, as if he feared Mona might tumble out.

Using the freight elevator was an excellent idea. When they arrived in the basement, Sargent carried Mona to the Oppenheimer Gallery, leaned her against the wall, and uncovered her.

"Have fun!" he whispered.

"Thank you, Sargent."

Mona was looking at him with such gratitude that Sargent was suddenly tongue-tied. "You're going to love the movie, I promise," he finally managed to say.

As soon as she could see the lights were out in the Contemporary Gallery, Mona made her way to an oil painting on the wall opposite the screen. It was a landscape Mona had visited many times before, filled with fat fir trees she could hide behind if need be. Not that anyone was looking at her; they were all staring at the screen. Sargent glanced back, saw her there, and grinned.

The opening credits began with a soaring soundtrack. Mona almost shouted in delight. She hadn't known what to expect, but it definitely wasn't this. This was amazing. Then: an owl, a wizard, a giant on a motorbike, a baby who became a boy. The train trip to Hogwarts. Harry had friends, he played Quidditch. It was hard not to laugh when the others laughed, hard not to echo Adam when he shouted, "Watch out for Voldemort, Harry!"

There had never been anything finer than this moving picture. Several times Mona had to wipe away tears of happiness. Whoever wrote this story had written it for her. And when the residents of the pictures in Hogwarts spoke and moved about, and—most wondrously— interacted with the staff and students of Hogwarts, it was as if she'd been given a glimpse of what life could be like if only Max's rules were not so strict.

As with all good things, it ended too soon. She was back in the blank canvas when she spotted Dusk in a landscape a few paintings away. Did Max know he was breaking the rules? As if he sensed her presence, Dusk turned and looked in her direction. Then he disappeared, and she heard his footsteps coming toward her. She was about to run when she saw Sargent racing down the hall-way. Dusk's footsteps stopped abruptly.

"We gotta move before they look for me," Sargent said as he covered the canvas with the drop cloth. "Did you like it?"

"It was amazing," Mona whispered, hoping Dusk couldn't hear.

"There are more movies based on the rest of the books."

Mona sighed. "I wish I could see them all. It was like being in a fairyland."

Sargent hurried to the freight elevator. Upstairs, he slipped through the Canadian Gallery, placed the canvas under the desk, and removed the cloth. Mona stood in a sea of white, her eyes shining, her feet tapping. "I'll never forget the music," she said. "It was magical, as if the composer turned the story into musical notes, instead of words."

"That's the perfect way to describe it. I'll bring you to every movie if I can."

More movies! "Thank you! I felt—" She stopped, uncertain if she was revealing too much.

"What?"

"I felt like a real girl again, not just a girl who lives in a painting."

"But your world is amazing, too! I'd give anything to step inside a painting, see what it's like to be in there, living in those amazing works of art. You're so lucky."

"I suppose . . ."

"No, you are lucky, Mona. Seriously, you can go into

any of the paintings here, see places created from the imagination of the world's greatest artists. It's so cool." He paused when he saw the pained look on Mona's face. "Maybe it's not that simple, but I do think your life is amazing."

Mona smiled. Her life would be amazing if someone like Sargent lived there, too.

They could hear voices in the distance. "I have to get back," Sargent said. "It was cool knowing you were watching the movie with us. With me." He touched the spot on the canvas where her hands were, whispered, "Good night," and ran off.

Dazed, Mona made her way back to her portrait. Sargent's palm on the canvas had been like a jolt of electricity. For an instant, Edmund's earlier words echoed in her head: "He will leave at the end of the summer. He will grow old. You will not. The path you travel guarantees nothing but heartache."

Edmund was right. This couldn't end well.

Ignoring the rule that residents could not leave their paintings during the sleepover, Clem arrived a few minutes later. "My parents are furious," he said straightaway.

"How furious?"

"As furious as I've seen. I'm mad at you, too."

Mona bit her lip. Of course Clem was angry. He was dying to see a movie, too.

"Oh, Clem, I'm so sorry! I should have invited you."

Clem's voice caught. "You went without me. Even Papa wished he could go."

Chastised, Mona nodded.

Clem dropped down to the floor by her stool in case a camper passed by. "Promise you'll bring me next time."

"I promise"

"Good. Now tell me all about it."

For the next fifteen minutes Mona reenacted the movie for Clem's benefit. Once or twice, she forgot a detail and had to improvise, but in general, she managed a true telling of the story.

"The end," she said finally. "Except Sargent says it isn't the end."

"I wish we had a library painting," Clem said. "Someplace we could go to and read. I think the only painting with any books is Max's painting. But his books are boring—all about politics and World War II. Hey, maybe Max could get us a painting of a movie theater!"

Mona nodded. A library and a theater would be amazing. "There's going to be another movie next week. I'll ask Sargent to sneak you in, too."

"My father will insist on going. . . ."

"I thought you were joking! Sir Charles truly wants to see a movie?" The thought of fussy Sir Charles watching a movie was almost too funny to believe.

"He's dead keen on it. If you want to assure his support and silence, he needs to come along, too. Is the canvas large enough?"

"I think we can all squish in."

"Okay, I'll let him know. That should chill him out." Clem hopped up, forced Mona to give him a high five, and hurried home to deliver the news. Sir Charles stood up, bowed deeply in her direction, and granted her a rare smile. Mona nodded, and hoped Sargent wouldn't mind.

CHAPTER TWENTY-FIVE

The campers spent most of their night in the museum talking, thanks to Troy getting his second wind around midnight. He assumed the role of sleepover ringmaster, leading them in rounds of Never Have I Ever and Three Things You Would Take with You to a Desert Island. That game ended when Alice said she'd bring a phone and call someone to get her off the island.

"On that note, time for sleep," Janice said. "Anyone need to go the bathroom?"

"Me!" Adam said. "But no way am I going by myself. This place is creepy at night, like all the paintings are watching you."

"I'm not leaving this comfy sleeping bag to hold your hand," Troy mumbled sleepily.

"I'll go with you," Sargent said.

The hallways were gloomy, for the daytime fluorescent lights were switched off in favor of very dim recessed light fixtures that saved electricity. While Sargent waited for Adam, he swiped his card and poked his head through the doorway that led to the staff area, checking to see if Sneely was still working. Hearing voices, he propped the door open and went to investigate, surprised to discover the workroom was inky black, its door closed. Had he imagined the voices? He was about to turn back when heard a man speak inside the workroom. He pressed his ear to the door.

"I'd appreciate an explanation. I know you are up to something, but I have yet to understand what you hope to gain from your actions."

A different man responded. "I owe you no explanation. I keep my own counsel. Always have, always will. You act as if you own this place. You don't own me."

"There is a lot of talk."

"Not my concern, what people think of that blowhard."

"It takes one to know one."

"Your wit slays me. If you think I will suddenly share all of my secrets with you, you are dreadfully mistaken.

And your threats are meaningless. I have been punished enough."

"You could be punished more."

"Could I?" The second man's voice cut like an icicle. "I don't believe so, little man. You think you can control everything? You can't control me."

Sargent's heart began to race. Was he hearing real people or paintings talking? He reached for the doorknob and tried to turn it, but it was locked.

"Sargent?" Adam whispered.

Sargent jumped. The workroom went silent. Reluctantly, Sargent tiptoed back to where Adam stood waiting.

"Sorry, I was just looking around. Let's go back."

"You gave me a heart attack, man. This place is so weird at night, like one of the people in the paintings might jump out at you and grab you."

"It sure feels like that," Sargent said, wishing he could tell Adam the truth.

The next morning, Isaac and Janice took a bleary-eyed Sargent out for breakfast. Sargent attacked his pancakes, oblivious to how Janice kept twirling her ring.

"You haven't noticed the new ring Janice is wearing," Isaac said, putting particular emphasis on the word "ring." Janice held up her hand for Sargent to inspect it.

Sargent took another bite. "Nice," he mumbled, his mouth full of pancake and syrup.

"I gave her the ring," Isaac said, emphasizing the word "I."

Sargent took a gulp of orange juice. "You're getting married?"

Isaac seemed relieved that he'd finally caught on. "Yes!"

"Oh! Congratulations, I guess."

Janice and Isaac exchanged a look that Sargent couldn't decipher. "We were thinking we'd do it at the end of the summer, before you go back to New York City," Isaac said. "Just a casual affair with close friends and family. We thought we'd have the ceremony and a champagne reception at the gallery."

Sargent knew Mona would be thrilled. "Good idea."

"Of course, I'm going to need a best man," Isaac said.

Sargent looked up. Isaac was staring at him, his eyes shiny. "Me?" Sargent squeaked.

"Yes, if you'll do it."

"Um, okay!"

Isaac and Janice appeared to glow from within. Sargent was glad for them but wondered if they would have more kids, like his mother and Bill. He pushed his plate away, suddenly not hungry anymore.

CHAPTER TWENTY-SIX

Sargent knew that one of the most important techniques an artist can master is perspective, the ability to make a painting look three-dimensional. It had taken Sargent two years of intense practice to create mountain peaks that appeared to rise out of his pictures rather than look like they'd been flattened by a tornado, so he wasn't surprised when Janice announced that the theme of the camp's second week was using perspective in art. Nor was he surprised by the groans of the other campers. Perspective was hard.

"If you're going to have the proper perspective in your work, you're going to need a horizon and a vanishing point," Janice said. "Perspective is where art meets mathematics, guys. When done correctly, our eyes enjoy looking at the painting because it seems natural, realistic."

"My perspective sucks," Adam moaned. "It always looks lopsided!"

"But that's life!" Janice cried, circling the room as if Adam's comments were rocket fuel. "How often have you thought your perspective on a situation was correct, only to discover you were missing a crucial piece of information, or in the case of a drawing, a crucial calculation?"

Sargent wasn't quite getting the analogy. "But there are rules about perspective. All you have to do is follow the rules, and you're able to trick the eye."

"But sometimes our eye wants to take us to the horizon, but the artist wants us to look elsewhere. Like how the Renaissance painters wanted to point at the Virgin Mary's womb."

Troy stuck his finger in his mouth like he was going to throw up. "Gross! I don't think my mother would want me to talk about the Virgin Mary's belly."

Everybody, including Janice, cracked up. She held up her hands in mock surrender. "All I'm saying is that artists can use perspective to draw our attention toward whatever they want us to see in their picture. And when they do that, we tend not to notice what they *don't* want us to see. Perspective is a sneaky tool you can use to trick your audience."

"What's this week's assignment?" Abby asked. She liked things to be orderly.

"We are going to trick one another!" Janice said. "Every day, you'll do a new drawing or painting. And every day, you'll do something different to the perspective. Sometimes you'll do it correctly, sometimes you'll move it around, and sometimes you'll screw it up. By Friday, you'll be masters of perspective! Now off you go to take a look at the different perspectives in the galleries. Then we'll meet back here in one hour and start today's project."

Sargent followed Troy and Adam out of the room. It was funny; perspective was supposed to make art three-dimensional, make it look alive. But now that he knew the paintings actually *were* alive, he'd lost all perspective. He'd spent Sunday thinking about Mona, who was the most amazing person he'd ever met. Sadly, she was also the most amazing person he could never tell anybody about, because their or other people's perspectives about art being alive might be way different from his.

At the top of the stairs, he took a quick detour to visit *Merrymaking*. He wanted to inspect it, study its brushstrokes, its colors, and everything else he could remember from Isaac's appraisal of the Gauguin. If he could just see Sneely's copy of Merrymaking, he might be able to tell if the guy was an art forger or not.

As luck would have it, he spotted Sneely taking Madame Juliette dans le Jardin off the wall. A docent was placing a card on the vacant space left behind: PAINTING BEING RESTORED.

"Hey, Mr. Sneely!" Sargent called.

Sneely forced a smile as he placed the painting on a small trolley. "Hello."

"I see you're taking Madame Juliette. Are you done with Hotel Bedroom?"

Sneely's voice was sharp. "Sometimes I work on two paintings at once. By the way, you still haven't visited me."

Sargent backed up. The guy smelled like dirty socks. What little hair Sneely had was plastered against his head in greasy tufts, and his eyes were bloodshot.

"Um, I guess I could come by this week," Sargent said.

"No doubt you're hesitant because of all the ghastly noise in that bloody workroom. The walls are paper thin. All day long, all I hear is talking and whispering."

Sargent's eyes widened. Were the paintings talking to Sneely? He thought of the voices he'd heard in the workroom the other night. What was going on?

Just then Isaac and Harmsworth came around the corner. Pushing the trolley, Sneely scurried off in the opposite direction. Isaac and Harmsworth didn't seem to notice; they were too busy chuckling at some inside joke.

Isaac smiled broadly when he spied Sargent. "Getting some perspective?" he joked.

"I guess," Sargent said.

"Well, keep at it. Mr. Harmsworth and I are on our way to a meeting."

"I've invited your father and Janice to go with me to an arts gala in Moncton on Saturday night," Harmsworth said. "Care to join us? There'll be lobster."

The thought of spending an evening with Harmsworth was more than Sargent could bear. "Uh, thanks, but I'm busy Saturday night," he replied, ignoring Isaac's quizzical look.

"Your loss, Sal," Harmsworth said, already moving on.

Isaac shot Sargent an apologetic smile and hurried to catch up. Watching them walk away, one thing was clear to Sargent: he had a definite perspective on Harmsworth, and it wasn't good.

CHAPTER TWENTY-SEVEN

Mona didn't have a chance to speak with Sargent for most of that week. Though she saw him daily, and he always waved as he ran by, the gallery was awash with tourists, thanks to a music festival and four days of rain that drove them inside. Meanwhile, the residents and gallery staff were abuzz with the rumor that Mr. Harmsworth had promised a significant donation to the Beaverbrook. Numbers ranged from one million to one hundred million, though Edmund told Mona that Max said the real number was twenty million. It was strange not hearing such news from Max directly, but Mona remained steadfast in her determination to ignore him.

She was ecstatic on Friday morning when Sargent whispered he'd be by to pick her up at eight thirty. With the other campers nearby, he didn't wait for her response, so Mona wasn't surprised by his shocked expression when he discovered that the blank canvas contained not only herself, but also Clem, Sir Charles, young Charles, and Lizzie Cotterell.

"I hope it's okay, Sargent," Mona whispered. "They were desperate to see a movie."

"Hi, Sargent," Clem said. "I'm Clem Cotterell. This is my father, Sir Charles Cotterell; my younger brother, Charles; and my younger sister, Elizabeth, who everybody calls Lizzie."

Sargent looked dazed as Sir Charles offered an awkward bow, thanks to how crowded the canvas was. "I know who you all are," he said. "I painted you last week."

"And a fine job you did," Sir Charles said. "It is generous of you to invite us to attend a moving picture. Are we seeing this Harry Potter fellow again?"

Mona giggled. "I told them all about last week's show." She watched Sargent, pleased to see delight creep across his face.

"We're seeing *Night at the Museum*," he said, covering the canvas with the drop cloth. "I think you're going to like it."

Two hours later, a dazed Cotterell family returned to their painting. Each of them had wished Sargent a happy life and thanked him again and again for taking them to the movie.

"I have not witnessed anything as wondrous in three hundred years," Sir Charles said, bowing deeply. "Truly, I thought the only magic in this world was paintings coming to life. But moving pictures are spectacular. Please, tell Mr. Ben Stiller that I hold him in the highest esteem."

Sargent laughed. "I don't actually know Ben Stiller."

"Then I shall write him a letter of congratulations and gratitude," Sir Charles said. He trailed after his children, who were already telling their mother about how wonderful it would be if they were able to step out of their frames into the real world, just like the characters in the movie.

"Thank you for allowing them to come along," said Mona, suddenly shy now that it was just the two of them again.

"I don't mind. They were so excited, and it was great you had someone to watch the movie with. Did you like it, too?"

"I thought it was wonderfully imaginative. I understand why Janice chose it."

"Yeah, she's got a theme going. Guess what? I checked Merrymaking. I am positive it's not a forgery."

Mona nodded. "I know. If it was, the residents of the painting couldn't have returned home. But it still doesn't mean he's not making forgeries of paintings to sell. Madame Rubinstein told me that some people think Mona Lisa was stolen so that the thieves could sell copies of her to evil art collectors who thought they were buying the stolen Mona Lisa." The color drained from her face. "You don't think Mr. Sneely is an art thief, do you?"

Sargent shook his head. "He put the original Merrymaking back on the wall, remember?"

Mona shook herself. "I'm being silly. You're right, Sneely is an odd man, and it makes the residents nervous. But he's not an art thief or art forger."

Sargent glanced over his shoulder. "I'm sorry, Mona, I have to go. Janice will come looking for me if I don't get back."

Mona nodded. "I wish we could talk longer. . . ." Her voice trailed off.

"Me too. I want to hear about before you were painted."

They were both silent. Mona was about to say good night when Sargent grasped the sides of the canvas and lifted it up so they were eye to eye. "I have an idea!"

"What?" Something about Sargent's excitement made her tremble.

"Isaac is going to some event in Moncton with Janice and Harmsworth tomorrow night, but I'm not going. That's a couple of hours away by car. What if you were in this canvas, right at closing, and I took you home with me? I'd bring you back first thing in the morning. We can hang out and watch movies and talk."

Mona bit her lip. "I haven't left the gallery in three years. Even then, I was wrapped and transported to another gallery. I haven't been outside, really outside, since 1915. But if you get caught, your father will be furious. Max will be furious."

Sargent's eyes were pleading. "We won't get caught. I'll show you around, we'll—"

"Yes," Mona said, ignoring every ounce of good sense she possessed. "Let's do it."

CHAPTER TWENTY-EIGHT

Sargent knew he should feel guilty. After all, he was about to steal a priceless painting. Well, technically, he was going to borrow *Mona Dunn* for twelve hours, though he wasn't sure the police or his dad would agree with the distinction. But as he'd watched Isaac and Janice drive away, all Sargent had felt was elated. Mona was going to get to see the real world again. They were going to get to hang out. That was worth the risk.

He arrived before the staff locked the doors at five o'clock. At 5:08, he stuffed Mona into one of Isaac's portfolio cases and followed two docents out the back door. The plan was to return before six thirty the next morning, so he could enter when the security guards switched for the day. He still had his security pass, but he wasn't sure it would work to get in and out of the building.

Outside, he crossed the pedestrian walkway behind the gallery and headed for the shrubs and trees that grew along the river, slithering down the steep bank until he was hidden from the passersby above. He unzipped the case and turned the canvas so Mona could see the river rolling by. She burst into tears. Mystified, he flipped the canvas to see her face.

"What's wrong? I thought you wanted to come outside?"

"Nothing's wrong, it's just . . ." Her voice trailed off. Panicked, heart sinking, Sargent stayed silent, afraid to upset her more. Finally she stopped sobbing and wiped her eyes. "It's just I forgot how much I missed this world. In the gallery, I can go inside paintings and feel the sun on my face, walk in the grass, swim in the ocean, but somehow it never feels quite like this."

Sargent turned her again so she faced the river and trees.

"The world in a painting doesn't feel really real," Mona continued. "I don't know why, maybe it's because I know it's not real, it's only someone else's interpretation of real. In the real world, you feel like things are happening in the moment, and when the moment's gone it's gone for-ever. I love *San Vigilio, Lake Garda,* but the sun will always be in the same place, the water will always be the same color. The people inside the paintings may change, but the world around us? It stays the same." She lifted her face toward the sun and sighed.

Sargent didn't know what to say, so he kept quiet. Taking Mona out of the gallery had been risky. But now, seeing how happy she was, he knew it was worth it. "We'll look at the stars later," he promised. "But we should go home now. I have the movies all queued up." Mona nodded, took a last gaze at the river, and Sargent zipped the case closed.

Mona oohed and aahed over everything, from Isaac's big-screen TV to the microwave. She was especially curi-ous about the artwork on the wall. "Have you tried to talk to them?"

"Yup. They never say anything."

"Are you're sure they're original works of art?"

Sargent nodded. "Pretty sure. My dad isn't real keen on copies."

"Maybe they're shy," Mona mused. "Or your father told them not to talk to you."

Sargent's laugh came out like a bark. "No way. Isaac doesn't have a clue."

"Maybe they just haven't woken up yet. Some paintings take a long time to wake up. Do you know when these were painted?"

"No idea. Can you jump into one of them and check?"

Mona tried to but found herself stuck. "They mustn't be awake. Max told me once that the passages between paintings don't open up until the people in the painting have woken up. But it's funny that none of these paintings are awake. I've never heard of that before. When I get back to the gallery I'll ask around. Perhaps someone has heard of a similar situation."

Sargent propped Mona up next to him on the couch, and they watched three more Harry Potter movies, chattering away about everything happening on the screen. After midnight, Isaac texted, "Just leaving Moncton. Home by one."

"If we're going to see the stars, we should go out now," Sargent said. He carried Mona onto the balcony, laying the canvas flat on the table so she could see the sky.

For several minutes, they stared up into space, lost in their own thoughts. Finally Mona broke the silence. "Tell me about your life, Sargent."

"Like what? I live in New York City, I'll be thirteen on November fifteenth, my parents divorced when I was a baby, and my mom remarried when I was eight years old."

"You said you didn't see your father again until you were six or seven. Do you know why he didn't come see you?" Mona asked.

"Nope. After that he'd visit a couple of times a year, take me out to shows or to museums. It was always tense, because I was so shy and so nervous around him, like if I did the wrong thing he might not visit again." Sargent coughed. Talking about Isaac made it hard to breathe.

Mona made a sympathetic chirp, and the tension in Sargent's chest eased a bit. It was strange, but nice, having someone to talk about Isaac with.

Sargent watched the yellow dot of a satellite whiz across the sky. "A few years ago I overheard my parents talking about me. My mom was saying, 'You have to learn to love the real Sargent, Ike, not some make-believe boy,' and then Isaac said, 'I don't know how to do that.'"

"Oh, Sargent." Mona sounded on the verge of tears.

"Yeah, it sucks, huh, finding out when you're eight years old that your father doesn't think he can love you." He took a ragged breath. "I was surprised when he wanted me to come for the summer. I was nervous to come, but I want to get to know him. It's hard, though. He's distracted with this Harmsworth stuff. Sometimes I think he—"

"Forgets you're even there," Mona finished.

"Yeah. And I just found out he's a really good artist and that I own a couple of his paintings. I tried to ask him about it, but he wouldn't talk about it. And Harmsworth's big donation? I heard about it from Janice, which made me feel stupid." Sargent shifted in his chair. "Hey . . . can we talk about you now? I'm sick of me."

Mona's laugh was like a tiny bell. "I think I already told you I had a younger brother, Philip, and a younger sister, Joan. I also have a half-sister, Anne, although she wasn't born until after I—" She paused and took a quick breath. "Until after I died."

"Does it feel weird to say that?"

"Not so much anymore. I've gotten used to it."

"Did you come to life right after Orpen painted you?"

"No, it was gradual. I just remember one Christmas morning waking up and seeing an older version of myself—she must have been fifteen or sixteen—pass by. At first I was confused and frightened; why didn't anyone in my family realize I was alive? I wanted to call out to them, but I was afraid. That night, after everyone went to bed, the inhabitants of the paintings next to mine visited me and explained what was happening."

"Were the paintings of your dad there?"

Mona shook her head. "He wasn't painted until the 1930s. Of course, it happened so long ago that now it seems like it happened to someone else. Gradually I got used to living behind a frame. When I came to the Beaverbrook, Max made me see that living in the world behind the frames was a gift, an opportunity to live another kind of adventure." She cleared her throat. "Your turn again. People say you're a talented artist."

Sargent sighed. "I guess."

"You don't believe it?"

"It's not that, it's just . . ."

"It's just that it's the only thing people say when they talk about you," Mona said. "I understand completely. When people talk about me, they only talk about who my father is, or my stepmother. I'm Sir James Dunn's daughter, not Mona Dunn."

Sargent smiled into the darkness. "I thought I was the only person who felt like that."

"Do you actually want to be an artist when you grow up?"

"Yeah, but it feels like it's the only thing my parents want to talk to me about."

"That's hard."

"Sometimes I feel like I don't really belong anywhere. I mean, if my own father wasn't sure he could love me, what does that say about me? And my mom has this other, perfect family. But I don't feel like that when I'm painting. When I paint, it's like the world goes away and

I'm the center of the universe, like I can make anything, do anything."

"I liked you before I knew you were a painter."

Sargent was surprised by how that happy truth spread through him like a sip of hot chocolate on a cold day. "Yeah, I guess you did."

"I liked you because you were nice and kind. And when I found out you were a talented artist, I was so happy. You know why?"

"Why?"

"Because the pieces of art you create will be lucky to have you as their creator. They'll have a piece of that kindness in them."

He'd never thought about it like that before, how it was an awesome responsibility, bringing art into the world.

Mona sighed. "At least you get to grow up."

Sargent pictured the return plane ticket tucked in his dresser drawer. When he left at the end of the summer . . . who knew when he would see Mona again?

"I'm sorry, Mona. I wish—"

Mona's laugh was strained. "No wishes. Thank you for this adventure. I will never forget it. You made me forget that I'm just a girl in a painting."

"You're not just a girl in a painting," Sargent said, his voice thick.

They continued to stare at the night sky. Now and then Sargent sneaked a look at Mona, whose features were blurry in the moonlight. They both started when Isaac's car door slammed in the driveway below. Sargent scooped her up then and shoved the canvas into the back of his bedroom closet.

The rest of the night flew by. After saying good night to Isaac, who was too tired to notice his portfolio case leaning against the wall, Sargent propped Mona on a chair and they whispered until dawn, when he carried her the two blocks to the gallery and smuggled her inside. Frank, the security guard, fell for his story about forgetting his phone at the front desk and needing to return his father's portfolio. After Sargent had placed the canvas underneath the desk, the two friends stared at each other in the watery early morning light.

Mona's lips trembled. "I will never forget this night for as long as I live. And that's a long time." With a sobbing gulp, she was gone.

Sargent's head throbbed the whole way home. Adam and Troy and Alice and Cory were great, but Mona was different; he could talk to Mona about anything. But their friendship was hopeless. At the end of the summer, he would have to say good-bye to Mona Dunn forever.

CHAPTER TWENTY-NINE

Sunday mornings were lazy at the gallery. The staff usually arrived close to eleven o'clock for the noon opening. They'd saunter in, cups of coffee in hand, and stand around the front desk chatting before heading to their respective posts for the afternoon. Mona liked to listen to them talk about their lives. It was another window to the outside world.

She was surprised on this Sunday morning when neither Edmund nor the Cotterells raised an eyebrow when she returned to her frame. No doubt they assumed she'd been at Lake Garda and forgotten the time. She settled in, content to spend the day thinking about her magical escape from the Beaverbrook, only half listening to a conversation between Amy and Frank.

"Is it true Mr. Harmsworth is donating twenty million dollars to the gallery?" Frank asked.

"That's what I heard."

"I hope they put some of it into enhanced security."

Amy laughed. "Frank, you *are* enhanced security. I hope they put some of it into a new coffee machine; the one we have is lousy. Oh, hi, Mr. Sneely. I wasn't expecting you today."

Mona frowned. Sneely didn't usually work on Sundays.

"I've come for *Mona Dunn.*"

Edmund raised an eyebrow at Mona in surprise. Clem mouthed, "What the—"

Mona swayed slightly on her stool. No one had told her she was going downstairs today. Paintings were supposed to receive at least a few days' notice in advance of restoration. Surely Max wasn't so displeased with her that he could forget to mention something as important as that? If she was in the workroom, she wouldn't be able to see Sargent. Nor was she likely to be able to slip out to watch the next movie.

"Pardon me?" said Amy. "We were told you were working on *Hotel Bedroom* and *Madame Juliette dans le Jardin.*"

Mona waited for Sneely to respond. He said nothing.

"I don't think Mr. Singer would like three master-pieces in the basement at the same time. . . . ," the docent continued. Mona could hear the protest in her voice.

"I don't believe you're paid to think about what Mr. Singer would or would not like. Could one of you please prepare a card that can be hung on the wall once I've taken her?"

His request was met with silence. Mona held her breath.

"Fine. If you won't help me, I'll do it myself. And then I shall be sure to communicate to Mr. Singer just how obstructive you have been."

"Now there's no need for that, Mr. Sneely." Frank was the gallery peacemaker. "Amy will make up a card."

"Thank you, Frank. Now could someone please page Barney to bring up the trolley?"

Amy's voice was shrill now. "Mr. Sneely, it's Sunday. Barney Templeton doesn't work on Sundays. Maybe you could wait until tomorrow."

"Never mind, I shall transport her myself. Can some-one fetch me a trolley?"

Sneely came around the corner. Seeing him made Mona want to cringe. The eccentric Englishman who'd stood before her on his first day at the gallery was now a wild-looking creature. Frank trailed behind, keeping a respectful distance, looking over his shoulder now and then at Amy, who hovered in the doorway.

"Mr. Sneely, you look awfully tired," Frank said. "Why don't you take the day off and come back tomorrow? You don't have to work seven days a week. It's not healthy."

Sneely rounded on him. "I've had enough advice, thank you very much," he snarled, stalking toward Mona. "I've got my orders. When and how I work is no business of yours."

"Your orders?"

Sneely faltered for the briefest of seconds, then drew himself up in such a way that he seemed to grow taller as he spoke. "Did I say orders? I didn't mean to say that. I meant to say I've got my way of working, that's all."

It was then that Mona spotted Sneely's feet. He was wearing what had once been expensive needlepoint slippers, which were now caked in mud and so punctuated by holes that his left baby toe was sticking out. Alarmed, Mona waited for Amy and Frank to intervene.

Frank tried. "You're right, Mr. Sneely, I don't know anything about art restoration. But I like to think I know when a fella looks tired. If you don't mind me saying so, you look beat."

Mona waited for Sneely to snap at Frank again. Instead,

he seemed to crumple a little, as if Frank's soothing words had hit their mark.

"I am weary," he half sobbed. "But I must get this painting downstairs." He gave Frank a pleading look.

"Then how about you let me fetch a trolley and I'll get her downstairs for you? After that you can go back to the hotel and take a nap. If you still want to work once you've slept and showered, then by all means, come back. How does that sound?"

Sneely thrust out his lower lip like a petulant toddler. "I suppose that would be acceptable."

Frank left and returned with the trolley, carefully lifting Mona off the wall. On her way to the trolley, Mona floated past the shocked faces of Edmund and the Cotterells. Then she was wheeled away: through the Canadian Gallery, into the freight elevator, down a hallway, and through the workroom door, where Frank placed her gently on the worktable. Sneely shuffled along behind, admonishing Frank to be careful, to walk slower, to show Mona's painting respect.

Finally the two men left, switching off the light as they went, which made the windowless room dreary. Mona stared up at the tiled ceiling in shock. Worst of all, Frank had left her like a turtle on its back, only able to see bits of things with her peripheral vision. She squeezed her eyes shut, trying to calm the nerves that were feeding her sense of dread. Surely Amy would call Director Singer and he would come and take her back upstairs. Then she'd swallow her pride, go see Max, and beg him to postpone her restoration until another art restorer could be found.

"Mona?" Juliette sounded frightened. "Why are you here, ma chérie? Your work was not to begin until the work on my painting was finished."

Hearing Juliette's voice made Mona too emotional to speak. She was surprised when Dusk responded on her behalf.

"Mona is not supposed to be here. She's not supposed to be restored until August," he whispered, mindful that it was daytime; gallery staff would be coming and going all afternoon.

"Then why am I here?" whispered Mona.

Dusk exhaled. "I have no idea. Something strange is going on."

"Mr. Sneely is unwell," said Mona. "He was belligerent to the staff, told them he'd been ordered to bring me downstairs. When Frank asked on whose orders, he said he'd misspoken."

"Only Director Singer could make such an order,"

Juliette said. "I cannot believe he wishes to have three of his most popular paintings out of commission at the same time. Mon Dieu, it makes no sense. I am sure Edmund will go see Max and straighten this out."

"I'll try to talk to Max—" Dusk was interrupted by a chuckle from high up on the wall. Mona had forgotten about Maugham. Squirming, she managed to position her head and body so she could catch a glimpse of his face.

"This is not amusing, Monsieur Maugham," Juliette scolded. "Mona's arrival is upsetting."

"My sincerest apologies, Madame Juliette," Maugham said, his voice a sticky combination of honey and vinegar. "I do not mean to be flippant. I laugh only because you all refuse to realize that you are subject to the whim of others. Could Mona stop Sneely and Frank from bringing her here? She could not. Could Lord Beaverbrook or Mr. Dusk have stopped it either? No."

"Now see here, Maugham. Don't bring Lord Beaverbrook or myself into whatever story you are concocting." Dusk bristled.

"Why shouldn't I bring you in, Mr. Dusk? You and your boss pretend to have control of the gallery, and yet here you and Mona are, trapped in this room with me, in complete defiance of Lord Beaverbrook's precious schedule. It appears Mr. Sneely is in charge. Even Director

Singer dares not question his world-famous art restorer. But ask yourselves: do you feel safe?"

Mona rolled over into her regular position. Maugham was right. She did not feel safe.

"Monsieur Maugham, you are frightening me," Juliette said.

"He's an addlebrained blowhard," Dusk muttered. "Director Singer will clear this up. In the meantime, ignore the disembodied head on the wall; he's hibernating here for a reason."

For once Mona hoped Dusk was right.

Sneely was whistling as he entered the workroom on Monday morning. Mona relaxed. Maybe things wouldn't be so bad after all. He leaned over her portrait and stared into her eyes.

"What are you doing here?" he asked her, his tone accusing.

It was all Mona could do not to reply that she had no earthly idea why she was here. Several more uncomfortable minutes passed. Finally Sneely stepped away from the table.

"I don't know where to begin," he muttered. "These are impossible working conditions."

Mona couldn't see what he was doing, but she heard

the rattle and clang of metal instruments banging together. Suddenly his face was over hers again.

"Time to get you out of that frame, Mona," he whispered. "There's work to be done."

Sneely turned Mona facedown, and she heard a series of tapping sounds as he worked to remove her portrait from its ornate frame. After several minutes, Mona could feel the frame being pulled away. Then Sneely lifted her canvas off the table and onto an easel opposite the easels that held Juliette and Dusk. Despite their silence, Mona could sense the tension emanating from them, a tension that only increased when Sneely crouched down in front of them.

"Absolutely no talking," he said sternly. "I will not tolerate it. Mona needs her rest." He looked at Juliette. "What do you say, my dear—ready to be copied?"

As he lifted Juliette off her easel, Mona saw the fear in her friend's eye, which only intensified her own. The walls of the room began to close in. The irony of a girl who lived in a painting becoming claustrophobic was not lost on Mona. Something was very wrong with Mr. Sneely, but would anybody help them?

CHAPTER THIRTY

Sargent couldn't resist running to see Mona first thing Monday morning. He darted into the Harriet Irving Gallery, halting in bewildered silence in front of the empty space on the wall where she should have been. He read the card: CURRENTLY BEING RESTORED. WILL RETURN SOON. It didn't make any sense—Sneely already had two paintings down in the workroom. Sargent checked his watch: fifteen minutes until camp began. More than enough time to find out what was going on.

He found Isaac and Sneely arguing in the hallway outside the workroom.

"Explain to me again why you need three masterpieces

down here at one time. It doesn't make any sense," Isaac was saying. "This is a busy time of year for tourists. They come here expecting to see our masterpieces, not empty spaces on the wall."

"I find it dull to work on one painting at a time."

"You worked on Merrymaking by itself," Isaac pointed out. "Unless you can provide me with a legitimate reason for having three of the masterpieces out of commission at once, you must put at least one of them back upstairs."

Relief washed over Sargent. Isaac would fix this.

"My contract." Sneely's tone was insufferable.

"Pardon me?"

"My contract states I can have access to the five paintings whenever I want them."

"Yes, but surely you don't mean to have all five paintings downstairs at the same time?"

"Of course not. I've returned Merrymaking."

"Yes, but—"

"But nothing. I am working as fast as I can. If working on three paintings at once helps me work faster, is that not better? Now, if there's nothing else, I'd like to get back to the paintings."

"But Mr. Sneely—"

"Do not 'Mr. Sneely' me. I see how poorly you run this gallery. You have ignored my needs and embarrassed me in front of others. The workroom is stuffy and loud. My supplies were late. Do not think I will forget such slights. If you do not allow me to complete my work in the manner I see fit, I will be forced to go to the board of directors and complain. I am a world-famous art restorer with an impeccable reputation. I believe this is your first directorship? Do not cross me, Mr. Singer, or you will be sorry."

Sneely turned and went into the workroom, slamming the door behind him. Isaac looked at Sargent and shook his head.

"You can't let him do that!" Sargent protested. How could Mona go to the movies if Sneely worked late on Friday night? How could they talk?

"I have to go," Isaac said curtly. "Remember, I'm helping Janice teach this week."

"But—"

Isaac ignored him and rushed off toward his office. Sargent began to pace, trying to think of what to do. Now and then he stopped in front of the workroom door, willing Sneely to come out and return Mona to her rightful place. But the door stayed closed. If Isaac wouldn't intervene, what could he do?

He ran his hands through his hair, trying to think. Sneely didn't seem to like Isaac, but he'd always been nice to Sargent. Maybe he'd listen to him, especially if he told Sneely he needed access to Mona for one of his summer camp projects. But could he be bold enough to just knock on the door and ask? Then he remembered Sneely scolding him for not visiting yet. Today would be the day.

Isaac seemed himself again when he began the morning's session.

"The self-portrait is a tradition in the art world. Since the first caveman picked up a piece of flint and scratched his image on the cave wall, artists have wanted to share not only their vision of the world; they also wanted to share their vision of themselves. Think of them as the first selfies." Everyone laughed as Isaac reached into his pocket, pulled out his phone, and took a picture of himself.

Smiling, Isaac clicked a button on his laptop, and a painting of a man sporting a ginger beard filled the blank wall behind him. "Probably the artist most famous for his self-portraits is Vincent van Gogh." He clicked again, and a series of van Gogh's self-portraits marched across the wall.

"Isn't it creepy that he did so many self-portraits?" Alice asked.

"Good question, Alice. There are a few reasons why van Gogh painted so many self-portraits. First, sometimes he couldn't find or afford a model to pose for him."

"Didn't he have any friends?" Troy said. He nudged Adam and Sargent, who were sitting on either side of him. "I'd pose for you guys. Just don't ask me to get naked or anything."

Everyone cracked up at that, even Isaac. "I'm sure Adam and Sargent appreciate that caveat, Troy. Van Gogh had friends, and he did paint them, but he also painted himself because at that time, portraits were popular and everyone wanted to buy them. Van Gogh was poor and needed money. Another reason was that these self-portraits allowed him to become a master portrait painter, because he could master his techniques and learn from his mistakes. But there's another reason people believe Van Gogh painted a lot of self-portraits. Anybody have a guess?"

Sargent raised his hand. "It was a way for him to learn about himself?"

"Exactly! The self-portrait helps us understand how we see ourselves. It's like a mirror to the soul. How we choose to portray ourselves may or may not be how we really are; it may be how we'd like others to see us. This week, your project will be to do your own self-portrait. And I'm going to challenge you all to be brave. Show us the real you!"

"With clothes, I assume?" Troy was on a roll.

"With clothes," Isaac confirmed, his mouth twitching. "But before I send you off to study faces and artists in advance of doing your own work, we need to talk about my two favorite Italian words: sfumato and chiaroscuro."

"Key-a-*what?*" Abby asked.

"Chiaroscuro. But let's start with sfumato. Sfumato is a technique that uses different tones of the same color, blending them together so there is no harsh line between the lighter and darker shades, so it looks natural. It's a useful tool for artists who want to show that the world isn't black and white. Leonardo da Vinci was a master of sfumato, and later we'll study the *Mona Lisa* to see how sfumato made her the mysterious superstar she is today. On the other hand, chiaroscuro is more heavy-handed. It actually means 'light-dark' in Italian, and artists use it to make their subjects stand out by illuminating them in a sea of darkness."

"Like *Mona Dunn*," Sargent said.

There was a split second where Sargent swore he could see Isaac remembering his failure to get Mona out of Sneely's clutches. "Unfortunately, *Mona Dunn* is currently being restored, but there are other examples upstairs. I encourage you to look for paintings that use sfumato and chiaroscuro. Remember, you need to be thoughtful about how you use these techniques. As in all things in life, sometimes you want to be subtle, other times you want to make a point. Both techniques, when used correctly, can have a profound impact on your work."

Sneely was working on his copy of Juliette's painting, when he suddenly stopped.

"Want to see?" he asked. "Of course you do!"

The paintings stared at him, waiting. The room was stifling hot, or so it seemed to Mona, who was desperate to get away. Mr. Sneely was acting more than strange; he was acting scary. He grabbed the canvas he'd worked on for the past hour and carried it around the room, holding it in front of each painting for several seconds, as if he wanted them to appreciate his talent. Mona was last. Sneely held it over her, the copy hovering in midair.

It was a lovely copy of Juliette, minus her garden. "This is worth a lot of money," he said. "I know people who would kill to own such a fine copy."

Mona didn't mean to, but she gasped out loud. She'd been right—Sneely was an art forger!

Sneely dropped the copy of Juliette and leaned over to look into Mona's eyes.

"I knew it! Say something," he ordered.

Mona remained silent.

Sneely's eyes narrowed. "I know you're in there! Say something!"

Despite her fear, Mona held herself together.

Sneely paused and rubbed at his forehead. "You think I don't know what's going on around here," he shouted. "But I do! You'll not get the best of Archibald Sneely!" He picked Mona up from the easel. "Now, Miss Dunn, let's begin working on you, shall we?"

CHAPTER THIRTY-ONE

"This is going to be hard," Adam moaned as he followed Alice, Sargent, and Troy up the stairs. "How the heck do I see myself? And now we have to think about this light-dark stuff, too."

"I could be abstract," Troy said. "Or maybe I'll paint my true self as a superhero."

"Life isn't all about comic books," Alice said tartly. "Mr. Singer wants us to dig deep."

"Alice, my self-portrait is going to be so deep it'll take a rescue crew days to pull you out of the depths of my soul."

He batted his eyelashes at Alice, who tried to look

annoyed, but eventually gave in to a fit of giggles. "Right, Troy. I don't know why I hang out with you."

"Animal magnetism."

Alice rolled her eyes and fell into step beside Sargent. "You're quiet this morning."

Sargent hadn't realized his distraction was so obvious. "I ran into Isaac arguing with the art restorer earlier. He's mad that Sneely is working on three masterpieces at once."

Alice wrinkled her nose "I've seen him. He stinks. I wouldn't let him touch my paintings."

"He's supposed to be famous," Sargent said. "He sat beside me on the airplane. At first I thought he was just peculiar, but now I don't know what to think."

"He'd better take good care of Mona baby. Otherwise, there'll be a sequel to my comic book where an evil art restorer gets his comeuppance," Troy declared.

Sargent wandered along behind the others, chewing a ragged cuticle on his thumb. Troy's comment nagged at him. He should check on Mona, see if she was all right.

"I'm gonna run downstairs for a sec," he told his friends. "I'll be right back."

Alice cocked her head, studying him. "You okay?"

Adam poked her in the ribs. "Lay off, Alice—he's going to the can. We'll be in the McCain Wing," he added, corralling a worried Alice while trying to stop Troy from making monkey faces at Lord Beaverbrook's portrait.

Sargent dashed off.

There was no answer when Sargent knocked on the workroom door. He looked left and right, and then turned the knob. The door opened, and he slipped inside.

Unlike the first time he'd visited Sneely's workroom, when the art restorer's tools were laid out with the precision of an operating theater, the room he entered now was helter-skelter. Candy wrappers and torn bits of canvas littered the floor. Paint splatters on the walls and table had dried into a crusty mess. *Hotel Bedroom* and *Madame Juliette dans le Jardin* sat on two adjacent easels, but Mona lay on the worktable, surrounded by crumpled-up hamburger wrappers. She looked smaller, more vulnerable, without her frame.

Carefully Sargent leaned over and lifted Mona off the table. The eyes that gazed back at him were startled, then relieved.

"You have to get us out of here, Sargent! It's Sneely, he—"

"What do you think you're doing?"

Sargent hadn't heard Sneely come in, and he whirled

around, face scarlet. "I'm sorry," he said. His legs shook. "I came to see you and spotted *Mona Dunn* on the table next to some garbage, so I thought I'd put her on an easel."

"You did, did you? Don't you think you ought to have asked my permission first? What if you'd damaged her? She's priceless."

Sneely snatched Mona from Sargent's arms and stalked across the room. He regarded Sargent with narrowed eyes, as if he thought Sargent might try to wrestle him for the painting.

Sargent balled his hands into fists and took a deep breath. Of course he knew Mona was priceless, and not in the stupid money way everyone else thought made her valuable! Still, he couldn't afford to be on Sneely's bad side while Mona was stuck here.

"I'm sorry, I was trying to help."

Scowling, Sneely placed Mona on an easel. "Help someone else. I have enough problems without you underfoot creating more work. The incessant noise is bad enough; I don't need to be bothered by young rascals, too."

Isaac's voice drifted in from the hallway. It sounded like he was on the phone. Sneely grabbed Sargent's arm. "It's time I told your father what a sneak you are." He pulled a shocked Sargent forward and flung open the door.

Isaac was on his phone. Listening intently, he seemed oblivious to the spectacle of Sneely hauling Sargent out into the hallway. He held up a hand for quiet.

"What do you mean, Harmsworth's checked out?" Isaac asked. His face was a blotchy, sweaty mess. "Did he leave a forwarding address? Look, I understand you're not supposed to give it out, but it's very important that I speak to him. Yes, I'd call his cell, but it doesn't appear to be working. I know it's not your problem. Thanks for nothing." He hung up and looked at Sargent and Sneely with a dazed expression.

"Harmsworth's vanished," he said, as if he couldn't believe it himself.

"Where'd he go?" Sargent said.

"I don't understand what happened," said Isaac.

"Does that mean he's not going to donate all that money?" Sargent asked.

Isaac, who'd been staring into space, looked at Sargent and winced. "I don't know. We were getting along. I don't know what went wrong, what I said that made him walk away. . . ."

Sneely couldn't restrain himself any longer. "Mr. Singer, I am lodging a formal complaint against your son."

"Excuse me?"

"I repeat, I am lodging a formal complaint against your son. I just caught him in my workroom, fiddling with the paintings."

Startled, Isaac looked at Sargent. "Is this true?"

"It wasn't like that. He told me I could come see him whenever I wanted, so I just stopped in to say hello. I saw Mona Dunn lying on the table, surrounded by garbage and stuff, so I picked her up to put her on an easel."

Sneely's smile was cruel. "I think you've got enough trouble, having to explain to your board of directors how you lost a wealthy patron, without also having to explain why your son is running wild in the gallery. Don't make me have to tell them about this little incident, Singer." Triumphant, Sneely added, "Stay out of my workroom, you hear me?" He turned on his heel and slammed the workroom door.

"I need to talk to you about—" Sargent began.

Isaac shook his head. "Just stop. I'm having my worst day ever and you go and do this? You know how hard I've been working to raise money. What's wrong with you? As of right now, you're grounded. I should send you home to your mother—you're just like her."

He stormed off, leaving a shaken Sargent behind. The words "you're just like her" crashed around Sargent's brain, the venom in Isaac's voice making him sick to his stomach. Isaac had ignored him when he was younger, but that was way better than being the focus of his anger.

Everything was ruined: his visit with Isaac, being able to hang out with Mona, his chance to figure out what Sneely was up to. And it was all Isaac's fault. Sargent ran to the bathroom, locked himself in a corner stall, and cried.

CHAPTER THIRTY-TWO

Half an hour after throwing Sargent out of the work-room, Sneely was still pacing. "Think, Sneely, think." He stopped and looked at Mona. "Do I tell them what I know?"

Mona was silent, frozen on the easel.

"I shall not be trifled with!" He whirled around, snatched his copy of Juliette, and bolted out the door. There was a metallic click when he locked the door, followed by the sound of footfalls hurrying away. Mona finally exhaled.

"Mon Dieu! He is mad!" Juliette whispered. "What is he up to?"

"I will go for help as soon as the gallery closes," Dusk said.

"Careful," warned Maugham. "You heard the conversation in the hallway. Do you want to get Director Singer and his son in more trouble? Sneely is strange, but he's done nothing wrong."

"He is worse than strange. He is ill!" Dusk countered.

"I don't disagree. But you saw the fine work he did on Merrymaking. Soon you will be back upstairs, too. The threat is not to us, but to Director Singer. Surely you do not want him fired?"

Mona shook her head emphatically. "Mr. Maugham is right. We are fine. We must stick together, support one another. We won't be here long."

Maugham chuckled. "I hope not. Much as I enjoy the company, you belong elsewhere."

"Sarge?"

Troy's voice caught Sargent by surprise. He'd lost track of how long he'd been in the bathroom.

"I'll be right out." He wiped his eyes. Troy was going to think he was an idiot.

The bathroom was empty when he emerged from the stall. Grateful, Sargent washed his hands and face and looked at himself in the mirror. There was no hiding the fact that he'd been crying. He took a deep breath and emerged into the middle of a Troy-Alice-Adam huddle.

Alice threw her arms around his neck. "We were so worried! Are you sick?"

"I—"

Troy pointed to the nearby cloakroom. "Emergency Beaverbrook Rat meeting."

Alice's arm still around his shoulder, Sargent followed Troy and Adam into the cloakroom.

"Look," said Troy. "Your business is your business. But when something bugs you, it bugs us, too. You want to talk about it?"

A fresh batch of tears began to form.

"You don't have to talk about," Adam added. "But if you want to . . ."

"We're here for you," Alice said.

Sargent took a ragged breath. "I just had a fight with my father."

"That sucks," said Troy. "I fight with my dad at least once a week."

Astonished, Sargent couldn't help but ask, "Like a real fight?"

Troy snorted. "Well, we don't go at it physically, but we sure get on each other's nerves. My dad's an engineer; he thinks my obsession with comics is a waste of time."

"He doesn't understand talent," Alice said.

"And my mom and I go at it sometimes," said Adam. He sounded sad. "She doesn't get why I want to be a set designer. She loves me, but she doesn't get me."

"Tell him about your parents, Alice," said Troy.

Alice smiled. "My parents want me to be a lawyer and the first black prime minister in Canada, but I want to do something artistic. But I don't fight with them. I just do what I want."

"No one fights with Alice," was Troy's solemn proclamation. "Not even me. I'm scared of her."

Sargent's laugh sounded thick. "Thanks, guys, but you don't understand."

Alice shook her head. "No—you don't understand, Sargent. We're telling you this stuff so you know you're not alone. So sometimes your dad's a jerk? Our parents are, too. But now you have us. You can talk to any of us about anything."

Sargent looked at each of them in turn. Could he? Could he trust them with his secrets? Not just about his parents, but about how lonely he was sometimes, how he was so afraid people wouldn't like him that he didn't even try to be friends. Could he trust them with Mona? Mona would need friends once he went away.

He stared down at his sneakers. "I don't have a lot

of friends," he said, "I don't think I'm good at being a friend."

"Are you kidding me?" Troy said, "You are an awesome friend! Sargent Sandwich!" The three of them encircled him in a giant Beaverbrook Rat hug. A few seconds into it, Sargent began to hug back. And then he told them about his relationship with Isaac.

Sneely did not return to the workroom at all that day. Late in the afternoon, Amy arrived and Mona's heart leaped—they would be rescued! But the docent simply stuck a large brown paper package into the corner and left without even glancing at Mona.

It was mind-numbing to be stuck in the workroom all day instead of up being stuck in her regular spot in the Harriet Irving Gallery. Mona hadn't realized how much she relied on the gallery's visitors for entertainment. To pass the time, Mona thought about her childhood. It was so long ago. Now when she remembered a particular incident, there was a faint hint of fiction about it. Was her dog named Pal or Ginger? Was the nanny named Gertie?

Once she would have been able to answer such questions with ease. Now she was a twenty-first-century girl who knew about computers and smartphones and space travel. Why, half the children who visited the gallery had earbuds permanently attached to their ears; it was impossible to ignore the bass of their rap, the crackle of their music. It was so different from the childhood nights she'd spent listening to the gramophone in the drawing room.

The week William Orpen painted her, the song everyone was singing had been "It's a Long Way to Tipperary." Without realizing she was doing it, she began to sing softly.

"It's a long way to Tipperary,
It's a long way to go,
It's a long way to Tipperary,
To the sweetest girl I know!
Good-bye, Piccadilly!
Farewell, Leicester Square!
It's a long, long way to Tipperary,
But my heart's right there!"

She'd been to Piccadilly Circus. Papa had taken her there via the Tube, the recently opened underground train, and it had been terrifying and thrilling all at once. She remembered being disappointed to discover there was no real circus in Piccadilly, that the circus was the name given to the roundabout that circled Shaftesbury Memorial Fountain.

The England she knew was probably all gone now.

Certainly the people were. It made her sad. She resolved to tell Sargent all about that world, the world where she'd been her parents' golden girl, had siblings who'd loved her . . . the girl who'd ridden ponies across fields and beside hedgerows, hair flying behind her like a wild thing. She'd make Sargent her memory keeper. That would make their parting at the end of the summer hurt less.

"I like that song," Somerset Maugham said. "I used to have a friend who lived in Leicester Square in the 1930s—clever chap. Those were the days. People pulled together, had manners."

"Speaking of manners," a muffled voice said. Surprised, Mona leaned forward, trying to figure out where the voice was coming from. At first she thought it was Mrs. Dusk. That would be exciting. Then she realized the voice was coming from inside the brown paper package Amy had left in the corner.

"Hello?" Mona called cautiously. "Who's speaking, please?"

"Patsy," the package said, as if that explained everything.

"Patsy who?"

"Patsy Ryder."

"Bonjour, Patsy," said Juliette. "My name is Juliette. Do

you know how you have come to be in this room? I do not believe we have met before."

Patsy's voice sounded far away, as if the paper covering her was a heavy dampening curtain. "I just arrived. I don't think I'm supposed to be here. I was dropped off to be appraised by Director Singer."

"Oh, dear, they've left you in the wrong place," Mona said. "They ought to have left you with Director Singer's assistant, Martine."

"I knew it. I hope they don't forget me here. It's stifling under this paper, and dark, except for the opened end where a little light comes in. I'm used to being in a bright room at home."

"Who's your artist?" Dusk asked.

"Jack Humphrey."

"Ah, a New Brunswick artist," Dusk said. "He was an excellent portrait painter."

His words seemed to please Patsy. "I am quite good," she said. "He used a lot of lovely grays and blues, really caught my essence."

"I'm sure he did," Mona said. "How old are you?"

"Fifteen."

"I'm thirteen. We're practically the same age."

Patsy sniffed, making it clear that thirteen and fifteen were not the same age.

"My name is Mona Dunn, and the others you hear belong to Madame Juliette, Mr. Dusk, and Mr. Maugham. Have you always lived in someone's house?"

"Yes. I'm a family portrait. Humphrey was a friend of my mother's."

"I wish I could see you, I'm sure you're lovely! How long ago were you painted?"

"I think around 1950, but I can't recall exactly anymore. Sometimes it seems sort of misty when I think of my life before the painting. . . ."

"It's like that for all of us. We shall keep one another company, and before you know it, you shall return home, none the worse for wear. But promise me one thing, Patsy."

"What's that?"

"Promise you won't make a sound when the art restorer returns. He's odd, best avoided."

Patsy's voice quivered. "I want to go home."

"I do too," Mona replied. "More than you can ever know."

CHAPTER THIRTY-THREE

In one of Sargent's favorite video games, he was an explorer, marooned on a distant planet that was infamous for the thousands of land mines left behind after a devastating war. Over time, Sargent had learned where the mines were hidden and was able to make his way to a long-abandoned spaceship, his character's one hope for escaping the planet. But early on, he always forgot where the land mines were and was forever blowing himself up. It wasn't so different from living with Isaac since the incident outside Sneely's workroom, like one false move on Sargent's part could ruin everything.

Isaac looked haggard as they ate supper the first evening

after he'd grounded Sargent. "I shouldn't have threatened to send you home. It was wrong of me to say that."

Sargent kept his head down and kept eating his takeout Greek food.

"What . . . you're not going to speak to me?" Isaac sighed.

Sargent, on the verge of tears, said nothing.

"Fine." Isaac jumped up, grabbed his takeout container, and retreated to the balcony.

Sargent's phone pinged.

"Everything okay?" It was Alice.

"Yup," he texted back.

A couple of minutes later, Adam texted him a video of a walrus doing sit-ups.

For the first time, Sargent had friends who cared. It was nice.

"Yo," Troy texted. "Hope you're okay. If you weren't grounded I'd come see you. Hang in there."

"Thanks, man. See you tomorrow." Sargent turned off his phone, stuck his half-eaten dinner in the fridge, and went to hide in his bedroom.

The standoff persisted all week. Except for mealtimes, when Isaac was too distracted to talk anyway, Sargent kept to his room. Janice led the rest of the week's sessions by herself. The campers were told the gallery director had unexpected business to deal with. Sargent knew the truth: Isaac was trying to track down Harmsworth or find another wealthy patron.

Janice stopped Sargent at the end of the day Thursday.

"Are you okay?" she asked. "I know this has been a rough week. Your dad told me you had a fight."

Sargent swallowed hard. Despite his efforts to remain calm, his voice shook when he responded. "We didn't have a fight. He yelled at me and wouldn't let me explain why I was in Sneely's workroom."

Janice looked surprised. "Oh. I'm sorry, Sargent. He's been under so much pressure. . . ."

Sargent shrugged. "He threatened to send me home."

"Oh, no! He didn't mean it, Sargent, I know he didn't. He's so happy you're here."

"He doesn't act happy," Sargent said. Not waiting for Janice to reply, he fled.

Sargent was surprised when Isaac showed up Friday afternoon to review the self-portraits.

"I'm sorry I wasn't able to spend more time with you this week," he told the group before he looked at their work. "The life of a gallery director is never dull."

When Isaac arrived at Sargent's self-portrait, he was

quiet. The work itself was impressive: Janice had told Sargent so several times, and all the other campers declared Sargent's work a masterpiece, although Alice had bitten her lip when she'd first seen it.

Painted in oils, the words WHO AM I? were written at the top. A jagged black line split the canvas into two halves, each one portraying a different Sargent. The one on the left was happy, a paintbrush in his right hand, face glowing from the soft golden light that surrounded it. His left hand held someone's hand, but whose would remain a mystery forever. He'd used the sfumato technique to great effect; he blended in effortlessly with his surroundings. Meanwhile, the Sargent on the right was chalk faced, surrounded by inky darkness, streaky slashes of purple running down his face, the paintbrush in his hand dripping purple blobs.

Isaac gave Sargent a sideways glance. "This is good. Can you tell me about it?"

"It's self-evident," Sargent said, and walked away. He didn't see Isaac head back to his office.

The week had left Sargent a hollowed-out mess. He hoped Mona could go to the movie tonight. It would be awful if she couldn't. Janice had chosen *Superman Returns*, per Troy's suggestion, and he knew she'd love it.

Late in the afternoon, he passed *The Cotterell Family* while taking Amy a note from Janice.

"When are you picking us up?" Clem whispered as he went by.

Sargent stopped, shocked. "I hadn't planned to, I—"

"Please, lad," Sir Charles said, "I've promised Lady Cotterell and the other children, and Edmund wants to come."

Surprised, Sargent glanced over at Edmund, who winked.

"Do you think you can all fit in one canvas?" he asked.

Sir Charles would not be deterred. "We will fit. Regardless of the size we are in our own paintings, when we go into another painting, we are able to conform to its dimensions nicely."

"Cool. Is Mona coming?"

Clem spoke rapidly, for voices were spilling out from the lobby from the last tour of the day. "I don't know. Sneely's always there. When he's not, Dusk is. Will you pick us up at eight thirty?"

Sargent nodded. He wished he knew if Mona was okay and crossed his fingers that she'd find a way to go to the movie.

"Where do you think that you're going?" Dusk said

Mona had jumped into Juliette's painting. A few minutes prior, someone had opened the security door for a moment, and the sound of music had floated down the hallway. The movie!

"I'm going for a little walk," she said, trying to sound nonchalant.

Dusk stepped into Juliette's painting and grabbed Mona's arm.

"Monsieur Dusk!" Juliette was shocked that the gray man would lay a hand on her beloved Mona. "Unhand her this instant! *Vite!*"

Dusk tightened his grip. "You know we are not allowed to leave our paintings after eight thirty. Max's rules are very clear. He—"

"I don't give a fig about Max's rules!" Mona squirmed, struggling to get free. "I've not laid eyes on him in days. How do I know he's not down the hallway watching the movie?"

"Ha! I knew you'd snuck down there!" Dusk said, elated. "I was sure I spotted you the night of the first sleepover, looking more like a rat than a mouse."

In his moment of jubilation, Dusk loosened his grasp just enough for Mona to slip free and race from the painting.

"Mona!" Juliette shouted behind her. "We do not know when the art restorer will return! You should not leave!"

"Let Dusk explain where I am," Mona called over her

shoulder. "I cannot abide this room one second longer! It smells like Mr. Sneely and rubbish."

She ran to the Oppenheimer Gallery, jumping from painting to painting, the sound of the movie getting louder as she neared the Contemporary Gallery. She tried to slip into her regular movie-watching painting, but discovered it was bursting at the seams. Besides the entire Cotterell family, Edmund was there, as was Helena Rubinstein, all watching the movie with rapt attention. Sargent hadn't let her friends down.

Mona jumped to a painting on an adjacent wall, a small watercolor of a flower garden on the outskirts of a forest. She sat on a grassy patch near the front of the painting and searched the darkened room until she spotted the back of Sargent's head. He had been so heroic, storming into the workroom and putting her on the easel.

She settled in to watch the movie, unaware of the shadowy figure that had crept into the watercolor behind her. Superman was just reacting to kryptonite when a burly hand clamped itself over her mouth and dragged her farther back into the painting. Mona struggled frantically, pulling and yanking in an effort to escape.

"Be still, you," a man's voice hissed in her ear. "Or I'll break yer neck and then go find yer friend Juliette and break hers."

Heart hammering, Mona knew she must keep her wits about her. Max had once told her a story about fishing on the Miramichi River as a young boy. A black bear had happened upon him, intent upon his afternoon's catch.

"I had a choice," he'd told her, his booming voice reminding her of a snare drum. They were playing Max's favorite card game, whist. "I could pick up my fish and try to get away from the brute, who was a good four feet taller and a thousand pounds heavier than myself, or I could let him have my catch, play dead, and return to fish another day. Sometimes you have to pretend to give in if you want to live to fight—or fish—another day."

Mona stopped struggling.

"There's a good girl," her captor said.

Mona remembered noticing a bench in the shadows between the garden and the forest, and hoped her captor had not. She was sure he would bump into it if he didn't look where he was going. Fortunately, he didn't look, and his legs buckled against the bench. To keep his balance, he let go of Mona. That was all she needed. She shoved him and dashed away.

Mona wasn't sure where go, so she simply ran, dashing through portals and down passages on her way to *Santiago El Grande*. At one point, she caught a glimpse of Dusk, which only made her run faster. Flying past the horse and rider, she ignored their demands for a riddle, amazed to discover that the painting was passable without one.

Behind her, the sound of heavy footsteps indicated her attacker was getting closer. What she needed was a place filled with people where she could blend in and hide. Rounding a corner, she saw just the place: Merrymaking.

CHAPTER THIRTY-FOUR

Merrymaking, painted by Canadian Cornelius Krieghoff in 1860, was one of the most popular paintings at the art gallery, and Mona knew why: it was the perfect French Canadian Christmas card, thanks to the party at the White Horse Inn, the snow, and the sleighs. Mona had never been in the painting, but she'd spent many evenings outside the frame, listening to the lively accordions and fiddles, wishing she could go for a sleigh ride.

She took a tentative step inside and was immediately struck by the noise: singing from the inn when a door was opened, the jangling of sleigh bells, people shouting, the howl of a dog, and most disconcerting of all, the odd rifle shot. Next were the smells: horse manure, cooking pork, drying furs. It was terrifying and thrilling all at once. And it was freezing. She shivered in the brittle January weather. She'd need a coat to stay any amount of time.

"Excuse me, lad," she called to a young fellow who was about to wreak havoc on his friend with a slingshot and a rock. "Do you know if there is a place where I might acquire a coat and a cup of tea?"

The boy glared at her, then ran away.

Sighing, Mona turned to a young man wearing fur-lined deerskin, who was crouched down and attaching wooden snowshoes to his deerskin boots, a black dog by his side.

"*Excusez-moi*," she said.

He looked up, his frown turning to a smile when he saw her. "Do you need help? You don't look as if you belong here."

"I am in trouble," Mona said, relieved. "I am fleeing an unsavory character and have slipped into this painting to hide. But I do not have proper clothing for this weather. I could use your assistance."

The young man untied his snowshoes and stuck them in the sack on his back. "Let's go inside and get you a coat."

Mona eyed the White Horse Inn with trepidation. "I am not allowed to visit a public house. Could you fetch a coat on my behalf?"

"It seems odd to retain one's high ideals when one is freezing," the young man said with a bemused smile. He reached back into his sack and pulled out a furry animal hide. "Drape this over your shoulders. I'll find you a coat and then help you find a place to hide."

Mona took it gratefully, trying not to wrinkle her nose at the pungent odor of damp fur. It covered her shoulders, at least, and that was a start. "It is terribly fine of you to take care of me, but do hurry, for I am becoming a snowman!"

The young man sprang up the stairs toward the inn's entrance, dodging two men engaged in a spirited fistfight. Meanwhile, Mona took a seat on an overturned sleigh and waited. Her eyes flitted from the inn's entrance to the side of the painting where she'd entered. There was no sign of her pursuer, or of Dusk. Above her, a pale lemon gumdrop of a sun was being swallowed by a band of lilac clouds. Somewhere behind her, sleigh bells rang out, and she would have felt jolly were it not for the fact that the bitter cold was making her shiver violently. Resolving to send someone in after the young man lest she freeze to death, Mona stood up, only to find herself being lifted off the ground by a pair of strong arms leaning out of a passing sleigh. A flour sack was shoved over her head, and the sleigh began to pick up speed.

At first Mona was too shocked to speak, but then her survival instincts kicked in, and she began to thrash about, screaming for help until a massive hand muzzled her cries.

A sinister voice whispered in her ear. "Another sound out of ya and I'll slit yer throat." Mona recognized the voice immediately; it belonged to the man who'd grabbed her earlier!

Terrified, she remained quiet. As the sleigh continued on its bumpy way, its long runners slicing through the crunchy snow, the sounds of the inn faded until they were completely gone, replaced by the odd call of a blue jay and the strange creaky sound of cold branches waving in the wind. Mona tried to imagine why she was being kidnapped and wondered if Juliette would send for help when she didn't return. But that could be hours from now, and what would happen before then? And if she never returned, the secret of the paintings would be revealed by her empty frame. The thought made her woozy, as did the cold, for the hide the young man had given her had slid off her shoulders and lay puddled around her feet.

Through chattering teeth, she whispered, "Please, I am half frozen."

"Cold, are ya? Argyle, this midge here says she's cold. What do you think of that?"

"I say cover her up, you idjit! She's no good to us froze to death!"

Argyle? Of Argyle and Bertha and Rossi's Café? Why was Argyle kidnapping her?

A larger fur was wrapped around her, but Mona kept shivering, due not just to the cold, but to her predicament as well. No one knew she was in *Merrymaking* or that she was even missing. Papa had warned her about this; you couldn't be wealthy in England in the early part of the twentieth century and not know it was a risk. Kidnapping the children of wealthy families and holding them for ransom was not unheard of, and Mona had been taught early on to keep her wits about her and to go nowhere without a chaperone. Yet here she was, a hundred years later and a world away, foolishly thinking herself invulnerable to the greed and unhappiness of others. Would Max pay the ransom?

The sled came to an abrupt halt.

"Why'd ya stop?" the man closest to Mona said.

"Tree trunk lying across the track," Argyle Smith said. "Help me move it out of the way, Ryan."

The name Ryan seemed familiar, but Mona couldn't recall where she'd heard it before. The sleigh swayed as the two men jumped off. "Don't move, Mona," Argyle Smith ordered. "Keep yer mouth shut and you might survive this day."

As far as Mona knew, no resident had ever been murdered. Would she be the first? Was it even possible for one resident to kill another? She did know that when a resident was hurt while visiting a painting, they were always healed as soon as they stepped back into their own. But did that work if the person was dead? She had no idea. Her chest tightened as she listened to the men's boots crunching across the snow. She was kicking her legs to get the blood flowing again, when she felt a thump. Someone was beside her.

"Shh! Stay quiet!" It was the young man! She was saved!

Nodding, she heard him pick up the reins and give them an easy snap. The two horses began to trot, veering left. Mona could hear them breaking a fresh trail in the hard snow.

"Ho there!" Argyle Smith yelled.

The young man snapped the reins harder, and the horses picked up speed. There was a sound of barking, and a dog landed on the seat beside Mona, panting heavily. Head still covered by the bag, Mona had no idea if the men were close to catching them; their hollering seemed near indeed, and several times she was sure they were done for. But then the sleigh turned and the horses began to gallop, their hooves pounding over the packed snow. The angry voices grew distant, and Mona exhaled deeply. She hadn't realized she'd been holding her breath.

"You can take the bag off your head, you know."

"Oh." Mona pulled off the scratchy sack and looked back. Argyle Smith continued to chase them, but Mr. Ryan had stopped and was bent over, as if he was trying to catch his breath. Stunned to find herself truly saved, she looked over at her driver.

"How did you know where I was?"

"I was coming out of the inn when I saw them grab you," he said, easing off on the horses a bit.

"But that was at least a mile ago!"

"About a mile and a half ago," he agreed.

"However did you keep up?"

"I have a small sled I attach my dog to," he replied. "He's fast. I'd noticed the log across the trail on my way to the inn earlier today and knew they'd have to stop. We used a trail in the woods to stay out of sight, and when you stopped, I unhooked my dog and stole you back."

Mona stared at him, dumbfounded. Troy needed to meet this fellow—he was a real superhero. "Why, I don't even know your name," she said.

"Jacques."

"Jacques? But you don't sound French."

Jacques shrugged. "My mother was French, my father, English."

"Why did you help me, Jacques? You don't even know me." Now that her ordeal was done, the emotion of what might have happened overtook her, leaving her shaky.

"I know them," Jacques said, tilting his head back in the direction of the men. "Argyle Smith and Charlie Ryan have done this sort of thing before. Earlier today I heard them bragging about someone they were holding captive over at The Terror. I was afraid that's where they were taking you, too." The Terror was a painting located next to Merrymaking.

"My goodness, I wonder who it is? I know Argyle Smith. I met him and his wife, Bertha, a few days ago. He seemed so amiable. I cannot for the life of me understand why he would kidnap me."

"Argyle Smith does others' dirty work. Someone hired him to kidnap you."

Mona could not imagine who would want to kidnap her except perhaps Max and Dusk, though that seemed extreme, even for them. No doubt Dusk had gone to Max when she'd left the workroom, and Max was making good on his vow to send her away if she got out of line. But who was Max holding hostage in *The Terror*?

They rode along in silence, Mona lost in her thoughts, trying to decide what to do next. She was surprised to see woodsmoke curling above the treetops. They were almost back at the inn.

"Thank you for saving me," she whispered. Jacques nodded.

"Do you ever leave this painting?"

"Not much. I prefer the wilderness."

"Will you come and visit me sometime?" she asked. "I would be so pleased."

Jacques turned and smiled. "I could do that."

Before Mona could respond, she heard shouting. Dusk was headed her way, followed by a group of men and women carrying torches.

"Hurry—drive me over to the frame!" she urged. "I can't be caught again!"

Face grim, Jacques veered right. Mona could see the frame's gilded edge on the other side of a stand of silver birch, golden in the twilight. Dusk yelled something incomprehensible.

As Jacques eased the horses to a stop, Mona leaned

over and gave him a peck on the cheek. "I shall never forget you, Jacques. Thank you ever so much!" Then she hopped off the sleigh and jumped through the frame. Despite her desire to return home, she knew she must go into The Terror. Someone else was in danger, too.

CHAPTER THIRTY-FIVE

The canvas Sargent carried upstairs at the end of the movie reminded him of a book he'd had as a child. It had multiple buttons down the right-hand side that if you pressed them, would say another line from the story.

"Never was there a man so wonderful as that Superman," he heard Helena Rubinstein say, her voice muffled by the drop cloth.

"My stars, I was certain he would not survive the Kryptonite," Lady Cotterell exclaimed.

Clem shouted to be heard above the others. "I liked Lex Luthor—he was funny."

"I shall be sad when the moving pictures are no

longer," Sir Charles said. "They have made me happy beyond measure."

"We must talk to Max!" Lady Cotterell's voice was shrill. "He must find a way for us to see more moving pictures! He must!"

"'Tis not that simple," Edmund said. "Who amongst us wants to tell Lord Beaverbrook that we have been transported to a moving picture by a person who lives outside the frame?"

"Hello, I'm still here, you know," Sargent said. They were almost to the front desk.

"My sincerest apologies, Master Sargent. I did not mean to offend."

Sargent tucked the canvas under the desk and crouched down in front of it as he removed the drop cloth. He grinned. "None taken. I'm glad you enjoyed yourselves." He was rewarded by curtsies and deep bows, all the more impressive because of the canvas's restricted space.

As Helena Rubinstein began to depart, Sargent held up a hand. "Was Mona there? I didn't see her, but I thought maybe she was hidden behind someone else."

Mona's friends shook their heads.

"Should I try to go see her again?" Sargent asked.

Edmund looked grave. "I beg you—no. I believe such

action will only call more attention to her if you do. I hope that the art restorer completes his work soon. It is lonely for me without Mona and my beloved Juliette."

Lady Cotterell reached forward, as if she'd like to pat Sargent's arm. "There, there, Sargent, she's fine. Our Mona is a resilient girl. 'Tis a pity she could not attend this evening, but no doubt she will be present next week. Do you know what moving picture Janice has chosen?"

"Pray, do tell," Sir Charles said. "I have another letter to write this evening, thanking the actors for their performances!"

"I think you're getting to be a movie buff, Sir Charles," Sargent said.

Sir Charles looked befuddled. "To what does this term 'buff' refer?"

"I know it means someone who loves movies, but that's a good question. I'll look it up on the internet and get back to you."

"The internet," the group in the canvas said in unison. While they had never seen the internet, they were aware of its powers. It was all-knowing.

"I gotta go. See you next week!" Sargent crawled out from underneath the desk, taking a last look back at the now-emptying canvas. He wished he could follow them. It would be cool to live in their world.

Isaac was waiting for him at the bottom of the stairs. "Where were you?"

"I just went to the bathroom," Sargent said.

"The bathroom is down here. Why were you upstairs?"

"I wanted to stretch my legs. Is that a crime?" Even as the words tumbled out of his mouth he wished he could pull them back. He sounded defensive, snotty.

"You need permission. This gallery is not a playground. Just because you're my son doesn't mean you have the run of the place."

"I don't act like I have the run of the place." Sargent tried to ease past, but Isaac put a hand on his arm to stop him.

"No? I talked to Frank earlier, Sargent. He told me about you coming into the gallery last Sunday morning to get your phone. You didn't tell me you were going downtown."

"I didn't want to wake you. I needed my phone, and it was only two blocks."

"You can't just leave the apartment without my permission. You're only twelve years old."

"I'm almost thirteen, or can't you remember?" Sargent

couldn't bear to look at Isaac's concerned face, so he looked down at the floor instead.

"I remember how old you are. But you can't come and go like you own the place. I answer to a lot of people. I can't afford to get in trouble because of something you've done."

"I'll be leaving soon, so you won't have to bother about me after that." He turned away. "I'm going back with the others. I'm sorry if I've harmed your precious gallery." Sargent ran to catch up with the other campers, wishing he didn't feel like an idiot. He didn't look back.

CHAPTER THIRTY-SIX

The *Terror* was not the real name of the painting Mona now approached. Painted in 1838 by George Chambers, it had one of the longest names in the entire gallery: *The Crew of HMS "Terror" Saving the Boats and Provisions on the Night of 15 March (1837)*. That was simply impossible for anyone to remember, let alone say, so the residents of the Beaverbrook simply referred to it as *The Terror*. And why not: it was a dismal icy scene that chilled viewers to the core.

The painting portrayed a ship trapped in ice with a ghastly blizzard bearing down on it. The doomed ship was the color of crows, and in the forefront, dozens of men worked to extract their salvation: wooden rowboats, boxes of food, water, and matches. All around them, ghostly shafts of ice breached the surface, white tips slipping into inky bottoms.

If looking at the arctic scene was enough to fill one with glacial thoughts, Mona knew that stepping into the painting would be a hundred times worse. No wonder the sailors went to the White Horse Inn at night. Who wouldn't, after being stuck in such a painting all day? She wished she could have brought the fur wrap with her; she needed to find something warm to wear, fast.

Dusk, still in *Merrymaking*, was calling her name, so Mona climbed into *The Terror*, stepping gingerly onto the ice. The howling wind almost knocked her off her feet, tossing icy particles that stung her eyes. She moved timidly, testing the ice with each step. The wind whirled another cyclone of snow and ice, out of which stepped a man with a grizzled face.

"Lord thunderin', what are ya doing here? It ain't safe!"

"Please," she said, teeth chattering. "I'm told someone is being held in this painting against their will. Do you know anything about that?"

The man looked up into the storm. "Perhaps."

"If such a person was being held, where would I look for them?" said Mona, wishing she were the sort of person who could leave things alone, ignore injustices.

"The ship is comin' apart. The ice floe ain't no place for a little girl. I'm givin' you fair warning: go home before you get hurt. Being a rich little girl's no benefit in this world."

"You know who I am."

The man smiled. "Ours is a small world, Mona Dunn."

"I can't go home. Only moments ago, someone tried to harm me in *Merrymaking*. I fear they will try to do the same to whoever is being held here. Will you help me?"

The sailor shook his head. "I have my orders. I'm tellin' you again, for the last time, *leave*."

Mona held out her hands, which were now turning a plum color. "You have warned me. I understand I am placing myself at great risk and you cannot help me, either because you are working for the people who wish me harm or because you do not wish to be involved for fear of getting in trouble yourself. But please, have you extra clothing that might fit me? Once I am kitted out, I shall venture forth myself, unaided."

The man gave Mona an appraising look that bordered on admiration. "We keep some extra kit back by the frame, in case. There's a set of clothes what belonged to a cabin boy who fell overboard out in the Atlantic that might do. Awful tragedy. He was a jolly lad, only twelve years old, and sorely missed by the crew. I wish I could recall his name, but it's been so long now."

He led Mona over to a wooden trunk, dug around inside, tossing what he thought might work over his shoulder in her direction. The cabin boy's clothing fit Mona perfectly, and she pulled on sealskin pants and boots, buttoned up the heavy coat, shoved a heavy woolen hat over her head until it practically covered her eyes, and stuck her hands into a pair of sealskin mittens. She was as ready as she would ever be.

She followed the man out to the edge of the ice floe. Unlike daytime, when all hands were on deck, only a few men milled about at night. Everyone else had gone visiting, not just to the White Horse Inn, but to other paintings. The man pointed Mona in the direction of a tall sheet of ice in the distance, one so solid it looked more like a wall of rock than frozen water.

"Go past the ice, then keep on till you see a tent. What you're looking for might be there."

Mona took a deep breath and extended a mittened hand. "Thank you."

The man looked down at her hand and smiled, revealing a mouth lacking in teeth. "Reginald Oliver, miss. I be a sailor on this doomed mission. You are a plucky thing, you are, though you ought to know your mission is also doomed."

"You can't know that," Mona said.

"The sorts of men what be involved are not the kind of men who lose."

Mona looked to the distant horizon, hoping Reginald did not notice her shaking legs. "We shall see," she said, and off she went.

The ice that had looked flat and unbroken from outside the frame turned out to be quite different. There were broad chasms across the ice, places where the sea reared and forced the separation of two sheets of ice, leaving a deadly gap of churning water between them. Mona slipped and slid, almost losing her footing on at least two occasions, both of which would have resulted in certain death. Heart thumping, tears frozen to her cheeks, she soldiered on, telling herself this was yet another dragon.

She tiptoed between two towering walls of ice that groaned and creaked as if in pain. Each wall was at least fifty feet high, and they leaned toward each other precariously, as if they might topple over at any moment. Mona assumed they would hold, since Chambers had painted them to stay as they were, but now she realized she might be wrong. There was a wildness to this painting that, much like Merrymaking, defied order and rules. Perhaps the parts painted in the foreground were fixed, but beyond, who knew? The artist had imagined a chaotic and dangerous world, and the painting had delivered. She shivered and shoved her mittened hands deep into her coat pockets, giving a tremendous sigh of relief when she was finally beyond the ice walls and could see a tent in the distance.

When Mona stepped through the heavy canvas flap of the tent, she saw someone wrapped in furs, slumped against two oak barrels. The figure reminded her more of a bear than a person, and she gave it a wide berth as she sidled forward for a better look.

"Max!"

This was a beaten Max, with his hands tied behind his back and his face covered with cuts and bruises. He glanced up, saw it was her, and then closed his eyes as if the mere sight of her caused him distress.

Mona ran forward and crouched down in front of him. "Max, it's me, Mouse. I'll untie you, and then you must come with me. We haven't much time to get away before Dusk arrives."

"Dusk is coming?" he whispered, without opening his eyes.

"Yes, so we must hurry. Do you think you can stand up?"

Max shook his head. It cut Mona to the quick to see the mighty Lord Beaverbrook in such dire straits. She would have to fetch Reginald, beg him to help her get Max out of The Terror.

Max opened an eye. "We must wait for Dusk."

"We can't, Max, something's happened to him. He's been chasing me everywhere and he had me kidnapped. Surely by now you realize you cannot trust him! I'm only here thanks to a sympathetic sailor. I'm sure he'll help me get you out of this painting and back to your own portrait." She crawled behind him and began to untie the tight ropes.

Max groaned. "I ran into a couple of thugs late last night. They knocked me out and dragged me here."

Argyle Smith and Charlie Ryan. "I didn't know you were missing—"

"Would you have cared? You were awfully cross at me the last time we spoke, Mouse."

It was true; Mona had been avoiding Max for weeks. Her heart squeezed in her chest. She had been angry with him, but clearly she had been wrong. Sobbing, she flung herself at Max.

"Oh, Max, I am so sorry. I was convinced you were behind some awful plot with Dusk and the art restorer. I see now you have nothing to do with it. But you were acting so suspiciously. And when I overheard you talking to someone outside of the frame . . ."

"Director Singer. I was advising him about how to negotiate with Harmsworth. He'd never been involved in such a large deal before, and he needed my help."

Mona's jaw dropped. "You talk to Director Singer?"

She saw a flicker of guilt cross his face when he nodded.

"But I heard you say that paintings might be moved. . . ."

"Yes, eventually, if the gallery added a new wing. It seems you and I have not trusted each other, Mouse, and that distrust has cost us both."

The hands that patted her back were bruised and clumsy. Whoever had been holding Max in the tent had used him poorly.

"Please, Max!" Mona begged, clutching his fingers between her mittened hands. "We must hurry!"

"I do not think I can walk, at least not far. One of my ribs feels broken."

"Then I shall go for help." Mona scrambled to her feet. She pushed the tent flap to one side and stepped out, bumping squarely into Dusk.

CHAPTER THIRTY-SEVEN

How Dusk got himself dressed for the weather and found her so quickly was a mystery. He scowled when he saw her, and shoved her back into the tent so hard she tumbled to the ground next to Max.

"Dusk—thank heavens," Max said.

Mona eyed Max with alarm. He still didn't understand. "Max, there is no 'thank heavens.' Dusk is our captor."

"I most certainly am not!" Dusk protested, glaring at her. Wrapped in furs and wearing a cap, he looked less gray than usual. "I am here to rescue you both before it's too late!"

"Rescue us! But you've been chasing me all day!"

Dusk gave her a withering look. "Yes, I have, and thanks to you believing the worst of me, you almost managed to get yourself hurt twice. Max went missing yesterday, and I've been searching for him everywhere. I had a lead that he might be in Merrymaking, which is why I was going there. Imagine my shock when you ran in ahead of me. Really, you have been quite a bother, Mona Dunn. But Max said I must protect you at all costs, and so I will."

"I don't understand. . . ."

"We don't have time for this right now. Someone is trying to get rid of Max. We need to get him back to his portrait."

"I'm not sure I can walk, Dusk."

"Not a problem, Boss. I saw a sled outside the tent. I'll fetch it and pull you out of the painting. There's a crevasse about three-quarters of a mile past this tent where there's a shortcut to the frame. We'll slip out there."

"How do you know about that?" Mona demanded.

Dusk rolled his eyes. "Really, Mona. I'm Lord Beaverbrook's right-hand man. It's my business to know everything." He hurried to get the sled, looking grim when he returned.

"I saw at least six lanterns coming this way," he said. "We need to move—now."

"Will we be able to pull Max fast enough?" She eyed Dusk. Max wasn't huge, but he was twice the size of Dusk.

"I can manage," was Dusk's terse reply. "Hold the tent flap open and we'll be on our way. Hold tight, Boss!" Max grimaced in pain, but nodded.

When they emerged from the tent, Mona saw that the storm had centered itself overhead. Lanterns bobbed in the distance. Mona had no doubt that Argyle Smith and Charlie Ryan were in their number.

"Hurry!" she called to Dusk, who grunted and began to pull the sled across the uneven ice, bumping and jarring Max with each step. Mona grabbed the extra harness and pulled with all her might. With each step her shoulders ached more, and her hands burned, but she wouldn't give up. They must save Max. As soon as they were out of the painting, she would find Sargent. He would help. Max would have to let him help.

During the twenty minutes it took to pull Max from the tent to the crevasse, Mona's opinion of Dusk changed completely. He muttered and groaned with every step, but he never faltered. Now and then he would glance back and shout, "We're almost there, Lord Beaverbrook—hang on!" and Max would reward him with a weak smile of encouragement. It was inspiring, and though it pinched at Mona to admit it, heroic. Dusk was going to save the day.

Then: there was the frame, a glittery lighthouse guiding them home.

"You did it, Mr. Dusk!" Mona cried. "Hurray!"

They stopped and helped Max to his feet. He shuffled forward, leaning on Dusk and Mona, too weak to carry the fullness of his weight.

"I'll go first," Dusk said, "and then I'll reach back and help him over. Once you're out, Mona, run for help. I won't be able to walk him to his portrait by myself. He'll need to be carried." He stepped across, and Mona and Max hung back, waiting.

"Thank you, Mouse," Max whispered. "You're awfully small to help pull a brute like me across terrain like that."

Mona nestled under his armpit and hugged him tightly. "Wait till Papa hears about our adventure!"

A gray arm reached into the painting. Max took it, stepping carefully while Mona steadied him so he wouldn't lose his balance. When he'd cleared the frame, Mona followed. The first thing that registered when she reached the dimly lit passage was that Max and Dusk looked frightened. The second was that Argyle Smith and Charlie Ryan were holding knives to their throats.

CHAPTER THIRTY-EIGHT

Sargent was desperate for Janice to tell the campers it was time to bunk down for the night. Isaac hadn't spoken to him since they'd rejoined the others, but Sargent knew a glowering look when he saw one. All he wanted to do was go to sleep and forget about this horrible night. But Janice had something else in mind.

"I have a surprise for you," she said, pulling a DVD out from behind her back and holding it up for everyone to see.

"I love *The Wizard of Oz*!" Alice squealed.

"Me too! I was talking to Barney earlier this week, and he suggested we have a double bill tonight. Fun, right?

By the time it's over, maybe I won't have to tell a certain someone to stop talking and go to sleep." She gave Troy a significant look.

"What, can't a guy share his thoughts with his fellow man?"

Janice laughed. "Troy, I swear, you are eleven going on thirty."

"That's not bad. My mom says I'm eleven going on life without parole."

"You can't top him, Janice, there's no point trying," Adam said.

Janice threw up her arms. "I surrender!" She popped the DVD into the player, and everyone settled into their sleeping bags to watch.

Sargent wished he'd known about the double bill; he would have told the Cotterells. Nothing could be done now, so he allowed himself to be lulled by the clouds floating across the screen during the opening credits. He almost jumped when someone tapped him on the shoulder.

It was Janice. "Would you mind running to my office? I left a couple of bags of chips and a big bowl of M&Ms on my desk."

"No problem."

He ducked down and headed toward the door. Isaac

leaned forward as he passed by. "Come straight back," he said. Sargent didn't respond.

Instead of going directly to Janice's office, Sargent raced upstairs to the Harriet Irving Gallery. "We're watching another movie tonight—an amazing movie called The Wizard of Oz—and you guys gotta come!" he told the Cotterells and Edmund. "There's a tornado, a wicked witch, a girl and her dog, a talking scarecrow—"

"We're in," Clem said. He didn't need to hear anymore to know this was his kind of movie.

"But here's the thing: you'll have to find your own way down."

Sir Charles was already donning his floppy hat with its jaunty feather. "Never fear, Master Sargent, we will find a way. Besides, neither Lord Beaverbrook nor Dusk have been prowling around tonight. I'll gladly risk their wrath to watch another moving picture." He bowed deeply.

Sargent turned to Edmund. "Can you tell Mona?"

Edmund tapped his walking stick against the side of his right shoe, thinking. "I can make no promises. We shan't forget your thoughtfulness, Sargent. Thank you."

Sargent smiled. Before heading downstairs, he did a quick circuit of the various galleries on his way to the Vaulted Gallery, in case Mona was at San Vigilio, Lake Garda. When he passed the spot where Lord Beaverbrook's

portrait was supposed to be, he stopped. The painting was gone, replaced by a small white card that said
BEING REPAIRED. BACK SHORTLY. Surprised, he stepped into the
Vaulted Gallery, scanning the other paintings. Everyone
else seemed to be in place.

Then a flash of something in one of the paintings
caught his eye: a black boot disappearing into the side of
Lady Macbeth's painting. He froze, waiting to see if the
boot would emerge in the next painting. It did not, but
there was a flicker of movement three paintings down. A
man was shoving Lord Beaverbrook. Ahead of them, disappearing into the frame, were Mona's black slippers. He
tore down the gallery, checking every painting for signs
of life. After a few minutes of nothing, he gave up and ran
back to the Harriet Irving Gallery to tell Edmund. Lord
Beaverbrook and Mona were in trouble. He rounded the
corner at full speed, nearly knocking over Isaac and Janice.

Isaac stood there, arms crossed. "Go back down with the
kids, Janice. Sargent and I will be right along."

"Leave it for tonight," Janice pleaded.

Isaac shook his head. "I can't. Sargent, we have to talk
about an email I just received from Art Tomlinson of the
Albuquerque Museum."

Sargent's knees buckled slightly. He'd forgotten about

shipping Isaac's paintings to the Albuquerque Museum. Crap. He was in a world of trouble. He glanced at Janice, who looked stunned.

Isaac pointed toward the bench in the center of the gallery and Sargent shuffled over to it, slumping down. It was going to be awful to be chewed out in front of the Cotterells and Edmund.

"First of all, how did you even know that the Albuquerque Museum had asked me to participate in their show?"

Sargent stared at his hands, still slightly violet from the paint he'd used for his self-portrait. "I saw the letter on your desk when I was waiting for you a couple of weeks ago."

"Setting aside the fact that you read my private correspondence, why in the world would you send them my paintings?"

"Why do you think?" No way was he going to just roll over and allow Isaac to make him feel guilty for doing something helpful.

"Honestly? I haven't a clue. Why don't you enlighten me?"

Janice cleared her throat. "It's my fault."

Isaac stared at her, confused. "Your fault? How?"

"Sargent overheard me telling Martine that you

weren't putting your paintings in the exhibit because you didn't have them. I'm sorry."

"That was none of your business!" Isaac said, exasperated.

"Everything to do with you is my business, Isaac. We're getting married! I'm sure Sargent was only trying to do something nice for you."

"He's done the opposite of nice, as have you."

Janice shook her head. "Look, I said I was sorry. I'm going back downstairs. You need to apologize to Sargent. And if you're smart, tell him everything." She wheeled around and left.

Isaac began to pace. "What a mess."

Angry now, Sargent looked up at him. "Nice job offending your girlfriend. You know what I did after I read that stupid letter? I googled you and discovered you used to be somebody in the art world. I read about how people admired your paintings, wanted you to do more shows, saw how brilliant your work was. And I felt stupid, because I had no idea. I asked myself why you'd never told me you were an artist, especially when it's the one thing we have in common. But I knew the answer: you didn't tell me because you hate Mom and me."

"I don't hate your mother and I certainly don't hate you!"

"I thought Mom had the paintings and you were afraid to ask her for them, so I asked her. And then I found out I own the paintings. Me, not her, a fact nobody thought they ought to share with me. I thought you'd be happy they were in the show, because people would see them."

"You shouldn't have done that without asking me. It's not what you—"

Sargent jumped to his feet. He was a balloon whose air was escaping all at once; it was impossible to stop talking. "Like you shouldn't have forgotten to tell me about Janice? Like you shouldn't have forgotten about me?"

Isaac looked as if Sargent had punched him. "I wanted to see you, but I—"

"Whatever. I hardly know you. When you do come to town, all you do is take me places. We never just hang out. Sometimes you even invite Ashley and Ainsley to go with us."

"I thought you wanted that!"

"They have a father, okay? A father they see every single day. They live with their father and mother. You're supposed to be my dad, not theirs! You don't know anything about me. You don't know who my friends are, you don't know how sad I feel all the time because you abandoned me. Don't tell me off for trying to do something nice for you. Soon I'll be thirteen, and when

I'm thirteen I won't have to see you anymore. I know, because some of the kids at my school don't see their deadbeat fathers anymore either."

Isaac staggered backward. "Sargent . . . please. I know I've made mistakes. I invited you here for the summer so we could finally get to know each other better."

Sargent knew they were never going to get past this. He glanced across the room. Edmund looked visibly shaken and Lady Cotterell had tears in her eyes. Now he'd disappointed them, too.

"You don't even know what's going on in your own gallery, right under your nose!" he shouted. "All you care about is chasing after idiots like Harmsworth. I'm the one who's trying to help the gallery, not you!" Sargent fled, and didn't look back.

CHAPTER THIRTY-NINE

Mona, Max, and Dusk had been shoved and dragged on such a byzantine route, it was impossible for Mona to keep her bearings. Stranger still was that half of the frames they traveled through were empty. The clock on the wall read 10:05—no one should have been out of their paintings. Had other residents been kidnapped, too? Things were going from bad to worse.

Juliette gasped when the group stepped into Mona's empty frame in the workroom. "Sacré bleu! What is happening? Who are these men, Monsieur Dusk? And what has happened to Lord Beaverbrook?"

Charlie Ryan silenced Dusk with a cuff to the side of

the head. "No one speaks less I say so."

Leaning wearily against the frame, Max chose to ignore him. "I am hurt, madame. I was kidnapped, beaten, and held under inhumane circumstances within *The Terror* this past day."

"He's very weak, Juliette," Mona added. She turned to Argyle Smith. "For all that is holy, please allow Max to return to his painting. He'll be able to heal quickly there."

Argyle Smith shook his head. "He stays here."

"Shut it," said Charlie Ryan. "All of youse."

Max collapsed onto Mona's stool with a groan. Mona reached down and retrieved the coverlet she sometimes used to wrap her chilly feet and draped it around Max's shoulders.

Dusk looked across the room at his wife. "You have us here, what do you plan to do with us?" he asked.

Argyle Smith's smile was akin to a crocodile's: wide and sharp and cunning. "Why, that depends on what the boss tells us to do, doesn't it?"

"The Boss will tell you to return to whatever hole you crawled out from," Dusk said.

"Not that boss, you ninny—*our* boss." Argyle Smith pointed to the wall. Somerset Maugham was watching them.

"Mr. Maugham cannot possibly be your boss," Dusk

said. "He never leaves this room."

"Don't he? Why, I've seen him at Lord Beaverbrook's meetings."

That was when Mona remembered where she'd first seen Argyle Smith. It had been at the meeting where Max had told the residents about the restoration schedule and Sargent. Smith was the man who'd complained about *Merrymaking* being closed. Mr. Maugham had been there that night, his head held in someone's arms like a jack-o'-lantern. She hadn't known who the man was at the time, but now she realized it had been Charlie Ryan, the same man Max had raged against at the next meeting.

"I feel honored to hear you discuss me with such patently uneducated theories," Maugham said, clearly enjoying himself. "It seems you and Dusk have overestimated your abilities and underestimated mine, Max."

"You're angry at being stuck in here," Max stated.

"Ah, Maxie, would it were so simple. But it was so much worse, was it not? Placing me, one of the greatest writers of the twentieth century, a raconteur of the highest order, in a workroom with few companions, when you knew all I wanted in life was to discuss ideas and literature. It was unconscionable."

Mona gave Juliette a questioning glance, but her friend seemed equally mystified.

"He's mad Max didn't keep him upstairs," Dusk supplied. "What he neglects to mention is what trouble he caused up there—the quarrels, the petty innuendos."

"Innuendos?" Mona said.

"He spread malicious rumors," Dusk said.

"But what does this have to do with us?" Mona pressed. "I understand you are furious with Max, Mr. Maugham, but why are the rest of us here?"

Maugham's laugh was triumphant. "There is an old saying, my dear: revenge is a dish best served cold. I had to bide my time until the stars were aligned. Many have wronged me in this art gallery. They are about to be punished." Seeing the confusion on Mona's face, he continued. "I have been in this room for ten long and lonely years. Even if I deserved to be punished, ten years is cruelty beyond measure."

Mona couldn't help but agree.

Something moved behind Maugham. The hand had slipped into Maugham's sketch and was turning somersaults, unbeknownst to Maugham, who continued to speak in a menacing manner. "During that time, I pleaded with certain individuals to intercede on my behalf: Edmund, Sir Charles, Sir James Dunn, and Mr. Dusk. Little did they realize the impact of their inaction."

The hand skittered away. Mona wished it was going

for help, but knew it was likely leaving to cause mischief elsewhere.

"Perhaps you are right to be outraged, Mr. Maugham, but you will have to let us go. The art restorer will return soon." Mona looked to Dusk for reinforcement.

"He will not return soon enough to save us." Dusk's voice was dull. "I have watched him these past days. He has become confused, odd."

Maugham practically crowed when he spoke. "Poor bloke. Once so full of himself, and now terrified that he is suffering from a breakdown after being whispered to by me these past weeks. I doubt he will return tonight. Even better, he will be the first person the police interrogate— for they will find it most suspicious that the missing paintings are the ones he was copying and restoring."

Confused, Mona surveyed the room. "But there are no missing paintings, Mr. Maugham."

"Ah, but there will be, my dear. Two gentlemen will arrive shortly. They will wrap you up and take you from this gallery. Wealthy art collectors have offered huge sums of money to purchase you. They will hide you in their fabulous homes and hang you on their walls where only a select few will see you. No one will ever find you again."

Mona's eyes widened. "I don't believe it!"

"You will see, soon enough."

Mona looked at Argyle Smith with disgust. "You have set Mr. Sneely up to take the fall. That story you told us at Signor Rossi's was a rumor designed to cast doubt on Mr. Sneely's character, wasn't it? By spreading the rumor that Mr. Sneely was an art forger, you deflected attention away from what was really happening."

Argyle Smith smiled. "Bertha and I was on the stage in London early in our lives. We had tremendous fun, wandering from painting to painting, whispering in people's ears. . . ."

Mona kneeled and looked into Max's eyes. "How do we stop him?"

Max shook his bruised and battered head.

"You can't stop them." Maugham's voice was contemptuous. "By tomorrow morning you will be gone, every last one of you, including you, Max."

"But, monsieur, I am to be wed!" Juliette turned to Dusk. "Can we do nothing?"

Dusk swallowed hard. "I don't think so. If people outside the frame take us away, we cannot stop them." He glanced over at his wife. "I am sorry, darling. I know you're happy here."

Stunned, Mona looked over at Hotel Bedroom. Mrs. Dusk was giving her husband an encouraging smile, which seemed to hearten him.

Max cleared his throat. Shoulders hunched forward, chin trembling, he looked at Dusk, Mona, and Juliette with tears in his eyes. "Normally, I would try to negotiate, but it is clear Somerset is not so inclined. Am I not right, old friend?"

Mona looked at Max in confusion. "You and Mr. Maugham were friends?"

"We were the best of friends. Two old dinosaurs living out our final years in the South of France. I begged, borrowed, and stole to bring the sketch of him to the Beaverbrook Art Gallery. We should never have fallen out, Willie."

Mona looked at Dusk. "Willie?"

"The W in W. Somerset Maugham stands for William," Dusk said.

Maugham's eyes softened for a moment and then became as hard as coal. "We should not have fallen out, Maxie. But you miss the point: it is a poor idea to leave an intelligent man alone for a decade. I may be a sketch on a wall, but I masterminded everything."

"But what about Max?" Mona said. "His frame's not here. And he was never on the list to be restored by Mr. Sneely."

"His frame will be brought here momentarily. Just as I

was banished, Max will be taken away from his beloved gallery forever. It is fortunate that the gallery director has been so distracted this week and did not notice that Max's frame was removed by Barney yesterday, as soon as we kidnapped him. And why should any of you care? He's been lying to you for decades. Do you know he has meetings with the gallery director?"

There was a shocked silence. Mona, Dusk, and Juliette turned to look at Max.

"You always said you just knew things." Dusk's comment was half comment, half accusation. "I thought you were magic. I can't believe you didn't tell me."

For the first time, Mona saw Max bow his head in shame. Everything made sense now. Of course Max spoke regularly with Director Singer. How else could he know everything that was going on at the Beaverbrook? For some strange reason, the thought comforted her. Max wasn't all-knowing after all.

Mona might be disappointed in Max, but she was not ready to give up. "You are the scoundrel, not Max," she said. "We can call for help, you know. There are people just down the hall." As if on cue, music filled the air. Someone had opened the security doors for a moment.

"Your tiny voices will not be heard all the way down in the Contemporary Gallery," Maugham crowed. "The

Wizard of Oz. How I loved that movie. What was the theme? Ah, yes. There's no place like home. How fitting."

Mona exchanged a heartbroken glance with Juliette. Mona would be stolen from the Beaverbrook Art Gallery, just like Mona Lisa, never to see her father, her friends, or Sargent again. Edmund and Juliette would never marry. She wanted to collapse, then remembered her father's words: show no weakness. She took a deep breath and did her best to hold her head high.

"All is not lost, Mouse. There is hope yet. I didn't help Winston Churchill win the war without believing the impossible is possible," Max whispered.

Mona nodded. She had to be brave so the others would think she'd be all right in the end, regardless of how things turned out. That was important. She tried a smile, leaned against Max, and closed her eyes. The security door must have opened again, for she heard singing in the distance. Its loveliness only added to her misery. All was lost.

CHAPTER FORTY

When he reached the basement, Sargent paused, emotionally spent after his fight with Isaac. He had to find Mona. He headed for the workroom. He didn't care if Sneely was there; he'd fight him if he had to. The lights were on, and Sargent tried the doorknob. It was locked, just as he knew it would be. Frustrated, he headed to the Oppenheimer Gallery, hoping to run into Edmund or Sir Charles. He'd just passed the back exit when the door opened. He ducked into the shadowy space under the stairs and waited. In stepped Barney and Harmsworth.

"I'm having second thoughts about this," Barney said.

"No, you're not." Harmsworth's voice was threatening.

What was going on? Was Isaac expecting Harmsworth? Hidden in the shadows, Sargent studied Harmsworth. His face was creepy in the dim light, all crevices and jowls. He'd traded his shabby suit for an old varsity sweatshirt and baggy sweatpants. Barney wore his work coveralls.

Harmsworth glanced down at his watch. "We don't have much time."

Barney nodded. The two men set off in the direction of the workroom and Isaac's office. Sargent crawled out from underneath the stairs and dusted himself off. Something weird was going on. He had to find Isaac.

Mona gasped when Harmsworth entered the workroom with Barney Templeton. She wasn't shocked that the obnoxious Harmsworth was involved—she'd disliked him from their first encounter—but the idea that Barney was part of this broke her heart. He'd had always treated the paintings with such respect and fondness. While Barney reached under the table and pulled out a roll of brown paper, Harmsworth drummed his fingers on the wall.

Hotel Bedroom was the first painting to be wrapped. Dusk had hopped back into his painting just as the door to the workroom opened, and he waited, stoic, for his fate. Tears ran down Mona's cheeks as Dusk and his wife, immobile, were closed off from the world by the thick brown packing paper. No one would ever know how heroic Dusk had been, dragging Max out of The Terror. When they remembered him, the paintings that remained in the gallery would no doubt recall him as Max's officious sidekick. Mona would never have the opportunity to tell the story and apologize to him.

Max was still in her portrait, as were Argyle Smith and Charlie Ryan. Harmsworth hadn't noticed them, but it was evident that Barney knew the paintings were alive. He'd nodded up at Maugham when he'd entered the room, a barely perceptible nod, but a nod nonetheless. Mona wondered how long he'd known the truth.

Harmsworth picked up Hotel Bedroom and opened the workroom door. "I'll take this out to the van." He turned back to Barney. "Toss me the keys, will you?" Barney threw the keys, and Mona watched Harmsworth leave, swinging the painting under his arm as he went, as if Hotel Bedroom was the equivalent of an umbrella.

Sargent ran to the Contemporary Gallery. Ahead of him on the screen, Dorothy had just stepped out of sepia-tinted houses into a colorful Oz. He scanned the dark room, looking for Isaac. He wasn't there. Maybe he was still upstairs.

The Harriet Irving Gallery was empty. To be sure Isaac wasn't somewhere else, Sargent dashed from gallery to gallery. Many paintings were empty, and not just the ones belonging to the Cotterells, Helena Rubinstein, and Edmund. Andre Reidmor was missing, as was Lady Macbeth, the two women in *San Vigilio, Lake Garda*, and the occupants of other paintings he barely knew. Stranger still, Lord Beaverbrook's portrait wasn't the only painting missing; *Merrymaking* was gone, too, only there was no card on the wall stating that fact. Something strange was happening.

Sargent took the stairs two at a time and slipped through the security door. The door to the workroom was open now. That was weird. Someone was talking. Sargent pressed himself against the wall and strained to hear.

"It won't take me long to wrap the rest up," Barney was saying.

Wrap what up?

Harmsworth stepped out into the hallway. His back was to Sargent, who held his breath.

"I'll carry this one out to the van," Harmsworth said, clutching what was clearly a wrapped painting in his arms. "Toss me the keys, will you?" A pair of keys flew through the air. Harmsworth caught them and headed toward the back door. Stunned, Sargent leaned against the wall. Barney and Harmsworth were stealing paintings!

Sargent dug his phone out of his pocket. A message popped up on the screen: 2%. He punched 911, hoping there was enough juice left for one phone call, and watched in horror as the screen went black. He needed to get help.

"Disrespectful idiot," Max muttered.

"Careful, Max, mustn't show how frightened you are." Maugham was enjoying himself. "Only a few more minutes, Barney, and then you will be a very rich man."

Max might be too proud to beg, but Mona was not. "Mr. Templeton, please! You can't allow Mr. Harmsworth to steal us! How did you even get involved in this?"

Barney turned and stared at her, as if he was just now noticing that there were four people in her portrait. "My wife is sick. My friend Mr. Maugham came up with a plan to help us."

Mona gave Barney a stinging rebuke. "A friend doesn't convince another person to steal priceless masterpieces that aren't theirs!"

"I supported Barney," Maugham corrected. "We've been friends for years. When that buffoon Harmsworth arrived, I knew he had connections and that it would be easy for Barney to sway him to the dark side. Harmsworth found a buyer who wanted masterpieces. And thanks to a decade of scheming, Director Singer's list of the paintings to be restored this summer included the exact ones upon which I wanted to exact my revenge. Of course your painting wasn't on that list, Max; I wanted your departure to be a complete surprise. It was simply a matter of keeping some of you out of the way until it was time for you to go. Thus, here we are."

Barney flashed Mona an affectionate smile. "Harmsworth says you're going to a lovely chateau in Switzerland, Mona. You'll make new friends."

"But I don't want new friends! I want to stay here with my old friends and my father!"

For a brief second, something flickered—guilt?—in Barney's eyes. "I'm going to miss seeing you every day, Mona. You were always a favorite of mine."

"Monsieur, please," said Juliette. "If you must send me away, send Edmund with me!" She began to sob as Barney lifted her off the easel and placed her on the table.

Barney shook his head. "I'm sorry, Madame Juliette. That's not part of the plan. Besides, Edmund's painting is too large to fit in the van."

Juliette started to cry in earnest. "Monsieur Barney, have mercy!" Barney began to wrap her up, avoiding

Juliette's desperate eyes as he did.

Mona cried out, "Take care, Juliette. I shall never forget you!"

"Nor I you, chérie," Juliette replied, her voice breaking. "À la prochaine."

"There will be no next time for Juliette." Maugham cackled. "I look forward to seeing Edmund's expression when he discovers her gone."

Mona buried her face in Max's jacket. "Is there nothing we can do?"

Max patted her back and remained silent.

The door opened and Harmsworth entered, whistling. "Got the next one ready?"

Barney pointed to the table. "Ready to go. I just need to run to the utility closet. I've stashed Beaverbrook's frame and *Merrymaking* there. I still can't believe Amy wasn't suspicious when I put the card on the wall yesterday morning saying Lord Beaverbrook's frame was being repaired and would be rehung shortly."

"What about *The Cotterell Family*? I told my people they'd have that one, too."

"The gallery director removed it this morning. I wasn't able to get it."

Mona was confused by Barney's lie. Then it hit her: the Cotterells were at the movie. Since Barney couldn't tell Harmsworth that, he'd made up a story. At least some of her friends would be safe.

Harmsworth cursed. "What? Where is it? Well, that's thirty million down the toilet! Whatever. I'll run this one out and you get the others. Hurry, though—we've ten minutes, tops."

Barney followed him out the door. The room was quiet for several minutes. It was Maugham who broke the silence.

"Charlie and Argyle, as soon as Barney returns with *Merrymaking*, jump into it. It'll be the next one wrapped."

"I didn't know our painting was leaving." Charlie Ryan's voice sounded a little dangerous.

"I ain't sure the missus will like movin'," Argyle added. "She's got a couple o' chums in other paintings what she's quite partial to. It'll be hard explainin' why we got to move."

"If you'd go for help, Mr. Smith, you wouldn't have to move," Mona suggested.

"Ignore her." Maugham's voice was frosty. "She's trying to trick you. But consider this: your new home has a view of the ocean and two other paintings with pubs for you to frequent."

That was all it took for Charlie Ryan. "Sounds downright hospitable."

"How could he possibly know that?" Mona cried. "He's lying to you!"

"I oughta cuff you," Charlie Ryan snarled, leaning over, fist near her face. "Mr. Maugham is a right honorable gent."

"If you touch a hair on this girl's head, I will break your neck," Max growled.

"Enough!" Maugham's voice was sharp. "You're making my head ache. Come to think of it . . . you stay with Mona in her frame, Argyle, in case she tries to make a run for it. I'll ask Barney to make sure you can jump into your own painting when you get to the van."

There was no escaping now.

CHAPTER FORTY-ONE

Sargent knew he didn't have much time. Once the paint-ings were gone it could be years, if ever, before they were found again. He needed to find Isaac now. Since Isaac wasn't upstairs or in the Contemporary Gallery, he must be in his office. Sargent couldn't take the quickest route—past the workroom—so he sprinted off in the opposite direc-tion, to the doors off the Oppenheimer Gallery. He was just swiping his card when someone hollered "Help!" in the Contemporary Gallery.

Barney was back. He put Max's frame and Merrymaking on the table.

Maugham grinned at Max. "Charlie, escort Lord Beaverbrook to his painting."

Charlie Ryan started to grab Max's arm, but stopped when Max shook his head and said, "I'm perfectly capable of going into my own portrait by myself."

Max looked down at Mona. "Mouse, let me offer you my sincerest apologies. I was so focused on securing a deal with that scoundrel Harmsworth that I failed to pay attention to what else was going on. I will regret that until my last day on this earth. I have done you, Juliette, Dusk, and the folk in *Merrymaking* great harm. Thank heavens the Cotterell family was moved."

Mona blushed. "They're watching the movie."

Max stared at her for a moment, and then nodded. "You have saved them, Mouse, thanks to your open heart and imagination. I see now I have tried too hard to control things. There is a price to pay for such hubris; I just wish I was the only one paying it. Bless you." He kissed her on each cheek and went to his own portrait, leaving a forlorn Mona behind.

Charlie Ryan hopped into *Merrymaking* and Barney wrapped it up, leaving one side open. Mona thought of Jacques, the young man who'd saved her earlier, and hoped he'd like his new home.

Max was next. Now that he was back in his own

painting, he was back to his robust self. "You'll never get away with this," he growled as Barney slid the brown paper under his portrait.

"I'm awful sorry, Lord Beaverbrook," Barney stammered. His hand shook as he cut the paper to size.

"Don't apologize, you idiot!" Maugham shouted. "Hurry up!"

Max roared as the paper closed over him.

Desperate, Mona took a last look around. Her eyes landed on the package propped up in the corner. And her heart leaped.

"Patsy, I know you've heard what's going on and you must be dreadfully afraid, but we need your help! Please, please, can you make it down the hallway to where the other residents are watching the movie? Tell them what's happening!"

"Who's she talking to?" Barney asked, looking around.

Maugham tilted his head to where Patsy's partially wrapped painting still waited to be appraised. "Blast! I forgot she was there. You stay put, Miss Ryder, or I shall have Mr. Templeton take you away. If you're really a Jack Humphrey, someone will want you."

"Patsy, please!" Mona begged. "You're our only hope!"

There was no response. Maugham's threat had silenced her. Mona's last hope was dashed.

"Patsy . . . ," Maugham's voice was low, threatening.

Silence.

"Check the painting, Barney," he directed. "I need to be sure."

Barney grabbed Patsy's portrait and unwrapped it.

The frame was empty.

"She got away!" Mona cried. "She's gone for help!"

"Has she?" Maugham's voice was acid. "How do you know she wasn't already gone?"

Mona's heart sank. She didn't know. There was no way to know.

"Why don't I go take a look-see?" Argyle Smith offered. "What's this Patsy look like, anyways?"

"Yes, for heaven's sake, run and check." Maugham's voice was strained. "She said she's about fifteen years old and painted in blues and grays. Barney will partially wrap Mona and you can jump in when you return. Be quick—Harmsworth will be right back."

Argyle Smith reached down and grabbed Mona's coverlet. "I think we'll keep this little Mona bird close to home while I'm gone." He twisted the blanket into a thick rope and tied her wrists and ankles to her stool. "Wouldn't want to lose another one."

Mona struggled, but it was no use. She watched in despair as Barney lifted her off the easel. As he carried her to the table, the last thing she saw was Somerset Maugham's triumphant face.

"I'm sorry, dear," Barney whispered. And then the paper covered her, eclipsing the Beaverbrook Art Gallery forever.

CHAPTER FORTY-TWO

Sargent hadn't known what to expect when he reached the Contemporary Gallery, but he sure hadn't expected this. The lights were on. All eyes—both inside and outside the frame—were fixed on a young girl Sargent didn't recognize, who stood in a painting of a garden, looking frantic.

"Please! They're stealing Lord Beaverbrook and Mona Dunn and Madame Juliette and Mr. Dusk!" she cried out, the names flinging themselves from her tongue in one breathless lob.

"What the—" Troy cried.

The movie continued to play as the campers and

Janice took in the fact that the paintings were filled with familiar faces who shouldn't be there, whose eyes were also blinking from the light. For several seconds, mouths agape, everyone looked at one another.

"I knew they were alive!" Troy crowed. Grinning with delight, he turned to his friends. "Didn't you always think they were alive?"

Everyone nodded, but no one else was capable of speech.

"Hurry!" the girl in the painting cried.

Sargent finally found his voice and looked at Janice. "Barney and Harmsworth are stealing paintings! They're taking them right now! We have to stop them!"

Edmund crossed from the painting he was in to where Patsy stood. "Where are they now?" he asked, his voice gruff with fear.

Patsy pointed behind her. "In the workroom! They've already removed Madame Juliette and Mr. Dusk from the building! We have to hurry!"

Frantic, Edmund looked at Sargent. "We need your help. We cannot save them ourselves."

Without taking her eyes off the paintings, Janice reached into her pocket for her phone and dialed 911. "I'd like to report an art theft in progress at the Beaverbrook Art Gallery," she said, struggling to retain her composure.

"Yes, I'll meet you at the back door."

She hit the off button and turned to the campers, who were huddled around the paintings, staring at the residents. Troy and Clem seemed on the verge of speaking. "You kids come with me. You're going to wait in my office until the police arrive and tell me it's safe for you to come out."

"I'll get Isaac," Sargent said.

Janice shook her head. "It's not safe; I should get your father."

"You need to wait for the police. I'll get him. I know to stay out of sight."

Reluctantly, Janice nodded. "Be careful! If you see Frank, tell him we need him. I don't know where he is. And have your dad take you to my office. Everybody else, follow me."

Sargent rushed back the way he'd come. When he reached Frank's security room, he stuck his head in the door. The room was dark, as were the monitors. Sargent flipped on the light and gasped. Frank was slumped over his desk. Sargent checked for a pulse and was relieved when he felt one. There were no signs of blood. Sargent wasn't sure what had happened to Frank, but he was pretty sure it wasn't life-threatening.

"It'll be okay, Frank," he whispered. "I'm going for help."

The reception area outside Isaac's office was dark, but a line of light underscored Isaac's door. Sargent gave a quick knock, then stepped inside. Something was wrong. Isaac's lamp lay on the desk, its emerald shade smashed into hundreds of glittering pieces. Ignoring the goose bumps that were fast covering his arms, Sargent ran forward. Rounding the desk, he tripped over something. He looked down and was shocked to find Isaac lying there, hands bound, a piece of torn drop cloth covering his mouth.

"Dad!" Sargent was on his knees in an instant. He pulled the gag down and began to fumble with the rope. "Are you okay?"

Isaac's eyes widened and seemed to look past Sargent. "Look out!" he shouted.

Confused, Sargent turned, and was lifted off the floor by Harmsworth.

"I wondered if I'd see you tonight," Harmsworth said, smiling at Sargent's bulging eyes. "Don't worry—I'm not going to hurt you. I just need to tie you up so you stay put. Then you'll never see me again."

Sargent tried to struggle, but Harmsworth twisted his arm so tightly he was sure it would break. "Sal, I don't want to have to hurt you, but I don't have time for this."

"Please, do as he says, Sargent." Sargent had never

seen Isaac look afraid before. It scared him. He stopped resisting and allowed Harmsworth to bind his hands.

"You won't get away with this," Sargent told Harmsworth. "The police are on their way."

Harmsworth shoved Sargent onto the floor beside Isaac. "Whatever, Sal. I'm leaving." He switched off the overhead light as he left, and the room went black.

"Let's go, Barney." Harmsworth was back. To Mona, trapped under the heavy paper, his voice sounded like he was speaking underwater.

"What happened?"

"I ran into Singer. I had to knock him around and tie him up."

"No one was supposed to be hurt! And now there's a witness!"

"Two. His kid arrived. I had to tie him up, too."

Barney groaned. "I knew when they changed the timeline, things would get messed up. Didn't I say there would be too many people around tonight?"

"Relax. No one knows you're involved. Let's get the paintings to the van."

"We should forget about it, throw ourselves on the mercy of Mr. Singer—"

"It's too late for that. Do you think we can walk away

now? We're dealing with people you don't say no to. Grab
the paintings. We're leaving."

"I need to straighten things up."

"We don't need to straighten things up, you idiot!"
Harmsworth's voice was furious. "I'll take Merrymaking
and the Beaverbrook portrait. You grab Mona Dunn."

Mona heard his footsteps hurrying away.

"Argyle Smith's not back yet, Mr. Maugham."

"Go ahead, Barney. You mustn't get caught."

"But I'll be separating him from his wife forever. She's
waiting for him in Merrymaking. If he doesn't make it back,
they'll never see each other again."

"You have no choice."

Barney grunted and Mona was airborne, her portrait bobbing up and down like a buoy on the ocean.
A tickle of cool night air slipped under the open flap of
her wrapping. They must be at the back door. The fresh
air reminded Mona of the night she'd watched the stars
with Sargent, and her misery was so fierce she was sure
it would scorch her canvas.

Suddenly there was shouting. Argyle Smith flew into
Mona's portrait and hollered, "Run!"

Confused, Barney stopped.

"What's happening?" Mona asked Argyle Smith.

"We're found out," Argyle Smith panted. "Patsy was

yelling for help. Janice called the coppers."

Patsy had done it! They would be saved! "I wish they'd caught *you*," she hissed at Argyle Smith.

Barney began to move again and Mona lurched back, bumping against Argyle Smith. "What's going on?" she heard the janitor shout.

It was Harmsworth who responded—Harmsworth, whose voice was getting closer and closer. "I hear sirens. We have to try for the front door, forget about the paintings in the van!"

Barney stopped. "Enough, Harmsworth. Let it go. There's no escape."

"Get out of my way!"

Mona felt her portrait being wrenched from Barney's arms. She was on the move again.

Argyle Smith pressed his mouth close to Mona's ear. "Toodle-oo! I'll take my chances elsewhere!" he said, abandoning ship.

"Scoundrel!" Mona called after him. Mona wanted to escape, too, but was still tied firmly to the stool. No amount of pulling would change that. She was going wherever Harmsworth took her.

CHAPTER FORTY-THREE

Neither Sargent nor Isaac spoke after Harmsworth left, trapped in the miserable realization that they'd failed the paintings.

Finally Isaac cleared his throat. "Sargent, I—"

Startled, Sargent asked, "Are you okay?"

He could sense Isaac wriggling next to him, trying to sit up. "I'll be fine. How about you?"

Sargent squirmed, trying to free his hands. "We have to escape—they're stealing paintings!"

"I know," said Isaac. "The stupid knots in the rope won't budge. Where's Frank?"

"Frank's out cold. Maybe Janice will come look for us."

"This is all my fault," Isaac moaned. "I invited Harmsworth here."

"Dad, I need to tell you something, something that's going to sound crazy, but—"

"The paintings are alive," Isaac finished his sentence.

All the air was sucked out of the room. "You knew?"

"I've known paintings were alive for years. The first night I arrived, the previous gallery director brought me to my new office, poured me a cup of coffee, told me the truth about the gallery, and introduced me to Lord Beaverbrook. Max and I talk daily."

Sargent tried to process what that meant. "Does he know I know they're alive?"

"He knows."

"Why didn't you tell me?"

Isaac sighed. "It's complicated. There was so much going on. . . ."

"Harmsworth."

"Yes, Harmsworth, but I was also getting to know you and getting engaged to Janice. I liked that you knew they were alive—it was something we had in common. It made me feel closer to you. Mostly, I thought it might make it less magical for you if you knew I knew they were alive, too. When I was a kid, I liked knowing stuff adults didn't know. I planned to talk to you about it before the end of the summer. I trusted you to keep the secret. And you did."

It hadn't seemed like Isaac trusted him. "The campers and Janice know they're alive now, too."

"Oh, no! No one is supposed to know! I don't even know the residents! My relationship is strictly with Max, always has been. That's what he prefers."

"They needed our help. They're nice, you know," Sargent added. "I mean, the people in the paintings are nice."

"Who have you met?" Isaac sounded wistful.

"Mona Dunn. She's become one of my best friends. And Edmund, Madame Juliette, the entire Cotterell family, Helena Rubinstein."

"You've met all of them?"

"Yeah. I snuck them into the movies. They get bored sometimes. When I came to find you, every painting in the gallery was full of residents watching *The Wizard of Oz*."

In spite of the perilous situation, Isaac laughed. "I can't believe it."

"They're cool, Dad. They're friends with one another; they visit at night after the gallery closes, and they even have meetings to talk about stuff. I can't imagine what it will be like for them if they're stolen. . . ." Sargent paused. The thought of never seeing Mona again made it impossible to speak for a moment. After several seconds, he managed to add, "Right before I ran into you upstairs, I saw Mona and Lord Beaverbrook being dragged through some paintings. I think someone from a painting is help-ing Harmsworth and Barney."

"I wish you had told me—" Isaac began, and then stopped. "Maybe you would have if I hadn't gotten so angry. I haven't spoken to Max for a couple of days, and his sketch on the wall here isn't talking." Isaac groaned. "This is the worst night of my life."

Sargent swallowed hard.

Isaac took a deep breath. "I'm sorry. I know you only offered the paintings to the Albuquerque Museum to help me. And you're right about me being a deadbeat dad."

Sargent was glad he couldn't see his father's face.

"You asked me why I never told you I was an art-ist," Isaac continued, his voice wobbly. "The truth is, I don't love painting. I love promoting other artists' work and teaching people how to appreciate art. Your mother didn't understand. She believed someone as talented as me had a responsibility to use that talent. When we broke up, I gave up painting."

"Is that why you hate each other?"

"We don't hate each other, but it's complicated. When your mom moved out and took you, I thought I was a failure." Isaac took a ragged breath. "And then a month or two later, I caught *Sarah in the Morning*—your mother—out of her painting. She was over in the painting I'd done of you as a baby, rocking you in her arms. I thought I was going mad. But then she talked to me. It was like the old, happier days. Suddenly I had my family back. This went on for months. At first it was wonderful. But then it became depressing, because I knew it wasn't real. I began to drink and stopped leaving my apartment. One night your mom came to see me, angry that I wasn't visiting you. That's when she discovered that the paintings were alive."

"Mom knows paintings are alive? What happened?"

"Nothing fazes your mother. She simply said, 'Ike, it is what it is. But you need to live your life going forward, not backward.' And then she took the paintings. I hit rock bottom for a while, but when I came out of it and got some counseling, she helped me get a job."

"Wow. Mom helped you."

"Your mother is a good person, Sargent. I think she felt guilty that I was obsessed with the past when she had moved on. I was sick for the first few years of your life, Sargent; that's why I didn't see you. Gradually, I built up enough trust with your mom that she let me take you, like when we visited Grandma Singer the weekend before she died. But your mother was always nervous I'd start drinking again, and I did, twice. You probably don't know that she stayed in a hotel in Albuquerque that weekend, in case something went wrong. And she was the one who suggested I only have prints at home, not original artwork."

That explained why he couldn't talk to the paintings in Isaac's apartment. Sargent willed himself to speak. "You told Mom you didn't know if you could do it when she said you had to love the real me."

Isaac sucked in his breath. "We were probably talking about my obsession with the paintings, Sargent. To be honest, those days are kind of a fog to me. Did you hear the rest of the conversation?"

If he did, Sargent couldn't recall. "No."

"The rest of the conversation was me telling her that even though I was having trouble letting go of baby Sargent in the painting, I loved you and wanted us to start over. I'm so sorry you heard that. You must have been so hurt."

Sargent digested the words he'd always longed for. "You should have told me. Maybe not when I was a little kid, but later. I would have understood. I thought you didn't care."

"I'm so sorry," Isaac said. "I was ashamed. And I guess

I still am. That's why I was frantic to get Harmsworth to invest in the Beaverbrook; I was afraid I might get fired if I didn't find a way to save the gallery, and that you'd be ashamed of me."

"How long since you've had a drink?"

"Four years."

"Does Janice know?"

"She knows I used to drink, but not about the paintings—until tonight. If you can forgive me, I'd like to start over, be a real dad."

Sargent's brain churned, equal parts anger, fear, and sadness. If he didn't forgive Isaac, would he carry this heaviness in his chest forever? He understood how Isaac had gotten caught up with his paintings; hadn't he done the same with Mona?

"I'd like to try again, Dad," he whispered.

"I promise I'll always be there." Isaac's voice cracked. "You are my son, the one who makes my heart sing."

A chunk of the hurt Sargent had carried for so long broke free and floated away. Things weren't perfect, but he knew his dad loved him. For now, that was enough.

The moment was broken by the door opening. Barney stepped into the room and switched on the overhead light. Isaac and Sargent blinked from the sudden brightness.

"Oh, Barney, what have you done?" Isaac asked. He

and Barney stared at each other, both on the verge of tears. "I trusted you."

"The police will be here any second. I'm sorry, Mr. Singer. I made a dreadful mistake. I'm going to turn myself in when they arrive." Barney leaned down to untie Isaac's knots and then Sargent's. "But Harmsworth's gone upstairs. Hurry—we don't have much time if we're going to save the paintings!"

CHAPTER FORTY-FOUR

Isaac and Sargent raced to the back stairs, Barney struggling to keep up. They met Troy and Alice at the bottom.

"You're supposed to be in Janice's office," Sargent pointed out.

"Harmsworth ran upstairs, and Janice and some of the other kids chased after him. We came to find you."

"Dear God!" Isaac cried. "Can you two let the police in?"

Troy nodded. "On our way."

"And tell them to call an ambulance," said Isaac. "Sargent says Frank's unconscious."

Barney hung his head. "He'll be okay. I just drugged his coffee to knock him out."

Isaac shot Barney a grim look, then headed up the stairs, Sargent trailing after him. When they passed through the Orientation Gallery, Sargent spied a crowd of residents huddled in *Santiago El Grande*.

"He's in the Canadian Gallery!" Helena Rubinstein called, waving her lace handkerchief at them as if she were watching a horse race. The other residents shouted words of encouragement, too. An astonished Isaac waved at them, and with a giddy laugh, kept moving.

Harmsworth was at the far side of the Canadian Gallery, near the almost invisible door that led to the storage area and the freight elevator. Janice and the other campers were across the room from him, still as statues, their faces aghast. Harmsworth was not going down without a fight. He'd ripped Mona's brown wrapping away and held her aloft with one hand. In his other hand was a lit cigarette lighter. Mona, still bound to the stool, was staring at the flame, petrified.

"Harmsworth!" Isaac shouted. "Give me the painting. None of the artwork is gone; as far as I know, there has been no damage. This doesn't have to end in tragedy. Please, if you love art as much as you say you do, don't do this."

"Please, Harmsworth," Barney whispered.

Harmsworth flicked the lighter on and off a couple of times. "I knew you were weak, Barney. Singer, I swear I'll set fire to this painting unless you let me walk out of here. Are you going to let me destroy Mona Dunn?"

Isaac's face was ashen. "Even if I let you leave, you won't get far."

Barney stepped forward. "Please, just give Mona back," he said in a hoarse whisper. "It's bad enough already. If you destroy a priceless painting, it'll be a hundred times worse. She doesn't deserve this."

Harmsworth gave him a quizzical look and clicked the lighter again. The small flame flickered near Mona's face. Shaking his head, he muttered, "The people who want these paintings won't just let me give up, Barney. I told you, it doesn't work like that. I want you to negotiate with the police, Singer. Tell them I'll destroy Mona Dunn unless they let me leave."

"I can't do that, Harmsworth," Isaac said. "I can't let you leave with Mona."

"You want me to destroy her, right here, right now? Because I swear I will!"

Heat tickled Mona's canvas, and a small patch of black paint puckered. Sargent recalled that on the night he'd taken Mona from the gallery, she'd said that paintings were only afraid of two things: being stolen and fire. It seemed one or the other would be her fate this night unless he did something.

The paintings in the Canadian Gallery were part of a visiting exhibit. None contained people, so everyone was shocked when they suddenly came to life.

"Let her go this instant!" Madame Rubinstein was standing on the porch of a ramshackle farmhouse, wagging a finger in Harmsworth's direction.

"You are a fiend!" shouted Sir Charles, shaking his fist from the peak of a weathered barn.

"Let her go!" shouted Edmund and Clem, who were sitting in a rowboat.

Max, still held by Janice, added to the chorus. "Every painting in the world will haunt you forever if you harm that girl!"

Harmsworth's eyes darted around the room, registering the impossible facts that the paintings were speaking to him and that no one else seemed the least bit fazed.

Sargent slipped from the gallery. He had a plan that just might work. Hurling himself down the stairs, he raced through the museum until he reached the freight elevator, which he rode back up. After creeping his way across the storage area, he opened the door a sliver and peeked in.

Harmsworth was pacing the gallery. "This is an interesting turn of events," he said, eyeing the paintings on the wall before he fixed his gaze on Isaac. "It seems the Beaverbrook has secrets even I didn't uncover. I wonder what would happen if I revealed to the world that your paintings are alive? Would they be seized? Taken apart? Dissected?"

"Harmsworth—" Isaac began.

"Seems there is more to this place than meets the eye," Harmsworth continued, smiling down at Mona. "Is the loss of one painting so terrible if it allows the rest to live their lives in anonymity, Isaac? What do you think?"

Sargent crept forward, keeping close to the wall, until he was able to catch Mona's eye. He smiled. She managed a weak smile in return. He mouthed the words "Say something." She looked confused for a moment, then nodded.

"Would you please stop talking, Mr. Harmsworth?" Mona's tone was imperious. Only those who knew her well would have recognized the slight quaver in her voice.

Surprised, Harmsworth looked down at her, almost as if he hadn't realized the painting he was holding must be alive, too.

"I'll go with you, Mr. Harmsworth," Mona continued. "I'm ready for a change. So long as you promise to keep what you've learned about us secret, I am sure Director Singer will oblige."

Isaac, who could see Sargent stealing up behind Harmsworth, guessed what was happening and played along. "But Mona, we all love you here. We don't want to lose you."

"Thank you, Director Singer, but it's clear that the good of the residents must outweigh my own needs. Barney says I'm moving to Switzerland, which is a lovely place." Sargent saw Barney staring at Mona. He hoped Barney wouldn't interfere. Then something nearly imperceptible passed across the janitor's face, and Sargent saw him give Mona a slight nod.

Harmsworth stabbed the air with the lighter. "See, Singer? She wants to come with me. Now let me go before the police arrive."

Isaac sighed and moved back slightly, as if to make room for Harmsworth to pass. Sargent had his chance. Darting forward, he wrenched Mona from Harmsworth's grip. Harmsworth pivoted, and lunged at Sargent, but was stopped by Barney, who threw himself at the burly man. Harmsworth and Barney crashed onto the floor, neither moving for several seconds. Finally, Barney stirred and rolled onto his back, too spent to stand up. Harmsworth was out cold.

"That's going to leave a mark," Adam said, wincing.

There was silence as everyone stared at Harmsworth on the floor, at Mona in Sargent's arms, and at Barney, who had covered his face with his hands. Before anyone could speak, Archibald Sneely poked his head into the gallery.

"There you are, Mr. Singer." Sneely's voice was cool, officious. He stepped forward and pressed an envelope into Isaac's hand. "This is my letter of resignation, effective immediately. I hope never to see the Beaverbrook Art Gallery again. Appalling place. Good evening." Before Isaac could react, Sneely spun around and stalked out the front door.

It was as if Sneely's arrival had broken the spell. Janice placed Max gently against the wall and hugged Isaac. Sargent, who hadn't taken his eyes off Mona, was suddenly woozy and had to sit down. Mona was crying openly with relief.

Soon they were surrounded by the others, who slapped Sargent's back and, calling from the paintings on the wall, congratulated Mona on her performance. The celebration was short-lived, interrupted by the *clump-clump-clump* of heavy boots pounding up the stairs. The residents froze. Seconds later, four police officers entered the gallery, followed by Alice and Troy.

"Everyone okay here?" the tallest officer, the one who appeared to be in charge, asked.

Isaac read his name tag. "We're all fine, Officer Barry, but the two men on the floor there—the large one and the one in the coveralls—have conspired to steal some of the most valuable paintings in the Beaverbrook Art Gallery. My name is Isaac Singer, I'm the gallery's director. These children are summer campers having a sleepover in the gallery tonight."

Officer Barry eyed Harmsworth with uncertainty. "How did that man come to be unconscious?"

"Barney tackled him in an attempt to stop him, and he was knocked out when he landed on the floor," Janice said.

"They took some paintings," Isaac said. "Did you find them?"

"We found a white van filled with paintings by the back door when we arrived," Officer Barry said. "Take a deep breath, folks. We're going to have to ask you some questions. You said you were having some kind of sleepover at the gallery tonight? Could someone call these children's parents and have them come to the gallery right away?"

Janice looked at Isaac, eyes fearful. Sargent knew she was worried about the Beaverbrook's secret being exposed. "I can call them," she said. "I just need to go down to the office to get their phone numbers."

Already, Troy had his sketchpad out of his pocket and was doing a likeness of the tall police officer, who was about to figure prominently in Troy's first graphic novel, tentatively titled *When Worlds Collide at the Beaverbrook Art Gallery.*

Officer Barry pointed to one of the other officers. "Could you accompany—?"

"Janice Hayes," Janice supplied.

Officer Barry nodded. "Could you accompany Ms. Hayes downstairs and help her make the calls? Some of the parents may want to speak to the police."

Janice, looking slightly queasy, nodded and headed downstairs.

"Are the paintings still out in the van?" Isaac asked. "They need to be kept in proper conditions, with the right humidity. The damp night air isn't good for them."

"I've called our forensic identification unit, and they're on their way. We should have your paintings back in the building within the hour. In the meantime, while my officers read these gentlemen their rights and take them to the station, is there someplace we could all go and have a chat?"

"I have a boardroom downstairs."

"Perfect. Lead the way."

Isaac glanced over at Barney, who was still lying on his back. Next to him, Harmsworth had come to and was groaning. "The man in the coveralls works for me," Isaac said softly to the policeman. "Can I speak with him?"

Officer Barry shook his head. "I think we need to let the justice system take over at this point. You're going to want to speak with the Beaverbrook's lawyer before you engage with an employee who's been charged with theft."

Isaac nodded reluctantly and led the police officer to the stairs. Sargent followed, still holding Mona, checking on her now and then. She appeared lifeless and was still tied to the stool. The other campers, following along like ducklings, were stopped by Troy at the top of the stairs. "Do you all swear never to tell the secret of the Beaverbrook? Because we can't, you know. Not ever, not even on pain of death and dismemberment."

Adam held up his hand. "I swear. But I want to talk to them."

"I swear, too," Alice said. "And I want to know more."

One by one, each camper made the same promise. It was a promise they would never break. Neither Officer Barry nor the other officers noticed the extra people in *Santiago El Grande*; they weren't familiar with who was supposed to be where. But as the campers passed, the giant horse whispered, "Well done." Everyone puffed out a bit at that.

"We might have to change our nickname to the Beaverbrook Lions now." Adam grinned.

"I thought I was lost forever," Mona whispered to Sargent. She closed her eyes. "I thought I would never see you again. It was terrible, imagining living for hundreds more years, knowing I would never talk to my friends and family again."

Sargent flinched. Mona's words weighed on him as if they were rock heavy. Yes, they were reunited, but not for much longer. Soon he would return home. The only comfort was that at least she was with people who loved her.

But he kept his thoughts to himself. Mona was safe; let her enjoy her relief. There would be time enough for regrets later.

CHAPTER FORTY-FIVE

The rest of the night was a blur. After the police interviewed Isaac, Janice, and Sneely, they talked to the kids, whose parents sat in with them. In addition to being charged with theft, Harmsworth would be charged with confinement of Isaac and Sargent, and Barney for administering a noxious substance to Frank, who was surprised, but none the worse for wear, when he eventually woke up.

Despite his role in the plot to steal the paintings, no one from the gallery was happy about Barney being charged. It was painful to think about what would happen to his wife if he went to jail.

It was nearly two a.m. before the interviews were finished. The campers gathered up their things to go home with their parents.

"Are we still having camp next week, Mr. Singer?" Troy asked, rolling up his sleeping bag. The others stopped and looked at Isaac, who rubbed the back of his neck, looking flustered.

"I don't know. . . . I guess it depends on your parents."

Alice's mother patted him on the arm. "The children are fine, Mr. Singer. If you hold a session next week, Alice will be here."

Other parents nodded. Overwhelmed by their support, Isaac clutched Sargent's shoulder to steady himself. "I appreciate you saying that. We love having your children here."

"Aw, let's go before it gets all mushy," said Troy. He mouthed. "I'll call you tomorrow" to Sargent and led the way out of the Contemporary Gallery.

Janice arrived just as everyone was leaving. "The police have returned the five stolen paintings. Six, if you include the Patsy Ryder painting," she told Isaac.

"Patsy Ryder?" Isaac asked.

Janice sighed. "Apparently she was dropped off for you to appraise last week and one of the docents accidentally left her in Sneely's workroom. If she hadn't have been there, Harmsworth might have gotten away. She and Sargent were the ones to raise the alarm about what was happening."

Isaac shook his head. "That's amazing. I'll appraise her tomorrow and thank her profusely for what she's done for us. Where are the paintings now?"

"They're in the vault for the night. The police needed us to secure the evidence. The Cotterell Family and Edmund are in there, too." When Isaac looked confused, she giggled. "Clem and Edmund insisted, and who was I to say no? The forensic identification unit took lots of pictures and pulled some fingerprints off the frames to send to their lab, but they want to look at them again first thing in the morning to make sure they haven't missed anything, especially after getting statements from Harmsworth and Barney. We should be able to rehang them tomorrow afternoon."

"It's like we're in a police show," said Sargent. Isaac looked ill. "Won't the police see the residents moving around in the paintings when they look at Frank's security feed?"

Janice shook her head. "Barney erased everything and turned off the recording device once Frank was knocked out. Isaac, I also gave the police the list of other gallery employees and volunteers; they're going to have to interview everyone over the next few days in case anyone has pertinent information. One of the officers said the case should be open and shut. Apparently Barney confessed to everything and provided details. I think Harmsworth's the problem—he refuses to tell them where he was taking the paintings and to whom he was planning to sell them. I overheard one of the police officers talking on the phone. The jet that was waiting for Harmsworth left right before the police got to the airstrip." She paused. "Could we talk about what happened tonight? I take it you knew the paintings were alive, Isaac."

Isaac's cheeks burned. "Yes. I'm sorry I never told you, Janice." He exhaled. "I wasn't trying to lie to you. It's a secret that every director has kept since the Beaverbrook opened."

Janice looked thoughtful. "I suppose it wasn't really for you to share, Isaac. But now . . ."

"But now that the genie is out of the bottle," Isaac finished.

"I won't be able to pretend they're not alive now that I know," she said. "I mean, I won't talk to them when other people are around or anything, but I want to talk to them."

Sargent jumped in. "They get bored," he said. "And they love movies. They want to be a part of things. I know

Lord Beaverbrook's trying to protect them, and I agree
with Janice; we can't talk to them in front of visitors. But
they live here, Dad. You guys just work here. More things
should be done to make their lives better."

It was Isaac's turn to look thoughtful. "I agree. Let me
talk to Max tomorrow. I think I can convince him that
it's time to loosen things up around here. But now, if you
don't mind, I'd like to go home. I'm exhausted."

"Could we—"

Isaac shook his head. "Not tonight, Sargent. Mona
must be beat, too. She's with friends in the vault. She'll
be fine."

CHAPTER FORTY-SIX

After the heavy door to the vault closed, there was silence for a few minutes. The paintings were grateful that Janice had left the light on. She'd also agreed to cover *Merrymaking* with padding at Max's request. No one wanted to see Argyle Smith or Charlie Ryan—not yet, anyway, and not until a decision was made about their punishment.

It was Max who spoke first. "I owe you all an apology."

"None required, Boss," Dusk said. He was sitting on the side of the bed in his painting, holding his wife's hand. "You didn't know what was going on."

"I should have. I left Maugham down there to languish for a decade, and his bitterness was almost the end of some of us. What happened tonight is my fault as much as his."

"I disagree," Edmund said. "Maugham ought to be hung—and not on a wall—for what he did to Juliette and the rest of you."

"I'm sure he's down in the workroom stewing because his plan to punish us has been thwarted," Dusk added.

"No doubt," Max agreed. "But the truth is, I've been too controlling, too quick to pass judgment, only interested in my own perspective. I wouldn't allow you to interact with the world outside the frames, and yet I did so myself, and I lied to you about that. Mouse has shown me I must change."

Juliette, who along with Edmund had joined Mona in her portrait in order to untie her, squeezed Mona's shoulder.

Max continued. "I propose that after this, a consortium of painting residents be elected to assist in the day-to-day operations of the gallery. Of course, I plan to nominate you and Lady Cotterell, Sir Charles, along with Edmund and Juliette, Helena, and Mona's father, upon his return. It will be cumbersome, but more democratic. People will have a voice in things. And the consortium will meet with the gallery director so there are no more secrets."

"*C'est incroyable,*" Juliette said.

"A wise decision," Edmund added.

Sir Charles bowed deeply. "And they say one cannot teach an old dog a new trick. I salute you, Lord Beaverbrook, and I will assist you to the best of my abilities."

"Hear, hear!" shouted Clem.

"Very generous, sir," Lady Cotterell said. For some inexplicable reason, baby Frances wasn't fussing, which Mona took as an omen of good things to come.

"Thank you, madame. But there is more. One of the first orders of business will be to work with Director Singer to develop activities for the paintings that connect them with the outer world in a more meaningful way. I'm not sure what form this will take—I still believe we must continue to be discreet. But I am sure we will think of something."

Sir Charles grew animated. "I could write to Mr. Ben Stiller, see if he might be interested in coming to speak with us about how moving pictures are made!"

Usually, Max would have shot down such an idea. This time he gave Sir Charles a genial nod. "We can certainly take that under advisement and see what Director Singer thinks."

"I cannot wait to see a moving picture." Juliette sighed. "I have missed all the fun, I fear."

"There will be more moving pictures," Sir Charles said. "Make no mistake, Madame Juliette, I will see to that personally."

Max eyed a still-pale Mona. "How are you, Mouse? It's been a terrible night for you."

Mona gave him a wan smile. "I was so frightened, especially at the end, when Harmsworth threatened to set me on fire. Thank heavens for Sargent!"

"I never thought I would say that, but I agree. The boy saved us, as did you, Mona. Sending Patsy off for help was brilliant," Dusk said. He and Mona exchanged a friendly smile.

"Patsy! I'd forgotten Patsy's with us, she's been so quiet!" Mona leaned forward and blew Patsy a kiss.

Patsy smiled shyly.

"Why, you are perfectly lovely, my dear," Juliette said, stepping out of Mona's portrait and going over to Patsy's to take her hand. "We owe you so much. You were tremendously brave."

"It was super cool when you just showed up and hollered," Clem said, giving the dark-haired girl the side-eye.

"I was terrified, but I knew I had to help Mona," Patsy said. "I'll never forget the looks on the faces of the people outside the frames. They were stunned."

Clem picked up the story. "It's like she tossed a bomb

in the room. But the most amazing thing—"

"Was how happy they were to discover we are alive," Lady Cotterell finished. "Not a one of them looked frightened; quite the contrary, in fact. It was most touching."

Her husband nodded. "I hope we will be allowed to interact with them again. They acted with tremendous speed and nobility in saving you all from Mr. Harmsworth."

"I look forward to that myself," Max said. "I want to talk to that lad who made the copy of my portrait. He used floral fabric for my face, cheeky lad! A boy after my own heart."

"And how weird was that when Sneely came in at the end and quit?" Clem asked. "He didn't even notice what was going on!"

"Do you think Mr. Sneely knows we are alive?" Mona asked Dusk.

Dusk nodded. "Yes. Maugham was muttering in his ear all summer and I think it was too much for him. No more restorations this summer."

"*Mon Dieu*, I will not miss him!" Juliette cried.

"And Sargent—will I be able to see Sargent now?" Mona held her breath. This would be the first test of Max's willingness to be more open-minded.

"I don't see why not."

"Oh, Max!" Mona was out of her painting and over at his, hugging him tightly until they both get a little teary.

Mona turned to Dusk. "I owe you an apology, Mr. Dusk. You are a hero. I hope we can be friends."

Dusk bobbed his head. Mrs. Dusk smiled. Whatever secret event or tragedy had resulted in her never leaving her bed, Mona was now convinced it was not due to Dusk.

"The world will never be the same, will it?" Juliette mused.

"The world will be better," Dusk said. "Trust Lord Beaverbrook to see to that."

Mona's smile was melancholy. Not everything would be better. Lord Beaverbrook was powerful, but even he wasn't powerful enough to stop Sargent Singer from going home at the end of the summer and growing up.

CHAPTER FORTY-SEVEN

August fifth was sunny. "Wedding weather," Lady Cotterell called it. Edmund was pacing in *Santiago El Grande*, oblivious to the chattering of his friends, who had divided themselves into two large groups to the left and right inside the painting. This left a wide aisle in the middle, down which Juliette would walk.

"Can you see if she's left her painting yet?" Edmund called out to Sargent, who stood outside the painting beside his father and Janice.

Before Sargent could respond, Alice nudged Troy, who ran to take a look.

He was back seconds later. "Max says she's almost ready!"

Edmund dabbed the perspiration from his brow with a fine linen handkerchief and looked down at Clem. "I wasn't this nervous when we fought the French," he whispered.

Clem slapped him on the back. "Buck up! Madame Juliette is nice. Besides, you can't change your mind now; everybody's here." He winked at his father, who stood holding the baby. Sir Charles hadn't held Frances once in four hundred years. Max wasn't the only one who was changing.

With a jangle of bracelets, Helena Rubinstein bustled into the painting. "She's coming!"

Sargent wondered what they would do for music, but he needn't have, for it turned out Adam was a fine flutist in addition to his artistic talents. As Max stepped into the frame and made his way to where Edmund and Clem stood waiting, Adam began to play a lovely Mozart concerto, which was met with gasps of delight from the wedding guests.

Then Mona stepped in. Before turning to go down the aisle, she looked at the small group forming a semicircle outside the frame. Her new friends. Her eyes met Sargent's, and she smiled. He returned the smile. How she wished he could step into the painting and be part of the party!

Then Juliette entered, escorted by Mr. Dusk. As long as she lived, Mona would not believe there ever was a more radiant bride than the young French woman who made her way toward her dashing British officer. She hoped Janice would look as lovely at her wedding to Director Singer the following weekend. When Juliette took Edmund's outstretched hand, the crowd erupted into cheers; the residents had gone through too much to worry about decorum.

Max led the couple through their vows, quoting Shelley and Tennyson, and admonishing them to follow the "holy ordinance of marriage," something the campers had to have explained to them at the reception that followed. Finally there was a kiss, and more cheering.

The party began in earnest then, spilling out into several nearby paintings. Sir Thomas Samwell had arranged for his painting to be hung next to the Dalí for the evening, and he led residents in multiple toasts to the couple. Merrymaking hung on the other side of the gallery, and a number of musicians from the White Horse Inn began to play jaunty airs that led to dancing in and outside the paintings, with Adam doing his best to keep up. Somewhere deep inside Merrymaking, Argyle Smith and Charlie Ryan were chopping wood as part of their punishment. All the campers except Adam and Sargent joined hands and danced in a circle, whooping and hollering with delight.

Sargent leaned against the wall, watching Mona dance with Patsy (who had been invited back to the Beaverbrook under the auspices that Isaac needed to check one more thing about her painting) and the Cotterells, wishing with all his heart that he could be with them, too. Now and then the dancers would part, and he would catch a glimpse of Somerset Maugham's head sitting on Max's chair, chatting amiably with Mr. Dusk, who stood nearby.

"It's funny they made up, huh?" he said to his father, who had come to stand beside him.

The sketch of Max's head that hung in Isaac's office had a new neighbor: Somerset Maugham. "I'll admit I was surprised when the residents asked Maugham to be part of the consortium," Isaac said. "They feel his actions were a direct result of being trapped in the basement for so long. They want to give him another chance. Apparently it was Max's idea. The two seem to have rekindled their friendship."

"It's amazing how much Max has relaxed the rules the past couple of weeks," Sargent said, never taking his eyes off Mona.

Clem extricated himself from the circle of dancers to respond. "I know! It's weird not to have to pass through

Santiago El Grande to go to the basement anymore, though everyone still does because the horse and rider got so lonely. It feels different to do something because you want to rather than being forced to do it, doesn't it?" Sargent nodded emphatically.

"I like to think that the wall separating those who live behind the frame and those who live in front of it has been erased," Isaac said.

Clem nodded. "Yeah, like last week when the campers stayed late and introduced us to the internet. My father is *addicted* to YouTube."

"It's true," Troy said, easing his way in between Isaac and Sargent and giving Clem a virtual high five. "Sir Charles swears he could watch videos of kittens forever!"

"And then there's the reading nights, the movie nights, the presentations on the arts and world events," Clem added, ticking off the growing list of activities with his fingers.

"It helps that I was able to let Frank in on the secret," Isaac said. Instinctively, they all turned to where the burly security guard was eating wedding cake and chatting with Helena Rubinstein. The drugs had had no lasting impact on Frank, who was thrilled that he now had people to chat with during night shifts.

"Are you looking for a new art restorer?" Troy asked.

Isaac shook his head. "Not yet. I think we could use some peace and quiet around here."

"The funny thing is, I think Sneely was the only person who couldn't handle the paintings being alive," Sargent said.

Isaac nodded. "I don't worry about him spilling the beans. I was worried about Harmsworth sharing what he knew, but when he told the police that the paintings were alive, during his interview, they thought he'd lost it. It seems the world isn't quite ready to believe in living art."

The party was winding down. Max asked Mona to dance, and he twirled her around the makeshift dance floor with surprising dexterity for a man his age.

"I suppose Sargent will be leaving soon, eh, Mouse?"

Mona's face clouded over. "Sargent Singer has become my best friend in the world. He's been here every evening since the night of the art theft. We've finished three of the Harry Potter books and *Anne of Green Gables*. He leaves August thirtieth. I'm not sure I can bear it."

"But he will return."

"He wants to, but . . ."

"But?"

Mona rested her head against Max's chest as they

continued to dance. "But when he returns, he will be different. He will be older. To be honest, I don't want to see him again after he leaves."

"That seems extreme, Mouse."

"It is extreme, but there is logic to it, and I have thought about nothing else these past weeks. Sargent will grow older, while I will always be my age. Someday he'll return and be so old that I'll be just another pretty child in a picture to him. I couldn't stand to have him look at me that way, Max. It will break my heart to see him leave, but it would break it more to have him return and not see me in the same way he sees me now." She lifted her head and looked into Max's face, searching for his support. "Does that make any sense at all, or am I being a goose?"

Max's smile was the smile of someone who'd experienced much heartache in his life. "Perfect sense. You know, if he hadn't come here, nothing would have changed at the gallery."

Mona looked past Max to where Sargent stood eating cake with the other campers, tears in her eyes. "He did it all, Max. If Sargent had never come, I'd be hidden away in Switzerland somewhere. He saved us, that night and ever since."

■ ■ ■

The Beaverbrook was silent when Sargent and his father arrived on his last night in Fredericton. It reminded Sargent of the first evening, when he and Isaac had popped in after supper. The first time he'd ever spoken to Mona. Everything that had happened in the eight weeks since made that evening feel like it belonged to another century, not the beginning of summer. Now the nights were cooler, school was starting soon, and tomorrow morning, Isaac would drive him to the airport. By this time tomorrow he'd be home, and missing the Beaverbrook Art Gallery more than anything.

"Max wants to say good-bye," Isaac said. "I suggested you use my office. Then you can go upstairs and say good-bye to Mona. I'll go chat with Frank and find you in an hour."

Sargent nodded, the lump in his throat so massive he could barely breathe, let alone speak. He'd said good-bye to everyone else the night before, and had avoided the gallery all day. He didn't want to leave the paintings. He'd come to love them all.

Max smiled as Sargent took a seat in his father's chair—a smile remarkable for the fact that Max's mouth was so large it threatened to split his face in two. Sargent noticed Maugham and the sketch of Max's head weren't in their frames and wondered if Max had wanted privacy.

"Tonight's your last night with us," Max began, never one to beat around the bush.

Sargent nodded glumly.

"You and your father—your summer visit achieved your desired ends?"

Sargent was surprised. He hadn't expected to talk about his father with Lord Beaverbrook. He nodded again, finding his voice this time. "I think so. It was hard, but then—"

"But then you learned the truth about each other and moved on," Max finished. "You know, I didn't agree much with my father. He was a tough old bird, a minister. Can you imagine me the son of a minister?"

"No," Sargent said truthfully.

Max snorted. "He was a good man, but strict. He didn't approve of the fact that I chased worldly pursuits, not spiritual ones. As soon as I was able, I left home and never looked back. I did everything a man could dream of, and yet in the end, all I really wanted was to return to New Brunswick and be loved and remembered here, in the land where I grew up. Now I am."

"Did you know paintings were alive when you had your portrait painted?" Sargent asked. He'd been thinking about that a lot, of how people were leaving little bits of their soul behind without even knowing they were doing so. Would people still want to be painted if they knew?

Max chuckled. "I had a great imagination, almost as great as my friend Willie's, and even I never imagined that. It's one of life's mysteries. It might not have surprised my father, for he saw the hand of God in everything. I can close my eyes right now and remember my mother handing me a present on Christmas morning in the early 1890s, smell the talcum powder on her skin, see her dark blue dress, hear her voice whispering, 'Merry Christmas, Max.' She's always with me, that moment is always with me, so why should I be surprised that the soul tucks itself into every nook and cranny it can find, like art or stories or our heads?"

Sargent contemplated Max's words. "I never meant to change your gallery."

Max's grin returned. "My dear friend Winston Churchill once said, 'Personally I'm always ready to learn, although I do not always like being taught.' You have taught me quite a lot this summer, Sargent, and I am grateful. Thanks to you, the gallery is thriving again. Did your father tell you donations and visits are up three hundred percent since the attempted art theft? Nothing like people realizing they might have lost something wonderful to decide they ought to take care of it. I even wrote the catchphrase for the gallery's new advertising campaign: 'Come to New Brunswick and See the Other Mona.' Change is good, Sargent. Never forget that. Now off with you—our girl's upstairs waiting for you. She's going to be a very sad mouse once you're gone."

Sargent stood up and headed for the door.

"Sargent." Max's low growl called after him.

"Yes?"

"Remember, you can always come home again. The only requirement is creativity, lad."

Sargent didn't have a clue what Max meant but nodded as if he did.

Mona was waiting for him on the rocky pier in *San Vigilio, Lake Garda*, her feet dangling in the water. She offered him a wan smile when she saw him appear around the corner.

"I've come to say good-bye," Sargent stammered.

Mona crumpled. "Do it quickly, Sargent. The longer you stay, the harder it will be."

"I—"

Mona held up her hand. He could see the wet blotches on her dress, ones that matched the blotches on his T-shirt. "Please don't say anything that will make me cry harder. You've become my dearest friend. We may never see each other again. Or if we do, you'll be different."

"I'll still be me!" he protested.

"No, you won't. You'll be a fifteen-year-old Sargent, or a twenty-year-old or even a seventy-year-old, and I will always be thirteen. You'll grow up and fall in love and marry and have children, and I will still be here, exactly as I am tonight. This must be the last time you and I ever speak, Sargent. I couldn't bear to talk to you once you've changed—"

"But I'm coming back, Mona!"

She ignored him. "Thank you for everything: saving my life, helping Max change. They're probably already writing songs about you down at the White Horse Inn."

In spite of his sadness, Sargent laughed.

"Because of you, we will all get to live interesting and exciting lives. You did that for us, and you should be very proud. And even though it breaks my heart to see you leave, know that I don't regret meeting you. Your friendship has been a gift to me."

"Yours has been a gift to me, too. You taught me how to be a friend. Remember when you told me that leaving the building made you feel like a real girl again?"

Mona nodded.

"I want you to know that you're the most real person I've ever met, Mona."

The sound of Isaac and Frank's voices coming up the stairs told them their time was up.

"I'll never forget you, Mona Dunn," he said. "We'll see each other again—I promise."

"I'll never forget you either, Sargent. Be happy."

Before he could respond, she was gone. Isaac came around the corner and found Sargent leaning against the wall. When he saw him, Sargent ran and buried his face in his father's chest. They stood there for several minutes, neither speaking. Had they looked around, they would have seen all the residents in the nearby paintings watching sorrowfully, some dabbing their eyes.

Finally Sargent took a deep breath. It was time to go. He followed his father out of the gallery and didn't look back.

As they walked back to Isaac's through the late summer evening, Sargent kept hearing Max's voice in his head, telling him he could always "come home." What a strange thing to say. They were climbing the stairs to the apartment when Sargent finally understood.

"Is it okay if I go to my room for a while? I have something to do."

Bewildered, Isaac nodded. "Sure. Need help?"

"Nope, this is something I have to do for myself."

THE BEAVERBROOK ART GALLERY

It was close to midnight. From where he stood, Sargent could barely see the outline of the Canadian Gallery. The gallery director, Dawn Gilbert, moved to turn on a few low lights. Three easels stood in the center of the room. Too excited to speak, Sargent watched his father and Ms. Gilbert place three large paintings on them.

"Tomorrow morning, before the ceremony, staff will set up the chairs and the podium in here," Ms. Gilbert said. "There'll be lots of press. It's not every day a world-famous artist donates one of his paintings. And two of his father's paintings," she added, smiling.

Isaac and Ms. Gilbert stared at the massive painting in front of them. Titled *Summer*, it was a collage: images of Sargent's favorite childhood books floated across a library that seemed to stretch forever into the distance; a slash of blue wound through the center, past a golden building; and in the center, the artist had collaged a watercolor painting of a smiling boy.

"It's so beautiful," Ms. Gilbert whispered. "Do you have many friends coming tomorrow, Isaac?"

"Quite a crowd: my wife, Janice; Sargent's children, Noah and Jillian; his wife, Martha; his sisters; and three good friends who attended summer camp with him here."

"Oh, yes! I'm excited to meet Adam. I understand he did the set design for that Broadway show everyone's talking about."

"They were a talented group. Two others, Troy and Alice, are married and run a comic empire." He stood back, satisfied, then smiled at Sargent. "Time for us to head downstairs."

Sargent nodded. He was ready.

"You've been gone a long time, boy," the horse said as Sargent passed through *Santiago El Grande*. "And you're behind the frame now! How did that happen?"

Sargent grinned. "That's a riddle for YOU to solve!" he said, and ran on, delighting in the squawks and protests that echoed behind him. He knew they'd be fussing all night about how he'd gotten behind the frame.

When he jumped into Mona's painting, it was empty. Across the room, Edmund, Juliette, and the Cotterells were playing cards. Juliette saw him first and cried out. Clutching Edmund's arm, she stood up, her cards fluttering to the floor. Sargent waved.

"She's in *San Vigilio, Lake Garda*," Edmund called. "Come back and see us when you find her! We have a lot to talk about!" Juliette was too busy wiping her eyes to wave.

"Yeah, like how you pulled this off," Clem added. Sargent snickered and kept going.

The sun was shimmering across the water, tiny flickering diamonds, as he stepped into the painting. It was different being inside—he could see everything John Singer Sargent had seen on the day he'd done the painting. Except there was one person the artist hadn't seen on that day: the young girl sitting at the end of the rocky pier, her back to Sargent, staring out at the water.

It had been a long time. Maybe she'd forgotten him or grown tired of waiting. Then she turned. Mona stood up, her face a kaleidoscope of changing emotions.

"You found a way." Four words conveying a world of emotion.

"I said I would."

Mona shook her head in wonder. "I'd given up hope."

Sargent grinned. "You're stuck with me now."

"Really?"

"Uh-huh. Max had it written into the donation contract we did with the Beaverbrook. Our paintings can't be separated. Where you go, I go."

Two pink splotches appeared on Mona's cheeks. "They agreed to that?"

"Yup."

For several minutes they simply stared at each other, exchanging giddy grins. Finally Sargent walked to Mona and took her hand. They began to laugh. They had never touched before.

"Do you want to go and say hello to everyone?" Mona asked.

"Would you mind if we just sat and talked awhile? We have a lot of catching up to do."

Mona nodded. For the first time, they had all the time in the same world.

■ ■ ■

A few hours later, Sargent and Mona visited the Canadian Gallery. He wanted her to see *Summer* and introduce her to his mother. Sarah had left her painting and was rocking baby Sargent in his. Helena Rubinstein was looking over Sarah's shoulder, cooing at the baby. When Sarah looked up and saw Sargent and Mona, she waved. Meanwhile, the Cotterells, Edmund, and Juliette were wandering through *Summer*, marveling at the images. Max and Dusk stood near the edge of the frame, watching the scene unfold, smiling.

"The boy who brought us the moving pictures has come home," Sir Charles said. He bowed deeply, and Sargent bowed in return.

"We are so proud of you," Juliette said.

"You didn't forget us," Clem said.

"You did not forget Mona," Edmund added.

"I could never forget you," Sargent said. He pointed to his heart. "You're always here."

"What took you so long, lad?" Lord Beaverbrook asked.

"I had to wait until I woke up," Sargent answered, looking a little sheepish.

A throat cleared. In the corner of the Canadian Gallery sat a man, watching them.

"We did it," Sargent said to him.

"We did it," the man confirmed.

Mona blew the man a kiss and whispered, "Thank you."

The man smiled and stood up. "I'd better get some rest; tomorrow's a big day. Be happy, you two."

And they were.

Revised Rules for the Residents of the Beaverbrook Art Gallery

As written by the Inaugural Beaverbrook Art Gallery Resident Consortium:

Lord Beaverbrook

Helena Rubinstein

Madame Juliette Nugent

Lieutenant Colonel Edmund Nugent

Lady Cotterell

Sir Charles Cotterell

Somerset Maugham

Sir James Dunn

1.   First and foremost, it is the belief of the Beaverbrook Art Gallery Resident Consortium that all residents are equal, regardless of the status of their artist, or their status in life.

2.   Issues requiring attention should be directed to the Beaverbrook Art Gallery Resident Consortium.

3.   Consortium meetings are open to all residents and approved gallery personnel. The gallery director assumes the role of secretary in perpetuity and is responsible for all minutes and records of decisions.

4.   Consortium membership shall be for a five-year period, renewable should the residents agree, via secret vote, that the individual(s) in question should retain their post(s).

5.   The exception to rule four is Lord Beaverbrook, who, as founder of the Beaverbrook Art Gallery, shall have membership in the consortium in perpetuity.

6.   Rule changes shall be presented to residents and subject to secret vote before adoption.

7.   Issues requiring sanction or censure shall be brought to the consortium, which retains the right to create a panel of residents to hear both sides before a final decision is made.

8.   No resident shall be moved or banished against their will. Decisions as to loaning paintings to other galleries shall occur in consultation with the paintings in question.

9.   Painting residents may only interact with humans preapproved by the Beaverbrook Art Gallery Resident Consortium in consultation with the gallery director.

10. Painting residents accidentally interacting with

humans must immediately advise the Beaverbrook Art Gallery Resident Consortium.

11. Paintings are free to move about except during public visitation hours at the gallery or during other special circumstances, which shall be explained fully to the residents, ideally in advance.

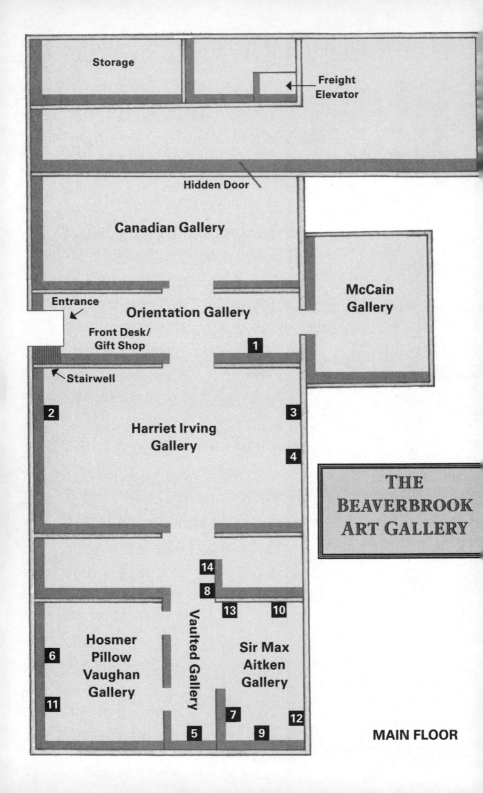

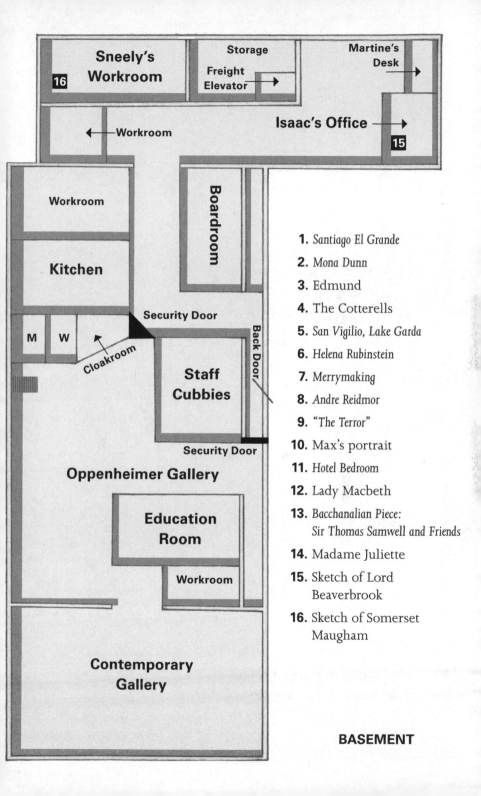

Sneely's Workroom `16`

Storage

Freight Elevator →

Martine's Desk →

Workroom ←

Isaac's Office → `15`

Workroom

Boardroom

Kitchen

M W

Cloakroom ↗

Security Door

Back Door

Staff Cubbies

Security Door

Oppenheimer Gallery

Education Room

Workroom

Contemporary Gallery

1. *Santiago El Grande*
2. *Mona Dunn*
3. Edmund
4. The Cotterells
5. *San Vigilio, Lake Garda*
6. *Helena Rubinstein*
7. *Merrymaking*
8. *Andre Reidmor*
9. "The Terror"
10. Max's portrait
11. *Hotel Bedroom*
12. Lady Macbeth
13. *Bacchanalian Piece: Sir Thomas Samwell and Friends*
14. Madame Juliette
15. Sketch of Lord Beaverbrook
16. Sketch of Somerset Maugham

BASEMENT

LORD BEAVERBROOK

While many of the people in the paintings included in this book were real, none casts a longer shadow over the Beaverbrook Art Gallery than Max Aitken—Lord Beaverbrook—himself. Max grew up in Newcastle, New Brunswick. New Brunswick is a small province in Atlantic Canada, but there was nothing small about Max's ambition. He was a born entrepreneur. By age eleven he was writing and selling his own community newspaper. As a young man, he pursued careers in the financial and legal worlds. But what he did best was use his imagination. He was famous for finding ways to meet the right people and for making money creatively.

In 1910, Max moved to England, which at that time was considered the center of the universe for a Canadian. Thanks to connections with other New Brunswickers who'd arrived ahead of him, Max got into politics, and befriended future prime ministers, including Winston Churchill. But politics is a tricky business, and Max being Max, he made mistakes and enemies. He was eventually forced out of politics during World War I, although he was rewarded with a lordship for supporting the government.

But Max, now Lord Beaverbrook, didn't fade away. Instead he returned to his journalistic roots and bought newspapers, one of which, the *Daily Express*, was the most-read newspaper in the world by the end of the 1920s. When World War II erupted in 1939, Winston Churchill called Lord Beaverbrook back into service and made him minister of aircraft production. It was an important role; many believed the war would be won or lost in the air. Churchill wrote to him in 1941, saying, "I want to point out to you that I am placing my entire confidence, and to a large extent the life of the State, upon your shoulders." Max rose to the challenge.

After the war, Beaverbrook turned his attention to giving back to his home province. While he continued to live at his estate in England, he visited New Brunswick often. His greatest legacy was the Beaverbrook Art Gallery, which he built and filled with priceless masterpieces, most chosen by him, including *Mona Dunn*; *Lieutenant Colonel Edmund Nugent, 1764*; and *Santiago El Grande*. When the gallery opened in 1958, Max gave it to the people of New Brunswick, although he actually kept a bedroom in the basement of the gallery for his use when he visited.

In 1964, Max died in England at the age of eighty-five. At his request, his ashes were returned to Canada and placed in a bust erected in his honor in the town square of Newcastle, New Brunswick. He was home again. But then, he never left the Beaverbrook Art Gallery, did he? For more information, visit the Beaverbrook Foundation online www.beaverbrookfoundation.org, read David Adams Richard's wonderful biography, *Lord Beaverbrook*, and visit the Beaverbrook Art Gallery online www.beaverbrookartgallery.org.

COLLECTION: THE BEAVERBROOK ART GALLERY, FREDERICTON, NB, CANADA/COLLECTION: LA GALERIE D'ART BEAVERBROOK, FREDERICTON, N-B, CANADA:

- ▣ Andre Reidmor
- ▣ Bacchanalian Piece: Sir Thomas Samwell and Friends
- ▣ Lt. Colonel Edmund Nugent
- ▣ The Crew of the MHS "Terror" Saving the Boats and Provisions on the Night of 15ᵗʰ March
- ▣ Lady Macbeth Sleep-Walking
- ▣ Merrymaking
- ▣ Madame Juliette dans le Jardin
- ▣ San Vigilio, Lake Garda

Courtesy of Wendy McLeod MacKnight:

- ▣ Patsy Ryder

ACKNOWLEDGMENTS

Many people supported this book, but my heartiest of thanks go to the staff of the Beaverbrook Art Gallery: former CEO Terry Graff, whose own book and kindness were critical; current CEO Tom Smart, who got it right away and is so creative, as well as Sarah Dick, Jeremy Elder-Jubelin, Meghan Callaghan, Jessica Spalding, and Adda Mihailescu. Shout-outs to critique partners Mary Mesheau, Barb Fullerton, and Faith Knight; to artist Janice Wright Cheney for the inspiration; to my agent, Lauren Galit, for believing; to Dawn and Don and Wendy Wheaton, for loving Mona. Finally, special thanks to everyone at Greenwillow Books, especially Virginia Duncan, Katherine Heit, and Tim Smith, whose hard work and vision has made this book a true work of art.